"What makes you think I'm angry?" Ethan asked.

Abigail tipped her head to one side. "For one thing, you're about to snap that pen in two."

His hand stilled. He hesitated, then slid the pen into his breast pocket. "I'm not angry," he said quietly.

"Please tell that to the vein on the side of your head," she quipped.

Moxie, he thought, as his irritation began to ebb. "Ms. Lee," he said, fighting an unexpected smile, "you don't think I'd believe that you had no idea what kind of reaction you were going to get from me, do you?"

Her lips curved into a soft smile. They were the full, kissable lips that generally drew his notice. "I had an inkling."

MacKENZIE TAYLOR

My One and Only

AVON BOOKS
An Imprint of HarperCollinsPublishers

This is a work of fiction. Names, characters, places, and incidents are products of the author's imagination or are used fictitiously and are not to be construed as real. Any resemblance to actual events, locales, organizations, or persons, living or dead, is entirely coincidental.

AVON BOOKS
An Imprint of HarperCollins*Publishers*
10 East 53rd Street
New York, New York 10022-5299

Copyright © 2002 by P.R.S., Inc.
ISBN: 0-380-81937-6
www.avonromance.com

First Avon Books paperback printing: May 2002

Avon Trademark Reg. U.S. Pat. Off. and in Other Countries, Marca Registrada, Hecho en U.S.A.
HarperCollins ® is a registered trademark of HarperCollins Publishers Inc.

Printed in the U.S.A.

10 9 8 7 6 5 4 3 2 1

One

Of all the attributes the woman had to recommend her—and there were many—what appealed to Ethan Maddux most about Abigail Lee was her moxie.

Ethan momentarily tuned out his assistant's list of rapid-fire reminders and concentrated on the woman standing serenely amidst the chaos in his office. She silently studied the Mark Rothko hanging over the fireplace while his staff buzzed around in their usual near frenzy. With his flight to Prague for an international economics summit less than two hours away, and his clients demanding his attention, his staff had their hands full managing the breakneck pace of his life and his business.

The arrival of the indomitable Ms. Lee on the

scene had the impact of a nuclear bomb. He narrowed his gaze to study her profile. Sunlight streamed through the enormous plate-glass windows of his thirty-second-floor office in downtown San Francisco. Limned as she was by the bright glow, he could understand what Harrison Montgomery saw in the woman. Her conservative business suit barely disguised generous curves—the kind of curves Ethan personally believed were designed to drive a man crazy. She'd pulled her hair into a complicated-looking style. Twisting the ends into a circle, she'd held it in place, barely, by a pencil at the nape of her neck. He especially liked the pencil. Its chewed eraser told him she wasn't nearly as calm as she looked, and the temptation to pluck it out and send that mass of honey-colored waves tumbling down her back had his fingers twitching.

"Ethan?"

Though he'd seen the woman only a handful of times in the past several years, something about her had always intrigued him. Probably, he conceded, it was the contrast between a pencil with a chewed eraser in her hair and a less-than-innocent reputation when it came to her relationship with Harrison Montgomery. In Ethan's experience, ambitious businesswomen didn't generally style their hair with battered pencils.

"Ethan?"

He had to be a first-class fool, he decided, for

even giving the woman a second look. But there was something oddly fortuitous about her unexpected arrival today. A week ago, he had endured a theatrical breakup with his fiancée of six months. Pamela had flung a string of accusations at him—everything from "dissociated" to "socially dysfunctional."

It wasn't her accusations that bothered him.

What she *hadn't* said had been enough to make him swear off messy relationships. She had carefully dodged the subject of their sex life, which had turned intense and unusually heated over the past several weeks. She hadn't mentioned that Ethan had begun to loosen the reins of his formidable reserve and let his fiancée—the woman who was a week away from committing the rest of her life to him—see the raw passion he'd worked for years to subdue. She had carefully avoided saying that he'd terrified her when he'd finally shown her a glimpse of the side of himself he kept carefully locked away.

He couldn't blame her for that. He feared it too.

He'd inherited that passionate wild streak from his mother—and from Harrison Montgomery.

Ethan had watched that wildness destroy his mother, then slowly erode whatever respect he might have had for his father. As a very young man, he'd vowed to bury the reckless sensualist inside him beneath an implacable calm and sound reason. Therein lay the path, he'd discovered, to security and peace.

Generally, he succeeded so well at taming the beast that he'd earned a reputation for emotional ruthlessness and unshakable calm. That reputation had helped him build a financial empire on seemingly reckless gambles and risks.

On occasion, however, the curse of his genetics got the better of him. In those moments a stark, raging passion surfaced. It forced him to wrestle with it until he slammed shut the door of the interior vault in which he held that side of himself.

Unfortunately, in an unguarded moment he'd allowed Pamela to see a portion of it. Wise woman that she was, she'd run as far and as fast as she could.

And he'd vowed never to let it happen again.

Which definitely meant he had no business looking at Abigail Lee as anything other than a likely nuisance and a potentially serious problem.

"Ethan!" Edna's voice held a rare exasperation.

Reluctantly, he pulled his gaze from Abigail and forced a smile for his secretary. "Helmut Zeiterling is meeting me at the airport, Edna. I got it."

She frowned at him. "You aren't listening to a thing I'm saying."

"Don't be ridiculous." Ethan tossed several more files into his briefcase. "You know I hang on your every word. Did you pull the Connolly file?"

"Of course." She tapped the red folder on his

desk. "You can review it on the plane. Edward is expecting your call tonight."

"Edward's an ass," he said, and added the file to the stack.

Lewis O'Kane, Ethan's vice president of legal affairs, choked. "Ethan, you can't ignore this. My source at the Justice Department says they're very serious about prosecuting him."

"I'm not going to ignore it. I'm just going to tell Edward he's an ass. What the hell was the man thinking?" Ethan glanced at his public relations assistant. "Which reminds me. Maggie, please make sure that any statements we issue specify that Maddux Consulting only worked with Edward Kinsey's domestic technology affiliates. What he did with his import-export interests was his own business."

"I've already written that into our releases," she replied. "Do you still want to wait until questions are asked before issuing the statement?"

"Absolutely." Ethan flipped through the stack of pink messages Edna handed him. "Send flowers to Letty. Something expensive and tasteful"—he crumpled the top message—"a case of scotch to Charlie—" the next message hit the wastebasket—"tell Meyerson he can damn well wait until I get back from Prague"—the third message followed the previous two. Ethan froze when he reached the bottom of the stack. "And tell Harrison

Montgomery," he said flatly, "that he can screw himself."

The room fell silent. Abigail Lee turned slowly from her examination of the Rothko painting to face him. Intelligent hazel eyes squarely met his gaze. Innocent eyes, he thought. Innocent and gutsy. He cursed himself a thousand times for a fool. She couldn't possibly be what she appeared. He saw her draw a deep breath, as if gathering inner resources.

"That would be my cue," she said, her voice as soft and warm as a summer breeze. "I assure you, Mr. Maddux, I didn't know Harrison had called you, or I never would have requested an appointment."

He studied her for several long seconds as the silence in his office stretched uncomfortably. Finally, he made a characteristically quick decision. Slamming his briefcase shut, he clicked the latches. "Walk with me, Ms. Lee. I'll give you ten minutes."

Beside him, he heard Lewis mutter, "Ethan—"

"I can take care of myself, Lewis. I assure you."

"At least let me—"

"No." Ethan rounded the desk, keeping his gaze pinned on Abigail. "Let's go."

She nodded and preceded him out his office door. Neither of them spoke until the elevator doors slid shut, cocooning them in a shroud of quiet. She released a long breath.

Ethan leaned one shoulder against the burled

walnut paneling and pinned her with a piercing look. Damn the woman, he thought. She had the temerity to look serene. This would be easier if she found him as intimidating as everyone else did.

"What the hell," he said, his soft voice belying the river of fury that was slowly raising his blood pressure, "made you think I would even consider helping Harrison Montgomery?"

Her clear hazel eyes never wavered. Another point in her favor. In fifteen years of business, Ethan could count on one hand the number of people who looked him in the eye.

"There's no need to get angry, Mr. Maddux." She clasped her hands in front of her. "Harrison's in trouble. He needs help—his company needs help. And you're the best corporate savior in the business."

He shot her a wry look. "Thanks for the plug."

"I did what anyone would do in my situation. I researched my options, and concluded that you were our best choice. I had no reason to believe you'd be angry over a simple request for an appointment."

Despite himself, Ethan felt the corner of his mouth twitch. "What makes you think I'm angry?"

She tipped her head to one side, and the motion sent a curl skittering across her forehead. "For one thing," she replied, even as a hint of mischief entered her expression, "you're about to snap that pen in two." With a delicate wave of her hand, she indicated the iron grip he had on the Mont Blanc pen he was idly tapping against his thigh.

Ethan's hand stilled. He hesitated, then slid the pen into his breast pocket. "I'm not angry," he said quietly.

"Please tell that to the vein on the side of your head," she quipped.

Moxie, he thought again as his irritation began to ebb. He'd nailed it. "Ms. Lee," he said, fighting an unexpected smile, "you don't expect me to believe that you had no idea what kind of reaction you were going to get from me, do you?"

Her lips curved into a soft, natural smile. They were the full, kissable kind of lips that generally drew his notice. The top one met the bottom one in a generous flare. Accented with a tasteful pale lipstick, they were apparently accustomed to smiling. "I had an inkling."

"But you came anyway."

"I felt strongly about it."

"Obviously."

"And besides, if you think *you're* angry, wait until I tell Harrison."

"He doesn't know you're here." It wasn't a question.

"Are you kidding?" Abigail shook her head and another curl bounced, then settled itself in a new position. Something about that fascinated him, as if her hair were likely to explode from the confines of the coil at any moment. "He'd kill me."

"And you risked it anyway?"

"Your father is about to lose his business. You know how everyone in the family depends on him."

"What a travesty if the Montgomerys had to find gainful employment."

Her eyes sparkled. "There aren't a lot of job openings for formerly wealthy and overly pampered socialites."

Ethan ignored that. "I've seen his stockholder reports. If Harrison sells now, the financial impact will be difficult, but not disastrous. He's got enough liquid assets to survive. It's not going to leave him destitute."

"Just devastated," she said quietly. "I'm more interested in saving his pride than his portfolio."

"Would it surprise you to learn I don't give a damn about Harrison's pride?"

"No, but you probably give a damn about yours."

"Look—"

She interrupted him. "You're probably the only person on the planet who could save Harrison's company." Warming to her topic, she leaned toward him and rested one hand on the wall of the elevator. The move gave him a tantalizing glimpse between the lapels of her black suit. Lace covered a narrow expanse of rosy flesh, peppered with a generous number of freckles.

He found the contrast between her sophisticated

business clothes and her spray of freckles intriguing. "Why the hell would I want to?"

"There would be a certain satisfaction in—"

"When I was eighteen years old, I swore I'd never speak to the man again."

"But that was almost twenty years ago. I had hoped that time and age—"

"Would have mellowed me? They haven't. The day I walked out of his house, I wrote him off. I don't care if the bastard rots; he's not worth my energy."

Her eyes widened, and Ethan stifled a curse. He had to struggle for a few seconds to slam shut the door of the vault again.

Here, surrounded by the benefits of his personal success, he was constantly reminded of what he'd come from and the role Harrison had played in that journey. Ethan cast a quick glance at the lights above the elevator doors. Eight floors to go. Eight floors before he could walk away from Abigail Lee and everything she threatened to do to him.

"Mr. Maddux—"

There was conciliation in her tone. He'd heard it from most of Harrison's family on dozens of occasions. If only they explained, they thought, they could make him see reason. Abigail Lee was obviously suffering from some latent delusion that there was anything about Harrison worth admiring. He saw no reason not to disabuse her of the notion.

"Has he ever told you what happened between us?" Ethan asked quietly.

"He never married your mother." Somehow the soft look in her eyes spiked his anger higher.

His short laugh was harsh. "That's one way of putting it."

"We haven't talked about it much. I tried a couple of times, but he made it clear that the conversation was off limits. I work for the man. I run his charitable foundation. I'm not his shrink. I try not to pry."

What the hell did she call this? he wondered. She'd flown halfway across the country to seek his help without even informing Harrison of her plans. She'd raised the art of prying to an entirely new level.

"Then, in the interest of time, and for the waning ten minutes I promised you, let me give you the simplified version." He couldn't keep the bite out of his voice. "Harrison used his father's power and wealth to seduce my mother. She was an employee at his father's company. When she got pregnant, he lost interest. My grandfather had my mother fired so no one would know Harrison had sired a bastard. Since her boss was forbidden to give her a reference, she had a hard time getting a good job. Harrison didn't feel the need to help with the expenses, so she supplemented her income however she could."

Ethan paused to let the meaning sink in. He could feel his shoulder muscles knotting, but he forged ahead. "Not surprisingly, her health began to fail. She was terrified of putting me in foster care, so she did the only thing she could think of. She took me to Harrison and made it clear that if he didn't put a roof over my head, she'd sue him for child support. The only thing my grandfather hated more than the idea of Harrison's bastard son living in his house was the idea of Harrison's bastard son being paraded through the newspapers. When he realized he couldn't intimidate my mother like he had before, he finally gave in.

"I was six when we went to live there. My mother died a year later. Harrison couldn't make the funeral, but he did pick up the tab for the medical bills."

Abby opened her mouth to respond, but Ethan cut her off. "I stayed with him and my grandfather because I had no choice. And as soon as I was old enough, I left."

"I'm sorry," she said, the truth of her words reflected in her eyes. The elevator doors slid open.

He stared at her for a second longer, then exited the cramped space. This would be easier if she'd attempted to persuade him that Harrison wasn't such a bad guy, easier still if she'd looked at him with pity or disbelief. The empathy he saw in her expression was worming its way under his skin.

"Don't be," he said over his shoulder. "It can't be changed."

Abby followed him down the narrow hallway, through the security door, and onto the roof of the building. Ethan checked the sky, then met her gaze once more as he waited for her response. He'd just handed her the perfect opportunity to send his rage to the moon. All she had to do was step into the trap, begin offering him reasons to put the past behind him, and he'd have all the excuse he needed.

"No. It can't be changed," she said softly. Abby's face scrunched into an oddly pleasing look of frustration. "Sucks, doesn't it?"

Something inside him went perfectly still. "Excuse me?"

"I said it sucks. No wonder you haven't given the guy the time of day."

"Ms. Lee—"

"Geez, if I were you, I probably wouldn't have exercised quite this much restraint."

"Restraint?" His chest had started to hurt. In the distance he heard the approach of a helicopter.

"Sure. I mean, look at you." She indicated him with a wave of her hand. "I knew your reputation before I came out here. Your father's in the computer business, so naturally I knew what you do. Everyone in the industry thinks you work miracles. That merger you negotiated last year for

DataTran—well, people are still talking about it. And obviously"—she looked around—"you get paid pretty well for it. Your own helicopter pad? Very impressive." The noise grew stronger. She was forced to raise her voice.

He had a strong suspicion she was mocking him. "It's practical."

"I'm sure it is." The approaching helicopter had caused the wind to pick up. She shaded her eyes and held his gaze. "Your office furniture probably cost more than I make in six months. Everything you do reeks of success and achievement. Even this junket to Prague—aren't you going because the President asked you to?"

He gritted his teeth. "Yes."

"See, even *he* knows how good you are at this." She was shouting now. From the corner of his eye he could see the helicopter settling on the pad. The gusts from the blades carried across the wide rooftop and beat against them. Abigail's hair was whipping around her head in a mad froth of curls that managed not to look untidy despite the pencil that now sat slightly askew at the nape of her neck. "And with your contacts and your skill," she continued, "had you wanted to, you could have put Harrison out of business years ago. Surely you've thought about it."

She had no idea. Montgomery Data Systems, Harrison's struggling family enterprise, was ripe for takeover. Low capital, high development debts, ever-narrowing profits made it a prime target. Ethan had watched the firm dwindle, seen its stocks sliding, and deliberately turned his head. To seek revenge, or even to give vent to his anger, would throw open the vault so wide, he might never get the door closed again. "Once or twice," he admitted.

"But you didn't do it. That's the difference between me and you, I guess. If I'd been you, and I had that many reasons for hating Harrison Montgomery, I'd have buried him."

Ethan's fingers tightened on the handle of his briefcase. She couldn't possibly understand. "Ms. Lee—"

She held up her hand. "All I wanted was ten minutes to state my case, Mr. Maddux. You still haven't given them to me."

He glanced over at his pilot. Holding up one hand, he halted the man's progress across the roof. "Whether I gave you ten minutes or ten days, what makes you think you can convince me to help Harrison?"

She shrugged. "Gut feeling, I guess. Don't you ever get those?"

The gut feeling he had right now told him that this woman was trouble—and that if he had a brain in his head, he'd get on that helicopter and never speak to her again. But something tugged—hard—on his resolve. He searched her eyes. Integrity. A hint of desperation. Grit. Moxie. That's what got him. Against his better judgment, Ethan released the tight rein he had on his resolve. "I won't be back for a week."

"I understand."

Five more seconds passed while he weighed the wisdom of his decision. The relentless pumping of the helicopter blades punctuated the thick tension. Finally, he drew a tight breath. "I'll call you when I get back. You can have ten minutes."

She visibly relaxed. "Thank you."

Ethan nodded. "You're welcome."

Abby tipped her head toward the waiting helicopter. "You'd better go. Your ride is here."

Ethan turned to leave, then gave her a final glance over his shoulder. "For the record," he shouted above the noise, "you got your ten minutes in spite of Harrison—not because. I'm doing this for you. Think about that while I'm gone. I'll call you in a week."

She did think about that while he was gone. Abby jammed her key into the lock of her town house in suburban Chicago. Good grief. *I'm doing this for you*. The words had haunted her all the way back from California.

The lock turned, and Abby entered the house with a slight sigh of relief. Safe haven. It always felt that way here. "Rachel," she called as she set her briefcase down in the small foyer. "LuAnne?

I'm home." She dumped her keys on the table. "Where are you guys?"

LuAnne—Abby's closest friend, personal confidante, mental-health advisor, self-appointed life-management consultant, and sometime beautician—came out of the kitchen drying her hands on a dish towel. Abby smiled at the sight of her friend's newly bleached hair. Against the Jamaican woman's mocha skin, the color looked fabulous. But then, most any color did. LuAnne changed her hair color like most people changed their clothes. "Sporting the Marilyn Monroe look these days, Lu?"

LuAnne shrugged. "Blondes have more fun, they say. I wasn't having a lot lately, so I decided it was time for a change." Her previous color had been a strange mix between purple and green.

"I like it."

"Thanks. I'm thinking I like it too."

"Where's my sister?"

"Upstairs doing her homework. And you'd better brace yourself, Abby. I think she's writing a research paper on how thirteen-year-olds don't need baby-sitters."

Abby laughed. "I'll bet. She didn't hassle you, did she?"

"No. Rachel never shows me anything but respect. But you'd better understand that she's starting to feel the need to exert some indepen-

dence. You hold on too tight, and she'll fight you."
LuAnne tossed the dish towel over the arm of the
sofa, then tumbled onto the overstuffed cushions.
"Dinner was fabulous, darling."

Abby nodded as she reached for the stack of
mail on the hall table. She wasn't surprised. In the
past two years, her sister had developed a keen interest in gourmet cooking. The cooking classes she
was taking, thanks to Harrison Montgomery's in-
fluence with a local restaurant owner, were doing
wonders for her skill—and for Abby's waistline.
"I think I've gained five pounds in the last two
months."

"You could stand to," LuAnne told her, blunt as
usual. "You work too hard, Abby. I told you six
months ago that no man is going to want a
woman who's got a figure like a bed slat."

"Hmm." She flipped through the mail, came to
one letter, and waved it at her friend. "Oh, look. I
may have won a cruise."

"You're trying to change the subject."

"Uh-huh."

"Want to tell me how your day was?"

Ethan's voice popped into her head again—*I'm
doing this for you.* "Surreal," she muttered.

"What?"

Abby dropped the mail on the table, stepped
out of her pumps, and began unbuttoning her suit
jacket as she walked across the living room. She

dropped into the armchair. "I said surreal. I had a surreal day."

"Oh." LuAnne leaned back against the sofa with a broad smile. She tapped her knee with one long red fingernail. "That good?"

"He agreed to listen to me anyway."

"You're kidding!"

"Nope. He's going to call me when he gets back from Prague. He's on his way to some international economics conference." She gave LuAnne a dry look. "He's representing the President."

"What president?"

Abby laughed. "Of the United States."

"Oh. Why can't the President represent himself?"

"Because Ethan Maddux knows more about international economics than he does."

LuAnne tucked her feet beneath her. "Well, that's comforting." She drummed her fingers on the arm of the sofa. "I'll bet he's having dinner with the King of Belgium or something."

"There is no King of Belgium," Abby said with a laugh.

"Whatever. Just give me the important stuff. Is he or isn't he as sexy as you heard he was?"

"It was business, Lu."

"Which doesn't mean there wasn't plenty of time for you to notice. You told me that Letty said he was lethal."

"Letty is his aunt."

"And don't you think it's fascinating that he won't talk to his own father, but his aunt thinks he's the hottest thing going?"

"Letty likes underdogs."

"Abby," LuAnne said skeptically, "a man who has dinner with the King of Belgium is *not* an underdog."

"No, I guess not."

"So come on, give, girl. I'm not leaving until you do."

Abby pictured him standing on the helicopter pad with the sun gilding the hard angles of his face. No one would dare call him handsome. There was too much power in his stance and his features were too perfectly carved to use any word as soft as "handsome."

"He's"—she searched for the right word— "dynamic."

"Potent," LuAnne said.

"Yes, I suppose so. You should see the way his staff scurries around him. And it's not terror either. They *adore* the man." Abby closed her eyes and tipped her head back against the nubby fabric of the chair. Lord, it had been a long day.

"How tall?" LuAnne prodded.

"Uh, over six feet, I guess." And solid as a rock, she silently added. With broad shoulders, a trim waist, and lean hips that tapered to impossibly long legs. He was the kind of man a woman simply knew remained in peak physical condition. Every plane would be muscular and hard.

"Hair?"

"Brown." Walnut, she'd call it, with just a touch of red. It was thick, with a hint of a wave. When wet, it probably curled at the ends. The sunlight on the helicopter pad had limned it, making it look soft and touchable.

"Eyes?"

"Um, gray, I guess." Too clear to be called anything as mundane as blue. Actually, what came to mind when she thought about the piercing way he'd studied her was "sterling silver."

"Bod?"

Hard, lean muscle that radiated with barely contained energy. Any word one usually used to describe the more perfect specimens of the male species would be out of place. "Attractive" was too ordinary; "gorgeous," too soft; "sexy," too unsophisticated. Ethan Maddux had a certain warrior/feline quality to him. Like a black panther, she had decided. He moved with an uncanny combination of grace, agility, and power. He seemed always in control. Every word was carefully chosen. Each movement was deliberate and contained. He wasted nothing, not even a fluttering eyelash. He calculated his surroundings and always, always, seemed to be lying in wait, ready to pounce when necessary.

Abby took a deep breath and forced herself to

answer LuAnne's inquisitive gaze. "He was wearing a suit," she said evasively. Although the flawlessly tailored navy blue serge had done little to disguise his physique.

"What size?"

"What?"

"What size suit?" LuAnne said, watching her with obvious glee.

"How should I know?"

"Take a guess."

"I don't know. Forty, forty-two maybe."

"Long or extra long?" LuAnne drawled the words.

At the not-so-subtle double entendre, Abby gave her a look. "Probably extra long—but I didn't check the label. He has very broad shoulders."

"I bet he usually dates Amazons."

"And you're basing that opinion on what?"

"Men like that normally do. They like to be noticed, so they pick women who complement them physically. I'll bet he hardly goes out in public without some gorgeous woman draped over his arm—and the two of them look like a matched set."

Abby laughed. "If he does, he probably feels right at home with the King of Belgium."

"I'd say he has a thing for blondes with big boobs, long legs, and great musculature. They all have that sophisticated bored look." LuAnne pursed her lips and lifted her chin. "You know, like they aren't secretly wishing they were alone with the guy so they could tear his clothes off and get at him."

"Well, whatever he likes or doesn't like, he didn't throw me out. At least he agreed to talk to me."

"Did he tell you why?"

I'm doing this for you. "No. Just said he'd call."

LuAnne nodded. "Well, it's something anyway. Do you really think he can bail Harrison out of this mess?"

"If anyone can do it, Ethan Maddux can."

LuAnne unfurled her legs from the sofa, stood, and stretched her arms high above her head. "I hope so. Look, I gotta go. Shop opens tomorrow at eight."

"I know."

"You coming in next week for your appointment?"

"Wouldn't miss it."

"Okay. I'll grill you some more then."

"There's something to look forward to."

LuAnne laughed as she retrieved her enormous purse from the end of the couch. "Get some rest, Abby. You look beat."

"It was a long day."

"I know." LuAnne squeezed her friend's shoulder as she passed the armchair. "Rachel's not really mad at you, by the way. Just frustrated with being thirteen."

"I'll talk to her."

"Good plan. I put a plate in the oven for you. Your dinner should be hot."

"Thanks, Lu. For everything."

"No problem." She headed for the door. "Oh, and if Rachel mentions anything about dying her hair green, it wasn't my idea."

Abby groaned. "Great."

LuAnne said good-bye and let herself out of the house. Abby relished the quiet for several minutes, then levered herself out of her chair. Lord, even her bones ached. She fought a wave of fatigue as she moved through the ground floor, retrieving her plate, a fork, and a glass of water before she set the alarm and headed upstairs. The spicy smell of the food was making her stomach growl. Between her flight schedule and her nerves, she hadn't been able to eat a real meal all day. She was feeling the effects of the two bags of pretzels and the Bloody Mary mix she'd consumed on the plane.

She reached her sister's room and knocked gently with the rim of the glass. "Rach—can I come in?"

"Yes." Terse, but not angry. A good sign.

Abby shoved the door open with her foot, but stayed just outside the room. Rachel sat at her desk, one hand on an open textbook while the other drummed a pencil on the edge. "Did you have a good day?" The computer monitor on the desk displayed a spiraling wave of color. Behind the screen saver, Abby suspected she'd find an open Internet connection with four to five instant messages waiting for her sister's attention.

Rachel looked up from the book. "It was okay."

"Mine was long."

"What time did you leave this morning?"

"Four-thirty."

"I was surprised when I got up and found Lu-Anne here."

"I told you I had an early flight."

"I could have gotten myself ready for school."

"I didn't think you should have to."

Rachel's jaw squared. The stubborn expression looked just like their father's. "I don't need a baby-sitter."

"LuAnne is not a baby-sitter."

"What would you call it?"

"She's just here in case you need something."

"I can take care of myself."

Abby drew a calming breath. "I know."

"Then why can't I stay here alone?"

"We've been over this, Rachel. I'm not comfortable with that."

"So? It's not like you're my mother."

Abby let the barb pass. "I'm sorry it makes you so angry, but I'm not ready to leave you here by yourself."

"I'm old enough to *be* a baby-sitter, you know. Lots of my friends do it."

Lots of her friends, Abby thought, hadn't seen

their parents being murdered while they themselves were hiding inside a closet. "I'm sure they
do."

"But I can't."

"Not right now."

"Why not?"

"Because I'm not ready for that."

"But I am," Rachel insisted.

Abby studied her sister's face in the glow of the
desk lamp. She'd inherited their father's coloring
and build. Her hair was a dark, rich brown. Her
eyes, wide and expressive, could easily have been
his mirror image. The familiar ache started in the
center of Abby's chest and spread outward.
"Look, I'm willing to talk to you about it. Just not
tonight. I'm tired. And it's late. I've got to go to
bed, and so do you."

"It's only eleven. Why do I—"

"Rachel." Abby's voice held a warning note.

Her sister knew better than to push her luck.
She slammed the textbook shut. "Oh, all right.
God, Abby, you're so uptight."

Probably. "Right now, I'm just beat." She held
up the plate. "And thanks, by the way, for dinner.
I haven't had anything but airplane food today."

Rachel's gaze flicked to the plate. "It's chicken
Tetrazzini. It's pretty good, but I think I used too
much sage."

"LuAnne said it's fabulous."

"LuAnne likes to exaggerate." Rachel jerked

back the covers on her bed and slipped between them.

Abby felt a slight pang. The days of tucking her sister into bed had sped by. She hadn't relished them like she should have. "Good night, Rachel. I love you."

Rachel mumbled something indecipherable beneath her breath. Abby hesitated for a moment longer, then flicked the light switch by the door. "I'll see you in the morning."

"Okay."

She closed the door of her sister's room and leaned back against the wall. A wave of longing overcame her as she thought about her parents. How she wished she could talk to her mother, ask her advice. Rachel's need for independence was growing, and Abby found it increasingly difficult to let go of her own fears and give her sister more freedom. The older Rachel got, the less able Abby was to provide the necessary parental care. This particular argument, about Rachel's desire to stay home by herself, had been brewing for weeks. And Abby was no closer to making a decision.

Incredibly weary, she made her way down the hall to her room. She ate what she could of her meal, went through the mechanical motions of getting ready for bed. By the time she crawled under the sheets, fatigue was squeezing her like a vise. She replayed her conversation with Rachel in her head, searching for clues, probing for anything that might make this transition easier.

But the voice she heard as sleep drew nearer wasn't her sister's. It was deep and husky and seductive, and it said, *I'm doing this for you.*

Two

"Abby?" Marcie Edwards, Abby's assistant, was watching her curiously two days later. "Earth to Abby."

Abby blinked. "Oh, sorry, Marcie. I guess I'm a little distracted."

"You could say that." Marcie leaned back in the chair across from Abby's desk and regarded her with a frank stare. "In fact, you could say you haven't exactly been yourself since you got back from San Francisco."

Abby winced. That much was true. Since her head-on collision with Ethan Maddux, she'd been hard-pressed to concentrate on business. "You noticed."

Marcie's eyebrows lifted. "Yesterday you asked me four times if I'd sent the contract to the caterer."

Abby dropped her pencil onto her desk with a sigh. "You ought to fire me."

That won a slight laugh. "As if. This place would go to hell in a handbasket without you."

"If I don't get my act together, it might anyway." Abby pushed aside the stack of papers on her desk. Among them were several pink message slips from Harrison's relatives. News was beginning to spread about the possible takeover of MDS, and the Montgomery clan was starting to panic. Abby reminded herself that while she could offer them empathy, how Harrison ran his family and, to a certain extent, how he ran his company were none of her business. "All right," she told Marcie, "what have we got on the schedule today?"

"You're supposed to confirm the hotel contract. I think you should call Hector and talk to him about the setup. There's some confusion about the union contract and how it's affected by the caterers needing to do their own table prep."

Abby nodded. "Okay. Have we got a report from Drysdale about the response rate?"

Marcie thumbed through the folder in her lap. She produced the report and passed it to Abby. "We have four hundred and fifty confirmed so far. We're way ahead of last year."

Abby scanned the report. As usual, their greatest response was coming from their $1,000-plus donors. "We've only sold three corporate tables."

"Roland is making phone calls this week. That'll

pick up once he contacts everyone personally."

"Good." Abby looked up from the report. "Is this my copy?"

"Yep."

She found the appropriate file folder in her drawer and inserted the report. "I've got to make some time this afternoon to do some calling myself. I talked to the administrator at Leland Ridge last night, and she's getting hassled by the VA hospital in Champlain."

"Big surprise there." Marcie rolled her eyes. "We've had problems with them since that new guy took over."

"I may need to go out there for a visit. We'll see."

"If you ask me, I think you should just be able to offer a gentle reminder that we give them over a million a year to make sure certain needs get met."

"Some people don't respond to subtlety." People like Ethan Maddux, Abby thought wryly. She glanced momentarily at the picture of her parents on her desk. "Dad used to say, 'Some people are determined not to give you the option of using diplomacy. They want you to go straight to artillery.' "

"Well, that definitely seems to be the case here. I don't know what else we're supposed to do, short of threatening him."

"Get me his number, and I'll set up a site visit." Abby leaned back in her chair. "Anything else?"

"One other thing." Marcie frowned. "Sorry, but I tried to prevent this."

"What?"

"Deirdre Montgomery is coming in today. She has some ideas she wants to discuss with you about the fund-raiser."

Abby groaned. As a favor to Harrison, she had agreed to let his sister Deirdre serve as honorary chairperson of the event. Coming off her fifth divorce, Deirdre was feeling a little fragile, Harrison had told Abby. The title, he'd said, would give her self-esteem a boost.

As far as Abby and her staff could tell, Deirdre's self-esteem had gone from launch pad to orbit in record time. Within days of receiving the invitation, Deirdre had descended on the office with a list of demands—including an office where she could conduct her "duties." Abby had taken the matter to Harrison, who had asked her to be indulgent. Against her better judgment, she'd succumbed.

Though Abby generally liked Harrison's sister, she realized that the power had gone to the woman's head. As Deirdre's demands had escalated, Abby's patience had waned. "What does she want this time?" Abby asked.

"Something about the entertainment. I don't know. I try not to listen too closely to what she's saying."

"Me either," Abby concurred. "When is she coming in?"

"At one."

"All right. Call upstairs and ask Ellen if Harrison is free to join us for the meeting."

Marcie snorted. "Like he would. He doesn't want to be around the woman either."

"Yeah, well, he created this problem for us, so he can solve it."

Three hours later, Abby frowned at Deirdre Montgomery and made a mental note to wring Harrison's neck at the first opportunity. "I understand why you'd see it that way, Deirdre, but this is—"

"Abigail." Deirdre leaned forward in her chair and pinned Abby with a hard stare. "Am I or am I not the chairperson for this event?"

"I've explained that," Abby said, trying not to grit her teeth. Ethan Maddux might not appreciate hearing it, but he definitely had some personality traits he'd inherited from the Montgomerys. His aunt was just as irascible and inflexible as he was.

Deirdre pursed her lips. "And I explained to Harrison that I was not going to take this job if it was merely some title with no responsibilities. For God's sake, Abby, my name is on this foundation. Surely you can see why I have an interest in making this event spectacular."

Turning it into a spectacle was more like it, Abby thought irritably. "I'm not arguing that," she said, keeping her voice calm. "I'm just saying that I'm not sure you understand the solemnity of the occasion. We've always—"

"I know, I know. This is the way you've always done it. I just want to bring a little spice into the thing."

"Donors who are paying fifteen thousand dollars for corporate tables expect a certain level of . . . dignity."

Deirdre frowned. "If I were forking over fifteen thousand—"

"It would be fifteen thousand of my money," Harrison said smoothly from the doorway. "Hello, Deirdre."

His sister started to stand, but Harrison held out his hand. "Don't get up." He glanced at Abby. "Feeling any ill effects from your trip to San Francisco?"

Abby studied him through narrowed eyes. This was the second time since her return from California that Harrison had mentioned the trip. As far as everyone on her staff knew, she'd made the trip to meet with two of the foundation's high-dollar donors—which she had, the same day she'd met with Ethan. Harrison's interest in the trip wasn't necessarily unusual. He generally took a personal interest in the workings of the foundation. But there was something she couldn't quite decipher in his usually benign expression—something that told her he at least suspected she was hiding something from him.

"Not too bad," she said carefully.

He looked at her for a few seconds, then took the seat next to Deirdre. "Now," he said smoothly, his implacable façade back in place, "let's talk about this business with the banquet."

Ethan settled into his first-class seat on the return flight from Prague. Irritated and exhausted after a grueling four days, he admitted that he had no one to blame but himself for the extent of his frustration. He'd been unable to take his mind off Abby Lee. That wasn't like him. He never had trouble focusing, but since his arrival in Prague, he'd found himself plagued with memories of their brief encounter. Mostly he thought about the way she'd looked at him when he'd told her about his past with Harrison. She'd looked simultaneously irritated and empathetic. He wasn't sure how she'd managed that, but he hadn't been able to shake the image.

The e-mail indicator beeped on his laptop, attracting his attention. He accessed the waiting message with a few clicks. At the name on the sender ID, his eyebrows lifted. While in Prague, he'd contacted an investigator friend in Chicago, asking for some general background information about Abby and how she'd come to work for Harrison. Ethan had made a habit in past years of keeping a more-than-casual interest in his father's business and personal lives. Though Abby and her work with the Montgomery Foundation, were not entirely unfamiliar to him, he'd wanted to know more. He hadn't expected an answer this quickly. He opened the message.

Ethan,

Generally as you suspected. Went to work for Montgomery ten years ago. Promoted to Foundation Director two years later. Sister Rachel is thirteen. Parents ran a restaurant on the waterfront. Died in still unsolved murder. Harrison hired her two weeks later. I'll brief you when I have more.

Ethan frowned and reread the message. It was scant, not at all like Charlie's usual reports. A basic, bare-bones kind of report with one tantalizing piece of information that piqued his interest. Unsolved murder. Harrison hired her two weeks later. The news was simultaneously perplexing and intriguing. He sent a response to Charlie, issuing a couple of specific instructions, then switched off the laptop with a shake of his head.

He was too damned tired, he told himself, to let Abby Lee keep him from getting a well-deserved rest as his plane crossed the Atlantic Ocean. He did manage to fall asleep quickly. But he dreamed of Abby's hair and a pencil with a chewed eraser.

* * *

A week after her trip to San Francisco, Abby put her pencil down on her desk so she could bury her head in her hands. A throbbing headache had started at the nape of her neck that morning and worked its way around to her temples.

She'd known things were bad. She never would have gone to see Ethan if she hadn't suspected how desperate Harrison's situation was. She'd been getting calls for weeks—from his board, his stockholders, and his family—begging her to reason with him.

Trouble was, nobody seemed to agree on what was reasonable.

A solid majority of his board wanted him to resign. If he didn't do it voluntarily, they'd soon demand it. There were stockholders calling for a buyout, while others were demanding that Harrison fend off the takeover bid his competitors had appeared to launch several weeks ago. Stock prices were slipping, and most of Harrison's family were beginning to worry that the Montgomery purse was about to be tightened.

So she hadn't been completely naïve, but nothing had prepared her for this.

Harrison needed a miracle.

In the week since her trip, Abby had spent what available time she had pulling together the reports and financial statements for Harrison's sprawling corporate interests. Though she was no expert, her long tenure at the company gave her a broad understanding of its inner workings. The Montgomery Foundation, which she ran with a small hand-selected staff, operated completely independently of Montgomery Data Systems. That had isolated her from most of the grim news about the company's financial outlook. The foundation's nonprofit status ensured a certain degree of separation.

But she'd learned more about MDS and its internal structure in the past week than she'd ever wanted to know. With an employee base of nearly six thousand workers in three countries, MDS had an interest in half a dozen other technology firms. Harrison had gambled big, and recklessly, on a couple of technological innovations. The shifting market had left him behind, and now his third-generation empire teetered on the edge of a hostile takeover.

The company he'd inherited from his autocratic and unforgiving father was crumbling. And while Ethan was right when he said the buyout wouldn't leave Harrison destitute, the cost to his pride was more than the old man could afford. Abby was sure of that.

She leaned back in her leather chair and turned to survey the view from her eighteenth-floor window. Harrison had saved her life once. She'd never forgotten that. So how in the world was she supposed to tell him that she'd failed to save his?

When the buzzer on her intercom rang, she was tempted to ignore it. The last thing she needed was another member of Harrison's histrionic family demanding that she save them from the realities of fiscal ruin. After several moments had passed, she reluctantly pushed the button. Harrison had always been available to her family, and Abby had made a lifelong habit of returning the favor. "What is it, Marcie?"

"Abby, there's a call for you on line four. I think it's a prank. But he's really insistent."

"Who is it?"

"Well, he says he's Ethan Maddux."

Abby's eyes widened. She hadn't really expected him to call. And given the near-legendary proportions of his feud with Harrison, it was no wonder her ever-efficient assistant hadn't believed him. Abby almost hoped Marcie had hassled him as only Marcie knew how. "I'll take it," she said.

"Are you sure?"

"Yes." She pulled one of her clip earrings off and reached for the receiver. Gathering her calm, she pushed the button. "Hello, Mr. Maddux."

"You didn't think I'd call, did you?"

Blunt as ever, she noted. Abby twirled her pencil on her desk. "Frankly, no."

"I always do what I say. You'll learn that."

That sounded like a challenge, so she let it pass. "How was Prague?"

"Wet. It rained the whole time I was there."

"Oh. I'm sorry."

"Don't be. I was tied up in meetings. I barely noticed."

"When did you get back?"

"This morning."

Abby's fingers stilled on the pencil. If she hadn't expected his call, she certainly hadn't expected him to move her to the front of his back-in-the-States agenda.

"Ms. Lee," he said, his voice sounding simultaneously impatient and commanding. "I've got a full day today. I don't have a lot of time right now."

"I understand. I asked for ten minutes, and I can tell you by way of—"

"Not now." She could practically hear the gears turning in his head. "I'm free for dinner tonight."

"Dinner?" Abby had the vague feeling that she was tumbling down Alice's proverbial rabbit hole.

"Yes. Even I stop to eat, Ms. Lee."

Dear Lord, was that a joke? "Um, yes, I guess you do."

"And after a day of airport food, I plan to enjoy the experience. There's a great steak house down the street from my office."

"You're in San Francisco."

"Yes. What if I make reservations for eight?"

"I'm in Chicago," she said, her jaw starting to ache from grinding her back teeth.

"I'll send you a ticket. You can pick it up at Midway at your convenience. Or O'Hare if you'd rather. Your choice."

"I can't fly out there tonight, Mr. Maddux."

"It's the best time for me," he insisted.

"Well, it's not good for me." She forcibly relaxed her grip on the receiver. "I can't."

"Why not? Harrison got you tied up?"

There was nothing in Ethan's tone to suggest more than a polite inquiry, but Abby still bristled. "None of your damned business."

If she hadn't known better, she would have sworn she heard him smile. "No, I don't suppose it is. Sorry. I've got jet lag. I'm cranky. And talking about Harrison always makes me surly."

"Then why did you call me?"

"I told you, I'm doing this for you."

Abby drew a calming breath. "Mr. Maddux—"

"Let me explain that comment before you misinterpret it." The creak of his chair traveled across the phone line. She could easily picture him leaning back in that massive leather desk chair and propping his loafer-clad feet on the polished sheen of his ebony desk. "Despite what you might think," he said softly, "I have an enormous amount of respect for you."

Abby frowned. "Why? Because I was foolish enough to think you might be willing to help an old man who, for all his faults, took you in when you needed him to?"

"No." The gentle tone in his voice startled her. She'd expected fury. "It wasn't foolish."

"It felt foolish."

"Desperate, maybe. I'll give you that."

"That makes me feel better."

"As far as I'm concerned, your motivation carried weight with me."

"Motivation?"

"You did it because of your loyalty to Harrison. I might consider such loyalty misplaced, but that doesn't mean I don't admire you for it."

Abby traced the outline of her nameplate with her index finger. "Since when did you start admiring desperate women? I'm sure you meet your fair share."

His chuckle tumbled over her nerves with the soothing effect of hundred-year-old cognac. "There's desperation and then there's stupidity. I wouldn't put you in the latter category."

"Everyone who knows I went to see you does."

"Including Harrison?"

"I haven't told him yet," she admitted.

"Wise."

"Probably."

"Definitely. And that's another thing you have in your favor. You know how to admit that you're over your head. Harrison could learn a thing or two from you."

Abby pushed the nameplate away. "Look, I'm not really sure what you're getting at here, but I'm not going to get into a conversation about Harrison. I'm not comfortable with that."

"I can certainly understand why."

She let the comment pass. He had his reasons to be bitter, and as far as she could tell, they were good ones. "Look, Mr. Maddux, this is a really difficult day for me. I've got a major fund-raiser coming up this weekend, and I—"

"I won't keep you much longer," he promised. "Just let me make a proposition."

Her eyebrows lifted. "A proposition?"

"If the obstacle to dinner tonight is your sister, Rachel, then bring her along."

The question made her flesh tingle. "How do you know about Rachel?"

"I do my homework. How old is she—twelve?"

"Thirteen." Abby frowned. "I don't think—"

"Don't worry. I'm not invading your privacy. I just make it my business to keep informed about Harrison's life."

"Which means keeping informed about *my* life?"

He didn't miss the sharp note in her voice. "Put yourself in my place, Ms. Lee."

"I couldn't," she said honestly. "The Harrison you know and the Harrison I know are two entirely different men."

"And you think your Harrison is worth saving?"

Abby let her eyes drift shut. "I think it will kill him if he loses the business."

"Then convince me," Ethan said softly, the challenge unmistakable.

"I can't come to San Francisco tonight—not even if I bring Rachel. Tomorrow's a school day." Did that sound as ridiculous to him as it did to her? As if the only thing preventing her from flying two thousand miles to have dinner with the man was her sister's first-period class.

"Don't you think a day in San Francisco would be just as educational as a day at school?" His chair creaked again. She heard his feet drop to the floor with a loud thump.

Abby grimaced. "Why are we even having this discussion? If you want to meet with me in person"—she flipped open her calendar—"then how about next week? I could do it on Thursday."

"I can do it tonight."

"Are you always like this?"

"Like what?"

"Relentless."

"Absolutely," he assured her without a hint of remorse. "It makes me good at what I do."

"It makes you annoying."

"There are certain advantages to, ah, focus. In fact, I've heard it said that it's one of my assets."

Her breath came out in an irritated huff. "By whom?"

"Women."

Abby was glad he couldn't see the sudden flush on her skin. Blast the man. He was toying with her—and he was too damned good at it. Too late, she realized that her nervousness was making her fiddle with the top button of her blouse. She'd worked hard to break that habit, and now she forced her fingers to be still. "Look, Mr. Maddux, even if I wanted to, I couldn't possibly—"

"What if I meet you instead?"

"Excuse me?"

"What if I meet you instead? You can't come here, so I'll come there. I hadn't planned on the travel time in my schedule, but what the hell. I can catch up on my paperwork on the plane."

"I don't think—"

"*Now* what's the problem?" He was starting to sound exasperated. "Got a date?"

"That's not—"

"You're asking a lot of me, Ms. Lee. The least you can do is budge on a scheduling issue."

"You aren't—"

"If you have a date, break it. I'm sure he'll understand."

"I don't have a date," she spat out before she thought better of it.

"Ah."

Abby didn't even attempt to decipher that remark. "As it happens, my sister has a cooking class this afternoon. She has one every Tuesday afternoon, which I don't suppose your surveillance reports revealed about the details of my life. She cooks with a chef at four-thirty on Tuesdays, and she and I eat dinner together at six, after her class. So I can't break *that* date. And I don't even want to."

"With a chef?" he probed. "No kidding?"

God, the man was insufferable. He actually managed to sound interested. "Rachel's got kind of a flare for gourmet cooking," Abby said, out of some perverse desire to overburden him with information. "She wants to open her own restaurant."

"Like your parents had?" he asked.

Abby swallowed. So he knew that as well. There were few holes in his information, it seemed. "Yes. And actually, she's quite good."

"Good. There's nothing like an excellent meal to chase away the lingering effects of jet lag. I'll look forward to it."

"You can't come."

"Why not?"

"Because you can't." She realized her voice had risen several decibels, and reached for her patience. "Because you can't," she said again, more quietly.

"Ms. Lee, does it occur to you that I'm offering to fly halfway across the country and give you my undivided attention for the bulk of an entire evening? Do you have any idea how much people usually pay for that privilege?"

She did, and it was true that she'd have much longer than the allotted ten minutes to plead her case. A case that needed Ethan Maddux's magic touch. "Why are you doing this to me?"

"I'm not doing it *to* you," he insisted. "I'm doing it *for* you. I told you that."

"I don't think—"

"That's my final offer, Abigail." His use of her first name startled her. It sounded strangely warm, wrapped in the husky tone of his voice. "Take it or leave it."

She let several seconds tick by while she gazed at the jumble of reports on her desk. Harrison Montgomery, a quiet voice reminded her, had saved her life. Surely that was worth one dinner with Ethan Maddux. She fought an apprehensive shiver as she shifted the phone to her other ear, positive that he had an ulterior motive. No way was he going to all this trouble simply because she'd had the nerve to ask. Clearly, he wanted something.

And despite the insistent clanging of warning bells in her head, she couldn't resist finding out what it was. "All right," she said at last. "We'll see you at six. Don't be late." She hung up without bothering to give him directions to her house. Let his informants find that out for him.

Three

Several hours later, Abby warily watched Ethan across her kitchen table. He looked absurdly at ease with his suit jacket and tie slung over the back of a chair and his pristine white shirt cuffs rolled back to expose tanned forearms. He was happily devouring a second helping of Barbecued Salmon Gravlax while he plied Rachel with questions about the recipe. Abby took the opportunity to picture him wearing an apron and cooking. It made her feel better.

"The hard part," Rachel was saying, "was cutting the salmon. Monsieur Billaud makes it looks so easy."

"It tastes incredible," Ethan assured her.

"Thanks," she said wistfully, "but it's supposed to look good too. Monsieur Billaud says that presentation is half the success or failure of a dish."

Ethan slanted Abby an amused look. "Spoken like a true Frenchman," he drawled.

Rachel shook her head. "He's very good. His restaurant is one of the most popular in town."

Abby folded her hands on the table and tried hard not to be annoyed with him. Why did he have to be so damned charming? "Rachel's been studying with him for over a year."

"Yeah." Rachel nodded. "Next year I hope I can take lessons from Pio Baldovino, but I don't think Uncle Harrison knows him as well as he does Monsieur Billaud."

Abby noted the slight lift of Ethan's eyebrows at Rachel's mention of Harrison, but he said nothing. Rachel propped her chin on her hand and continued. "Monsieur Billaud says that if I do well enough in Baldovino's institute competition, I might have a chance."

"Competition?" Ethan pressed.

"Uh-huh. Every year Baldovino hosts a charity event where chefs compete for prizes."

"Most of them represent restaurants," Abby added.

Rachel shrugged. "It's very competitive. And everybody's older than me."

"Harrison agreed to sponsor her," Abby told Ethan. "But she has to accrue enough hours to qualify."

Ethan looked at her inquiringly. "How do you

get hours when you don't work in a restaurant?"

"Good question," Rachel said. "But actually, Abby and I figured it out. I'm doing the baking for the Montgomery Foundation's Memorial Day event and assisting the caterer for the annual fund-raising ball."

"Monsieur Billaud has agreed to account for her hours," Abby explained.

Ethan finished the last of his meal, then set his napkin down. "If it's all as good as this, I'm sure you'll do well," he told Rachel. "I can't remember the last time I had a better meal."

Rachel beamed at him. "Thanks. Want dessert?"

"You bet." He rose from his chair with fluid grace and reached for the plates. "I'll clear, you serve."

From the corner of her eye Abby noted her sister's near swoon. Rachel had been falling under his spell from the moment the man walked in the door. Which, she thought irritably, would leave *her* with a hearty mess to clean up once he took his charm and sophistication back to California. The last thing she needed in Rachel's developing war for too much independence too soon was a lethal crush on a man like Ethan.

Abby placed a gently restraining hand on Rachel's shoulder as she got up. "Sit, Rach. I'll get it."

"It's in the refrigerator," Rachel told her. Her

gaze strayed to Ethan, who was putting dishes in the sink. Her eyes lingered, Abby noted, on his rear end. Not that she blamed her. He looked every bit as compelling from that angle as he had seated at the table. "I already put it on a plate," Rachel said.

Ethan continued a steady stream of casual conversation, politely answering Rachel's questions about his trip to Prague and what kind of food they'd served at the conference. Disaster didn't strike until they were all seated again. Abby had just swallowed a forkful of something rich and excessively chocolate when Rachel pinned Ethan with a shrewd look and asked, "So why do you hate Uncle Harrison so much?"

An uneasy silence descended on the kitchen. Abby raised her eyebrows and slowly slid the fork from her lips. Ethan leaned back in his chair and asked himself, for the tenth time that evening, just what the hell he'd been thinking of in making this trip. He wasn't interested in Harrison's business or his financial disaster. He especially wasn't interested in expending time and energy trying to dig the Montgomerys out of a hole of their own making.

He was physically and mentally beat.

Functioning on less than three hours of sleep and suffering a jet-lag hangover, he needed a hot shower and a soft bed. He flicked a glance at Abby, who was watching him closely. But for reasons he didn't even want to consider, he hadn't been able to resist seeing her, not even when she'd forced his hand by making him fly to Chicago.

On the flight, he'd carefully considered his strategy. He'd find out exactly who Abigail Lee was, what she did—or didn't do—for Harrison Montgomery, and then he'd inform her that hell would freeze over before he'd help bail out Harrison's company. He'd counted on her trying to change his mind. He'd counted on being tempted.

He had not counted on being quietly seduced by the patience in her gaze or the way she waited for him to make the first move. Nor had he planned on the decided effect that the sight of her clad in a faded sweatshirt and worn jeans would have on his travel-weary body.

And he certainly hadn't counted on an interrogation from her younger sister. Carefully, Ethan set his fork down and looked at Rachel. "I do not hate Harrison Montgomery." Despised, yes. Resented, maybe. But hate—that was too strong a word to describe the absolute empty feeling Ethan had when he thought about his father. Hate required too much passion. And Ethan had steadfast rules against excessive passion.

Rachel's eyebrows drew together in confusion. "Everyone says you do. Even Abby."

Abby gave her a sharp look. "Rachel—"

"Well, you do," her sister interrupted. "And I talked to Carlton." At the mention of his cousin, she looked at Ethan again. "And he says you and Uncle Harrison practically killed each other once."

Ethan quirked an eyebrow. "I suppose no one has ever told you that Montgomerys have a tendency to exaggerate."

"Well, yeah," Rachel went on, "but Carlton says things got really, really ugly and Uncle Harrison told you that you could never come back. I mean—"

Abby broke in. "It's none of our business, Rachel."

Rachel shrugged. "I just wanted to know, is all. I mean, what did he do to you anyway?"

"It's a long story," Ethan said.

Rachel frowned. "He's really a nice guy, you know?"

"You think so?" Ethan sat back in his chair.

"Sure. He kind of takes care of us."

"Rachel, I don't think—"

"Oh, come on, Abby." Rachel twirled her fork between her fingers. "He gave Abby a job after our parents got killed. Did you know that?"

Ethan nodded. His silver gaze now rested steadily on Abby's face. Her color was heightening. "Yes."

"She couldn't *do* anything."

Abby's patience seemed to snap. "Cut it out, Rachel. That's not true."

"Well, I mean, it's not like you could type or

something. You told me yourself you had no idea why he hired you."

"He felt sorry for me, that's why."

Rachel snorted. "I guess so." She looked at Ethan. "Abby had been interviewing all that day."

"He's not interested," Abby told her sister.

"Yes, I am," Ethan insisted.

Rachel took the cue. "It was pouring rain and she was late for her appointment with Uncle Harrison's personnel manager."

"I missed the El," Abby explained. "And I didn't have enough cash for a cab."

"She had to walk fifteen blocks up Michigan."

Ethan folded his hands on his stomach and studied her. She was uncomfortable, but hadn't tried to shut the story down again. "I remember the summer thunderstorms here. Frog stranglers, my mother used to call them."

"This one came off the lake," Abby said. "I was drenched. I had mud splashed all over my legs, and runs in my stockings. By the time I got to MDS, the security guard had left for the night." She shook her head with a slight laugh. "And it's a good thing too. If he'd seen me, he'd have thought I was a vagrant. Someone exited the building, and I slipped through the door so I could dry off in the lobby. I just sat down and started crying."

"Uncle Harrison found her like that," Rachel supplied.

Ethan waited. Abby continued. "He probably stopped to talk to me to make sure I wasn't planning to sleep in the building that night."

Rachel pulled her knees up to her chest and wrapped her arms around them. "Whatever. That's when he gave you a job."

"In the mail room," Abby said.

"And Abby went to work for him, and thanks to Uncle Harrison, I didn't get put in foster care."

Ethan's temples had begun to throb. "How generous of him."

Rachel nodded enthusiastically. "So now Abby runs his foundation, and he kind of, you know, looks out for us. It's like having a father, only not."

Ethan knew that feeling well. Abby laid her hand on Rachel's arm. "Rachel, I think that's enough."

"I just wanted to know what the big deal is between you," Rachel told Ethan again. She shrugged. "I mean, after what Carlton told me, I was expecting you to be a real jerk."

"Rachel!"

"Well, I was," she told her sister. She looked at Ethan again. "But you seem nice enough, and he's not like an ogre or something. It just seems weird, is all."

Ethan had to agree with her there. The benefactor of the Lee family bore little or no resemblance to the hard, distant man he remembered. He thought the matter over, then made a characteristically quick decision. "I'll make a deal with you," he told Rachel. Abby gave him a shrewd look.

Rachel's eyes brightened. "Okay."

"If I can have dinner here again, say next Tuesday night, we'll talk about Harrison." He let his gaze rest on Abby. "I'll tell you the whole story."

"Cool."

Abby frowned. "I don't think—"

Ethan cut in smoothly. "I'll need at least a week to go over the figures. I'm assuming you have them for me?"

She nodded.

"It's settled, then." He glanced at Rachel. "Dinner next Tuesday, and we'll see how many of Harrison's problems we can solve."

Abby's jaw clenched so tight he thought he might hear her teeth crack. "Rachel, do you have homework?" she asked.

Her sister gave her a cross look. "Is that your way of telling me to go to my room?"

"I just want to know if you have homework."

"Yes."

"Then you should go do it. It's getting late."

"What if I want to listen to you and Ethan?"

Abby said nothing. She merely stared at her sister for long seconds until Rachel made a frustrated sound and rose to her feet. "Fine." She scooped up a couple of plates. "But next week I'm staying until the end." She slid the dishes into the sink. "Next week we're having trout almondine. Is that okay with you?" she asked Ethan.

"Yes."

"Great. I'm pretty sure I couldn't have talked Monsieur Billaud out of it anyway. He's on this seafood kick." She turned to go. "Nice meeting you," she told Ethan.

"Nice meeting you, Rachel."

"See ya." She pushed through the swinging door. It glided shut with a swoosh in her wake.

Abby rose from the table and finished gathering the last few dishes. "I'm sorry she put you on the spot like that."

A smile played at the corners of his mouth. "If she decides to give up cooking, she can always consider journalism."

"Or espionage. She interrogates better than anyone I've ever known."

"I wasn't uncomfortable."

Abby shrugged but didn't respond. "You asked about the numbers. There's a file on the coffee table in the living room." She indicated the door with a tilt of her head. "What you need is in there."

He studied her for a minute as she tidied up the kitchen. She seemed tense, and unless he missed his guess, also anxious. This wasn't the confident woman who'd come to see him in San Francisco. She was scared.

Abby continued to busy herself at the counter. "I'll be there in a minute," she told him without meeting his gaze.

He hesitated, then stood. He'd lived with Harrison long enough to recognize a dismissal when he heard one.

An hour later, Ethan glanced at Abby over the top of the page he'd been trying to read for the past five minutes. She pretended to inspect the room, to look, he supposed, at anything but him as he surveyed the evidence of Harrison's pending financial ruin. Deliberately, he set the stack of papers aside.

He was about to make an irrevocable choice. And he didn't want Harrison's financial statements cluttering his mind. "There's something we need to talk about," he said carefully.

She took her time meeting his gaze. Slow and easy, deliberate and controlled, he noted. Something about her made most of the women he knew seem a little crass. He had a sudden vision of always-perfectly-dressed, always-perfectly-groomed Pamela. Abby made his ex-fiancée seem harsh around the edges. Though Pamela wouldn't have been caught dead in jeans and a sweatshirt, Abby wore them with an unpracticed elegance, which told him, somehow, that she'd have lace on underneath. She was that kind of woman—full of secrets.

"You don't have to sugarcoat this for me," she assured him. "Things are bad, aren't they?"

"You could say that."

She pressed her lips together in grim acceptance. Full lips. Lips he'd thought about innumerable times while in Prague. "I knew it." She sank more deeply into the heavily cushioned sofa. "It's disastrous."

He tapped the report with his index finger. "From what I've seen, that's an understatement."

"Is there anything . . ."

"I can't tell you that after an hour of looking over the numbers. I told you that I need a week."

"I understand."

He tapped one long finger on the arm of his chair as he watched her. He was trying to figure out just what it was about the woman that caused him to seriously consider having anything to do with Harrison's life. "If I did decide to do this, I'd have to give it my full attention," he said carefully.

"I'm aware of that."

"Can you give me a reason why I should?"

She swallowed, and her lips parted slightly. Ethan considered that a very good sign. She wasn't nervous, just aware of the undercurrent that ran between them. He'd suspected as much but hadn't had the chance, until now, to really watch for the signs. He'd kept his attention deliberately on Rachel during dinner, not wanting to bait Abby until he had her alone.

"You told Rachel you'd come back next week for dinner," Abby pointed out.

"I was seduced"—he deliberately cradled the word—"by that chocolate thing."

Her lips twitched in that charming little half smile that tickled nerve endings. How long, he wondered, would he have to know her before she'd smile that way when she thought about him? "She's good."

"She's excellent."

"If it makes you feel any better, you aren't the only one to cave in when faced with one of Rachel's desserts. I've made some pretty major concessions while she was waving a plate in front of my nose."

"Hmm."

"She does this cheesecake thing that's out of this world."

She was warming to the topic, he realized. When Abby was particularly lost in a subject, she used her hands a lot, as if she were manipulating the air in front of her to help make a point.

"Good?" he asked.

She rolled her eyes in exaggerated bliss. "God, you can't imagine. I think I put on four pounds that day."

His gaze dropped to the lush swell of her hips. The faded denim hugged generous womanly curves that made his hands tingle. There wasn't a sharp angle on her.

She chuckled, then continued. "Last year Harrison was going to see if he could arrange some lessons for her with a pastry chef. I had to threaten him within an inch of his—" She stopped suddenly and dropped her hands into her lap. "Sorry. I get a little carried away."

"You're very proud of her."

"Yes. It hasn't been . . . easy."

"I can imagine."

"I wish she'd known Mother and Dad."

The wistful note in her voice did Ethan in. Courage, depth, passion, grace; Abby was the complete package. And at that precise moment, he realized with a bit of a shock, he wanted her to long for him so deeply that she'd have that same note in her voice when she thought about him.

He didn't even dare take the time to analyze the intensity of his desire. For the space of a few heartbeats, he let restraint war heavily with it. Hunger was beginning to surge through the vault. Anger he was used to. Exhilaration, passion, even desire had occasionally gotten the better of him, but this gnawing hunger was new. And if he took the time to think about it, it would scare the hell out of him. He was tired, he told himself, and Abby represented something he'd left behind when he'd walked away from Harrison Montgomery. Naturally, he found her intriguing. This explanation satisfied him. He thrust the anxious feeling aside with the determination and skilled precision of a knight dropping his visor into place as he prepared to charge into battle. "You're nervous," he said softly, "aren't you?"

"Wouldn't you be?"

Did he mistake the slight intake of breath? "Depends."

"Six thousand people are about to lose their jobs. If I can't convince you to help—" She was clutching her fingers in her lap now. "It's a lot of pressure.

"I'm not talking about Harrison or his company. I think you know that."

"I don't—"

"Do I make you nervous, Abby?" he asked quietly.

"No."

No hesitation there, he saw. He raised an eyebrow. She shook her head. "You look like you don't believe me," she told him. "You don't make me nervous."

"That's a very good thing."

"I'd say the feeling I have is more like the slowest and fattest gazelle in the herd who knows the panther just woke up and realized he was hungry."

His lips twitched. "I'm not sure I'd have used 'fattest' and 'slowest' . . ."

"So you're more diplomatic than I am. How am I supposed to respond to statements like 'I'm doing this for you?' "

She hadn't forgotten. He put that piece of information in the Positive column of his growing balance sheet of this conversation. "You didn't actually think I'd do it for Harrison?"

"I don't know what I thought."

"You're probably the only person alive who could stand the man for as long as you have," he told her. "I'll admit that I'd kind of like to know what the attraction is."

She didn't flinch. He'd spent the two-hour flight to Chicago mentally ticking off all the reasons that he shouldn't do this. Those reasons had started to crumble the moment she'd opened the door and let him into this warm haven of her life. They now lay in ruin around his Italian leather shoes.

Abby shifted on the couch so she could tuck her bare feet beneath her jeans-clad legs. She slipped one of those honey-blond curls behind her ear. Every time she did that, it made him jealous. He'd been wanting to get his hands into her hair since he'd seen it confined by a pencil with a chewed-off eraser.

"It's not like I don't know the man has his flaws, you know."

"I don't think you're that naïve."

"But it's like Rachel told you tonight. After Mother and Dad were killed, it took months for the insurance to pay out. If Harrison hadn't hired me, social services would have sent Rachel away to foster care."

"How did you make your way from the mail room to running the Montgomery Foundation?"

A slight flush stained her cheeks, but the angry glint in her eyes told him fury had caused it, not embarrassment. "I worked hard. I did everything anyone asked me to, and more. I spent as much time as I could learning what MDS does, who we do it with, and how we do it. I studied, I did a lot of jobs nobody else wanted to do, and my managers appreciated it."

"No doubt."

"By the time Harrison moved me upstairs, I had already held managerial positions in three departments. When he started the Montgomery Foundation, I was naturally excited by the project."

The foundation, Ethan knew, supported a number of different charitable ventures, the most notable of which provided financial support, health care, and a variety of social services for Chicago's veterans. Abby's father, Ethan's research had told him, was a veteran of the Vietnam War. Before his death, he'd owned and operated a well-loved restaurant on the waterfront. The unique character of the place had made it a natural gathering spot for veterans to swap war stories and memories.

Abby had virtually grown up in the restaurant, helping her mother cook and her father serve and entertain. After her parents' death, their vast network of friends had responded to Abby and Rachel's loss with emotional, financial, and practical help. One friend had arranged Abby's fated interview with Harrison Montgomery. Ethan could well imagine why she'd warmed to the idea of being a part of Harrison's benevolence efforts.

Abby continued. "I asked to be brought on board with the foundation project, and Harrison accommodated me. I worked under the original director, Kaitlin Moses, for a year and a half before I succeeded her. Kaitlin went to Washington to work in the development office for the United Way. By the time she left MDS, no one was better prepared to take over the foundation than I was." Her hands had clenched the side of the chair. "And what ever else I do or don't do for Harrison is no one's damned business."

Ethan felt the blood begin to pound in his temples. He'd come here tonight prepared for many things. He'd come with an agenda and a plan, and with the sure knowledge that he wanted Abigail Lee. He had also come determined to learn the truth about her relationship with Harrison Montgomery—a relationship heavily rumored to be sexual. But Abby had wide, innocent brown-gold eyes. And Ethan couldn't make sense of a woman who looked guileless yet conducted a ten-year affair with a man like Harrison. He kept his tone deliberately bland when he said, "It's not like the man doesn't have a history of seducing his employees, you know."

She stared at him for a minute. When she said nothing, he bit out, "My mother worked for him once, too."

Her face registered a momentary shock, then softened. "I'm sorry." Her eyes mirrored the sentiment. "I didn't think. I've spent a long time fighting the urge to defend myself against people who don't know what they're talking about. At least you have a decent reason to be suspicious."

He waited. She studied him. In the distance, he could hear the relentless drumming of Rachel's stereo drifting down from her room. The sound matched the throbbing of his head. His hands were fisted against his thighs as he waited for her to say more. She was right. It was none of his business what she did for the man, but he couldn't fight a feeling of repugnance.

"I don't sleep with him," Abby finally announced. "I've never slept with him."

The throbbing in his temples abruptly stopped. He sat perfectly still. The simple statement made him feel like a bastard for dragging it out of her. No, he thought with sudden clarity, she'd made him feel that way for even thinking it in the first place. He'd been the victor in this small contest of wills, but the victory had left a sour taste in his mouth. The woman was tying his guts into knots. "People think you do," he said.

"People are jerks."

"Does it bother you?"

"Sometimes. Mostly only when some creep suggests that I wouldn't have my job unless I'd given Harrison a roll in the sack. That's pretty annoying." She pushed her hair over her shoulder.

"I can see why."

"At least you didn't accuse me so you could drag it out of me."

"Harrison has a way of bringing out the worst in me," he said by way of apology.

She started to reach a hand toward him, then seemed to think better of it. "Look, before I came to see you last week I only had a vague idea of what had happened between you and Harrison. It's like I told you. I tried to discuss it with him a couple of times, but he made it really clear the topic was off limits. And I had *no* idea he'd called you that day."

"It was the first time in several years."

Her gaze shifted to the papers on the coffee table. "If I'd known what you told me . . ."

"You believe it?" he pressed, needing to know.

"I believe that whatever happened, it left you feeling really bitter about him. He might have a few more details to add, but I'm sure the facts are basically true. No one in the family talks about it."

"Except Carlton, obviously."

"Carlton is twenty years old and barely even related to the Montgomerys. Letty is Harrison's sister, but Carlton is her stepson."

"I'm aware of that."

"I seriously doubt he's got a clue what he was talking about. He's a nice enough kid, but sometimes he acts like he knows more than he really does."

"Rachel seemed impressed."

"Rachel is thirteen. She's easily impressed by nice-looking boys these days."

"I can imagine." He watched her fuss with the papers on the table. "But there are any number of the Montgomerys you could have asked. Why didn't you?"

"It wasn't any of my business," she said. Her hands stilled on the papers. "I wanted to know once, so I asked Harrison. He made it pretty clear the topic wasn't open for discussion."

"So you asked me instead."

"You volunteered, if you recall."

"And you took my word for it?"

"Why not? You've got no reason to lie to me."

That statement probably shouldn't have satisfied him like it did, but he chose not to fight the feeling. "I'm glad you see that."

"Either way," she went on, "if I'd known, I might not have come to you. I'm not sure. All I know is, Harrison's in trouble. And if I can help him, I want to. But I can understand why you probably want nothing to do with this."

"So I'm absolved?"

"What difference does it make?" She shrugged. "My opinion hardly matters."

Ethan couldn't quite decipher her meaning, so he didn't try. He stuck with the topic he knew. "Harrison has always known he was never going to live up to his father's expectations. Nobody could have."

"I never met your grandfather."

"Consider yourself fortunate. He ran that entire family like a terrorist. Harrison never had the guts to stand up to the old man. Montgomery Data Systems is the last tangible link he has to him."

She nodded. "He's terrified of failure. I'm sure his father did that to him."

"Montgomery fathers have a way of screwing up their children's lives," Ethan said dryly. "I suppose it's a good thing that none of them stick around for long."

At his mention of the startling Montgomery divorce rate, Abby looked a little sad. "I've never known a group of unhappier people."

"And they're all like that. Even the ones you haven't met." The vast Montgomery clan, in his opinion, should be the poster family for dysfunctionalism. With a few notable exceptions, and usually among the "related-by-marriage" set, they were a colossal group of emotional basket cases.

And when it came to Harrison, Abby was right.

As the leader of the large clan, he had shouldered the behemoth of the Montgomery legacy at a relatively young age. His autocratic and critical father had died at sixty-two, leaving a forty-year-old Harrison his sprawling financial and personal empires.

Harrison had always feared disappointing his father. Losing the business would crush him. Ethan wondered why the idea didn't bring him more pleasure. He realized Abby was watching him expectantly. Something about her hopeful expression urged him to appease her. "Even if I wanted to—" he began, then shrugged. "It's probably too late."

She leaned forward. "Ethan, I know you have every reason to resent the man. He got himself into this mess by making some pretty rotten choices, but I don't think he deserves to lose everything he's worked for. Not if there's a way out."

"What if there isn't?"

"You can find one."

Her rock-solid faith shook Ethan a little. "What makes you think so?"

"Just a hunch." Abby met his gaze with a frankness that stole his breath. He couldn't remember the last time a woman had looked at him with such honest intent. "You could do it if you wanted to."

"And why would I want to?"

Her eyebrows knitted together. "I'm not going to say anything trite about family loyalty, so don't sound so cranky."

He frowned. "I am not cranky."

She ignored that. "There are two reasons I can think of that you might agree to take this on. The first is that you'd relish the idea of finally getting even with Harrison by proving that you can accomplish something he can't. The irony of making him rely on you to save his family business might be too tempting to ignore."

Something about the way she said this made his gut churn. "And the other?" he asked.

"The other reason is because you'd enjoy the challenge. I saw you last week in your office. I watched the way your staff twitters around you—"

"Twitters?"

"Like little drones."

That had him scowling. "My staff will be delighted to know you think they twitter."

She made a funny little motion with her fingers that told him she was definitely mocking him. "You speak, they listen. You command and it's done. Your success is astounding. You've gained international recognition as the tycoon who always delivers. As far as I know, you haven't lost a gamble yet."

"I've lost plenty of them."

"Not in recent memory, and not any that mattered."

He didn't respond. Abby rubbed her palms on her thighs. "I saw it that day in the elevator. You're bored."

"Is that so?" How, he wondered, did she manage to do this to his moods? She could take him from sour to content and back again in the space of a heartbeat.

"Absolutely. It's obvious in the way you talk about what you do. It's all too easy now, and it's lost its thrill. Besides, it's only been, what—a few weeks since your fiancée broke your engagement?"

Something inside him went still. "You know about that?"

"Carlton tells all," she quipped.

"How comforting."

She dismissed his sarcasm with a slight wave of her hand. "Whatever. My point is, it hasn't been that long, and from what I can tell, it didn't even affect you."

"You don't think so?"

"You don't look affected."

"Maybe I'm not the histrionic type."

"Or maybe you were just bored with her as well."

Too close to the mark, he mused. "Either way, it's not really any of your business."

"No," she conceded, "not any more than my relationship with your father is any of yours." She looked at him closely. "Unless, of course, your being here has nothing at all to do with wanting revenge on your father."

Ethan found himself oddly fascinated by the litany. From any other source, it probably would have annoyed him. What squelched his irritation, however, was the sure knowledge that Abby had spent time analyzing him. Lots of time. While he'd been in Prague, distracted by too-frequent memories of her lips and her hair, she'd been in Chicago, clearly distracted by trying to unravel his brain. That effort probably wouldn't have been his first choice, he admitted, but he found it gratifying to know that she, too, had been unable to forget their encounter. Things were definitely looking up. He steepled his fingers under his chin and did his damnedest to hide a smile. "Why do you think I'm here, Abby?"

"I think you're here because the idea of saving MDS challenges you, and nothing has challenged you in a while."

"Is that so?"

She hesitated, then nodded. "Yes."

Her eyelids fluttered when she said that. It was a bewitching little movement, almost imperceptible, and it goaded him quickly past whatever inner impulse had urged him toward caution. He was not a patient man. And he didn't want to wait much longer to see that same expression on her face when she said yes for altogether different reasons.

He leaned back in the chair and studied her through narrowed eyes. "Is it going to shock you to find out you've got this all wrong?"

He sensed, rather than heard, her slight intake of breath. "Wrong?"

"Um." He smoothed a wrinkle from his trouser leg. "Absolutely wrong. My being here has absolutely nothing to do with boredom." On the contrary, he couldn't actually remember the last time he'd felt so alive.

She had started to fidget, as if she knew where this conversation might be headed and desperately wanted to divert it. "There are easier ways to be entertained than to wrap up my business in Prague and then fly halfway across the country to have dinner with you and sift through Harrison's financial records."

"I see."

Oh, she definitely did, he thought. "There's a strictly personal reason why I'm here. I have something you want." He paused. "And you have something I want."

She wet her lips with the tip of her tongue. "I do?"

"Yes." He allowed the silence to stretch between them. Abby remained perfectly still, her gaze locked with his. When he swore he could hear the sound of her heartbeat in the too-still room, he bent forward and whispered, "I want you."

Four

Harrison stood with his back to her. That was never a good sign. Abby could see his reflection in the plate glass. He was staring out the large window of his twentieth-story office at a brooding Chicago sky, and the sky wasn't alone in its bad temper.

Harrison's secretary, Joanna Dugan, had given Abby a sympathetic look as she'd waved her through the front office into Harrison's private suite. Word of her meeting with Ethan was obviously out, and Joanna knew Harrison well enough to know that Abby had little chance of surviving the inevitable confrontation unscathed.

"Have a seat, Abigail," he said without turning to face her.

Abby grimaced and eased into the chair across

from his desk. She'd known the man for ten years
and only one thing put him in this mood. Three
days had passed since Ethan's visit. Three days
since he'd made that extraordinary announcement, then simply picked up the financial statements and walked out of her house. She'd had
three days to worry about what she should do
next; three days to listen to Rachel rhapsodize
over Ethan Maddux; three days to feel her stomach twist into knots every time the phone rang;
three long, horrible days to decide how she was
going to break the news to Harrison Montgomery
that she'd walked into the den of his enemy and
begged for help.

Evidently, someone had done the deed for her.

"I just got off the phone with your sister." Harrison's voice was as calm and smooth as a frozen
pond.

"Oh?"

"Um. She wanted to know if I'd buy a couple of
raffle tickets for her school's marching band."

"She's dating the first trumpet player."

"She's too young to date."

"I keep telling her that."

Harrison turned from the window. "She also
mentioned that she enjoyed meeting Ethan Maddux."

It was the second time in a decade she'd even
heard him mention the name. Abby didn't bother
to respond. Harrison gave her a wounded look

that made her heart skip a beat, then dropped into his desk chair. "Would you care to explain that?"

She took a fortifying breath. "I went to San Francisco to see him," she confessed. "The day you called him." Storm clouds gathered in Harrison's eyes, so she held up a hand. "I wasn't even sure he'd see me. I didn't see the point in bringing this up until I knew we had something to discuss."

Harrison was silent.

"I didn't do it to hurt you, Harrison. You know I wouldn't."

"For God's sake, Abby, Ethan Maddux? You told him I was about to lose my company."

She didn't have to ask how he knew that. "Isn't that why you called him?"

He gave her a look that said the question was off-limits. Abby knew better than to press. "I asked for his help," she said. "It's true."

"Without consulting me." His voice had taken on a hard edge.

"You would have said no."

"Damn right I would have."

"But you called him yourself, Harrison. You must have known."

"I called to tell him I'd heard a terrible rumor that you might be on your way there. If he—" He stopped. "I wanted to make it perfectly clear that if Ethan has something to say to me, it's best said to *me*. Not through you."

"You knew I was going—"

"I suspected. Ryan mentioned you were headed for San Francisco."

"I went out there to meet with Doris Claymont about the foundation's direct-mail program. Ethan Maddux was an afterthought."

"I'm sure he'll be delighted to hear that."

"Harrison," she said gently, "I've seen the numbers. Ethan might be your last hope." She let the words hang between them for several seconds. Then she deliberately lowered her voice. "He's the best in the business. If anyone can pull Montgomery Data Systems out of this trench . . ." She trailed off.

Frustrated, she began to pace the confines of the plush office. She'd been in this room hundreds of times. She had listened while Harrison planned the future of his empire. She had provided research and reports, analysis and input on projects and ventures that had carried the business steadily forward. She had learned more, seen more, and experienced more in this office than she could have imagined the day he'd hired her.

Always, he'd been in control of the conversation. He'd been both mentor and friend, but she couldn't fight the sensation that their roles were changing.

"Look," she said, "I wasn't trying to deceive you." At his skeptical glance, she winced. "No matter what it looked like."

"You knew how I'd feel about this."

"I have reports coming across my desk every

day that say there's no bailout in sight. Your field offices are calling in a panic that they aren't going to meet payroll. The stock is sinking, and at the rate we're going, a buyout is inevitable."

"I pay you to run the Montgomery Foundation, Abby. I wasn't aware you'd taken on financial analysis as a sideline."

She winced again. It wasn't like him to be acerbic. In the ten years she'd known him, she could count on one hand the number of times he'd spoken to her out of irritation. His biting sarcasm was one more sign of how deep were the wounds of his conflict with Ethan.

She sat down in her chair with a slight nod. "Point taken."

Harrison tapped the end of a fountain pen on his desk in a sharp staccato. "I ought to fire you for this."

"Probably."

"You had no right—"

"Harrison, can you honestly tell me that you'd rather lose your company than swallow a little pride and ask for Ethan's help?"

"Yes," he said without hesitation.

Stunned, Abby stared at him. "Oh."

He frowned at her. "You didn't think so?"

"Well, no, I—"

"I've spent my life building and developing this business. We've had some very good years, and I believe we'll continue to have good years."

When she would have interrupted, he held up a hand. "We will probably have those years under someone else's leadership."

"But—"

"Let me finish." He set the pen down and folded his hands on his desk. "Maybe I held on for too long. Maybe I should have started listening earlier."

"There are back taxes—"

"I see you've been talking to Robert."

"People are anxious," Abby admitted. "I've been under pressure to try to reason with you."

He leaned back in his chair and shot her a weary smile. "How many members of my illustrious family have called you in a panic?"

"Several."

He looked tired, as if the burden of his sisters, their husbands and ex-husbands, children and stepchildren, cousins, aunts, uncles, and the scores of in-laws had suddenly become far greater than he wanted to bear. "I'm certain they have."

"They're concerned."

He tapped his finger on the desk in a lazy rhythm. "Last time you counted," he said, "how many members of my family are gainfully employed?"

Abby frowned. "Not counting the ones who work for you?"

"Not counting those."

"Four, including Ethan."

"Hmm. No wonder they're anxious."

"Your board has been asking me to try to reason with you."

"And by 'reason,' they mean bring in Ethan to bail us out?"

"It's come up, but I approached him on my own."

"No one believes I can do it by myself."

The defeated sound of his voice struck a nerve. "Harrison—"

"Don't bother to deny it."

"No one's questioning that you've provided excellent leadership for this company."

"Please. Whatever you do, don't placate me. You, of all people, ought to know how I hate that."

"I'm sorry." For everything, she thought. That you're in this place and I can't help you. That your family is more interested in what you can do for them than in who you are. That you've never trusted anyone enough to let them love you. "I didn't know what else to do."

"You shouldn't have brought Ethan into this."

"I wanted to help."

"What did he say when he saw the reports?"

It had pained him to ask the question, she knew. "He confirmed what we already know."

"And?"

"He said he'd get back to me."

"The best thing that could happen would be for him to turn you down."

"Maybe he will."

He shook his head, his expression fierce. "I doubt it."

"I don't think he wants to hurt you, Harrison."

"You could never understand, Abigail. Trust me."

"If you'd only—"

He held up one hand. "Just make sure you keep me in the loop at least, will you?"

Abby sensed the dismissal and rose to go. She hesitated as she studied the haggard lines of his face. "If you tell me to, I'll call him and say I've changed my mind."

He thought it over for a minute, then shook his head. "It's too late for that."

"You're sure?"

"You have no idea what you're asking, Abby." He seemed slightly lost. "Things aren't always what they seem" he said enigmatically. His voice sounded flat and lifeless. "But the wheels are in motion now. There's no sense trying to stop them."

Abby hesitated. "Are you sure there isn't something you want to tell me?"

"I'm absolutely sure." He reached for a manila folder—her signal that the discussion was closed. "Let's get back to work, Abby. What's done is done."

She was halfway to the door when he interrupted her progress. "Tell Rachel I'll take ten tickets."

"I will." Abby paused, her hand on the doorknob. "Deirdre is coming in this afternoon. She wants to talk about this office issue again." Thus far, Abby had been able to persuade Deirdre that she didn't need an office in the MDS building to conduct her business. As the fund-raiser neared, however, Deirdre was pushing harder. "Do you want to come sit in on the meeting?"

The look he gave her spoke volumes. "Would you want to if you were me?"

"Hell, no," she assured him. "But she's your sister, and I'm only putting up with her because you asked me to."

His expression softened. "And I appreciate it. Deirdre's in a bad place. She needed something."

"So you gave her to me."

"You're the best I've got, Abby."

She felt cheered by the return of their usual banter. "Well, she's driving me nuts—and the rest of the staff along with me. That little scene the other day was just the tip of the iceberg."

"She's determined to have an office?"

"I think she wants mine."

"She does," he admitted. "She told me the other day that she thinks the foundation should be run by a Montgomery."

"If I hadn't heard you complain about how the woman keeps her checking account, I might feel threatened."

Some of the usual sparkle had returned to his gaze. "Believe me, you have nothing to fear. I love my sister, but I'm not stupid."

"Then can I count on you this afternoon?"

"Yes. Check with Joanna and make sure my schedule's cleared."

"Got it." She pulled open the door.

"Abby?"

"Hmm?"

"Are you planning to bring a date to the fundraiser this year?"

Abby managed a small laugh. "Good grief, Harrison, like I have time to think about a date!"

"It's a big night. I'd rather not have any surprises."

Ethan, she thought. He was worried that she would bring Ethan.

"No, I'm not bringing a date. And are you ever going to stop bugging me about my social life?"

"Lack of social life, you mean?" He shook his head. "When you tell me you've developed one, I'll stop asking."

"I'll keep that in mind."

He gave Abby the full impact of his gaze. "Thank you for telling me the truth, Abby," he said quietly.

She didn't have to ask what he meant. As their financial picture had grown bleaker, many of Harrison's advisors had attempted to shield themselves by concealing the more unpleasant facts from him. Since the day he'd inherited the business from his autocratic father, there had been a common misconception that Harrison's less imposing ways and more democratic leadership style meant he lacked his father's charisma and intelligence. Abby knew better. Harrison was a man willing to let others take the credit for his victories, while he alone accepted blame for his defeats.

She understood him very well—with the exception of one missing piece to the puzzle. The tension of his relationship with Ethan seemed starkly out of character. Soon, she vowed, she'd get to the bottom of what put that slightly haunted look in his eyes whenever he thought about his estranged son. And if she were lucky, he'd forgive her for it when it was over. "I'd never lie to you," she told him earnestly.

"I believe that," Harrison assured her.

"What do you think, Jack?" Ethan sat in his San Francisco office on Friday afternoon and regarded the two men across from his desk. Late last night, after looking over the bleak evidence of Harrison Montgomery's financial picture for the third time, he'd decided he needed a second opinion on what he was seeing.

Jack Iverson, Ethan's CFO and longtime friend, glanced up from the reports. "I think your father's got himself a hell of a mess on his hands."

"Hmm." Ethan shifted his gaze toward the other man. "Ted?"

Ted Conner, one of the security consultants Ethan used for special cases, looked up from his copy of the reports. "Either someone's robbing the man blind, or he's deliberately trying to run his company into the ground."

Definite possibilities, Ethan mused, along with another, darker scenario he wasn't willing to pursue yet. "Do you think they could face Chapter Eleven before he can negotiate a buyout?"

Jack gave him an affirming nod. "I'd say it's a distinct possibility."

"What's he got to negotiate with?" Ted asked.

Ethan shrugged. "Hard to say. I'd have to look at every division's assets separately, and I haven't put that much time into it yet. I'm not sure I want to."

Jack dropped the stack of papers onto Ethan's desk. "From what I can tell, it started as a trickle about a year and a half ago. Now it's a hemorrhage. I can look a little harder if you want—probably nail down the dates."

"I want to know exactly when the problem started and where. Which divisions started to lose money first, who runs those divisions, and why the problem wasn't addressed." He glanced at

Ted. "As far as you can tell, could there be fraud here?"

"Ethan, it can always be fraud."

"But is it likely?"

Ted shook his head. "No. The losses are widespread throughout the company. When you've got an embezzler, they're usually limited to one area of access to the company accounts. If someone's stealing money from MDS, it would have to be someone so high in the organization that he had a practically unlimited run of the place."

"So if it's not extremely bad luck, bad business decisions, and rotten timing on Harrison's part," Ethan said, "then it could be someone with legitimate access to these accounts."

"Or at least someone who knows how to get legitimate access," Ted pointed out. "Still, it doesn't seem likely. Montgomery is an old-school kind of manager. He's got a core of very dedicated people at the top of his pyramid. The rest are isolated in their own departments. That's part of the reason his company is falling apart."

"All right." Ethan placed his palms on the desk. "Ted, see what you can find for me on Harrison's top tier. Put out some feelers and see if anything turns up about his people."

"We've probably got some of that on file already," Ted told him. "When we were considering the stock option last year on Montgomery's Taiwan operation, we pulled a lot of that together. I'll see what else I can find."

"Ethan," Jack said, "are you telling me that we're going to get involved in this?"

"*I'm* getting involved," Ethan replied. He'd made that decision on his flight back from Chicago. He was definitely and completely involved with Abigail Lee. "I haven't decided yet whether Maddux Consulting is taking the case."

"Is this why you blew off the rest of that meeting in Prague?" Ted demanded.

"I was bored. Next time the President wants a representative at an international economics summit, I'm sending you."

"You were supposed to speak Monday night."

"They probably gave me a medal for being a no-show." He glanced out his window at the dreary May sky. "Is it supposed to stop raining soon?" he asked no one in particular.

"I heard," Jack said, "that they've had nice weather in Chicago lately."

Ethan slanted him a wry look. "I ought to fire you for that."

"Probably. Look, Ethan, it's not that I care if you want to take on this MDS thing—"

"I told you, I haven't decided."

Jack ignored that. "It's just that there will be certain speculations if we do. I'd like your permission to prepare the publicity department. They're already a little overwhelmed dealing with Edward Kinsey's mess. It's not a big deal, but I'd like to give them a heads up."

Ethan scowled. "Speaking of Kinsey, Lewis still hasn't briefed me on that. Are we going to be implicated?"

Ted shook his head. "I doubt it. We've cooperated with the Feds, and it's pretty clear there's no way we could have been involved with that side of Edward's operation."

Jack forged ahead. "Nevertheless, they've got their hands full down there, and if we're going to open a can of worms like MDS, then I think the least we could do—"

He stopped abruptly when the door to Ethan's office crashed open. "My God, Ethan!" The woman swept into the room like a ship in full sail. "Tell me it isn't true."

Ethan stifled a groan. "Hello, Pamela."

Both Ted and Jack politely stood. Ethan refused the small courtesy. His former fiancée, clad in a dramatic-looking red suit that had probably cost as much as a small car, advanced into the office and planted her manicured hands on his desk. "Did you really seduce Harrison's lover?"

The fragile rein on his temper snapped. He gave Jack and Ted an unmistakable look that sent them both hurrying from the room with mumbled greetings for Pam as they passed by. Jack pulled the door shut behind him. Ethan rose from his chair and rounded the desk. "Nice to see you, Pam."

She turned to face him. "Are you going to an-swer me or not?"

"I haven't decided yet," he told her. "But whether or not I do, don't you think that question was a little inappropriate to ask me?"

She frowned at him. "Since when did you start worrying about propriety?" she said with a pout.

This had been one of the most consistently irri-tating facets of their relationship. Though he had developed a reputation for a somewhat reckless approach to his business ventures, he preferred to keep his private life circumspect. Pamela had never understood the distinction. Initially, she'd felt challenged to bring out that side of him. When he'd refused, she'd pushed harder. When the rela-tionship ended, he'd had the grace not to point out to her that he'd been right all along.

But he had always found her histrionic streak annoying. During their engagement, he'd resigned himself to the fact that this would constitute the "worse" part of the for-better-or-for-worse arrangement of their pending marriage. Now that he was no longer obligated to endure it, he found his patience for it even thinner.

Pamela was watching him through narrowed eyes. "You did, didn't you? I couldn't believe it when I heard—"

Ethan held up a hand. "Stop right there. What the hell did you hear anyway?"

She looked flustered, and he could understand why. He had never raised his voice to her during their engagement.

"I was your fiancée for six months, Ethan, and we dated for two years before that. I have friends here."

"And I, obviously, have an employee loyalty problem."

She advanced toward him. "It's not like that," she assured him, her tone conciliatory. "I happened to stop by the afternoon you left for Prague. I was having lunch with—with someone. She mentioned that Abby Lee had been here to see you. I wouldn't have thought twice about it except that I called Edna for an address on Tuesday, and when I asked to speak to you, she mentioned that you were on your way to Chicago."

"So you, naturally, decided to storm into my office today and demand answers you gave up the right to have."

The barb hit its mark. She visibly flinched. Ethan felt a sting of guilt but didn't back down. "I was concerned," she said quietly. "I'm worried about you."

"I'm doing fine without you," he said. "You don't need to concern yourself."

She gave him a disgruntled look. "You could at least have the decency to appear a little devastated."

Ethan simply stared at her. She exhaled an exasperated sigh and slipped into the chair Jack had recently vacated. "Oh, for God's sake, Ethan, can't you take a joke anymore?"

Not about this, he mused. Not since he'd been waiting two days to hear from Abby Lee and she'd steadfastly ignored him. "I believe my lack of a sense of humor was one of your reasons for ending our engagement. It came after 'temperamentally maladjusted' and 'emotionally detached.' "

She waved a hand in the direction of the chair. "Would you please sit down? I'm getting a crick in my neck from looking up at you."

He hesitated, but finally acquiesced. "I've got an incredibly busy schedule today," he told her. "If this isn't something important . . ."

"Was it ever important enough for you to disrupt your busy schedule?" she asked, and he didn't think he imagined the hint of sadness in her tone.

"Pamela—"

"Never mind," she said, and gave him a slight smile. "That's behind us." At his censorious look, she nodded. "Really, Ethan, it is. I'm just here because I want to talk to you about this Abigail Lee issue."

"There is no issue—and if there were, I wouldn't be interested in discussing it."

"Well, I am," she insisted. She regarded him closely. "Are you seriously involved with her?"

"By your own count, I've seen her twice," he said evasively. "How serious can I be?"

"Depends. For some people, that's enough time to be completely captivated."

"I'm not like other people."

She ignored that. "For you, two times is all you need to have made up your mind. Usually, only once. I'm betting that you decided what you wanted to do with her that day in your office and that's what had you running off to Chicago the day you got back from Prague."

He wasn't sure if she was mocking him or not, so he said nothing. Pamela leaned forward and placed her hand on his knee. "I didn't come here to pick a fight with you," she said. "I just—actually, whether you believe it or not, I meant what I said. I really am worried about you."

"I've been taking care of myself for a long time."

"It's only been a couple weeks since we—"

"Since you informed me," he interjected smoothly, "that I was emotionally incapable of meeting your needs."

"You don't have to make it sound so harsh, Ethan. I was hurting at the time, you know."

He accepted that at face value. At least she didn't appear bent on causing another scene. He'd chosen Pamela because she had all the credentials to be his partner in business and in life. She was an impeccable hostess; she had ambition and drive, and the intelligence to match. She was sophisticated and charming, and other than the occasional bout of dramatics, she wasn't prone to make him uncomfortable. Things hadn't gotten messy until she'd wanted an emotional commitment. "I'm sorry you were hurt," he said.

She glanced toward the window. "But you don't think I had the right to be?"

He didn't know what to say, so he waited. When she looked at him again, her eyes were clouded. "Did you ever feel anything for me at all?" she finally said.

The question caught him off guard. "I care for you a great deal, Pam. You know that."

"But you didn't love me." It wasn't a question, so he didn't answer it. Pamela shook her head. "Never mind. I can see I'm not going to get anything out of you today."

"If I had time," he told her, "I'd take you to lunch."

She looked at him a little sadly. "You didn't have time when we were engaged, Ethan." She stood. "I guess that's really why I came by today. When I heard about your trip to Chicago. I wasn't sure I believed it. No woman likes to find out she's that easily replaced."

"Pam—"

She bent down and kissed his cheek. "It's all right, darling. I'm just having one of those moments you hate so much. I'll leave you alone now."

He walked with her toward the door. She turned to him when her fingers were on the latch. "For the record, Ethan, from what I've heard, I think you really might be in over your head this time. She's not your usual type."

"Thanks for the tip."

Pamela brushed a piece of lint from his shoulder. "People say that she's one of those really unreserved type of women—the kind who goes at things with both her emotional guns loaded."

"I'll consider myself warned," he said, and pulled open the door.

Pamela shook her head. "God help me," she said, "but I'm almost glad for it."

Five

"I want *you*?" At five-thirty on Friday evening, LuAnne pulled her now-blue hair into a ponytail and secured it with an elastic band. She pinned Abby across the kitchen with a shrewd look. "Was it like, I WANT you, or I want YOU?"

Abby took a long sip of her mineral water. "I'm not sure." It was Memorial Day weekend. LuAnne had come to help Rachel and Abby with the awesome amount of baking Rachel had volunteered to do for the annual party the Montgomery Foundation sponsored for the residents of the Chicago Metropolitan Veterans Center. To fulfill her requirements for the Baldovino competition, Rachel had agreed to oversee the preparation and distribution of 115 dozen cookies. When she'd signed the papers, Abby hadn't thought 115 dozen seemed insurmountable—until the bags and boxes of ingredients had begun to crowd out the space in her kitchen.

From the look of things, they'd be up to their elbows in flour and egg whites all weekend. And for her part, Abby was glad for the distraction. Between her growing preoccupation with Ethan Maddux and her confrontation with Harrison that afternoon, she was actually looking forward to the sheer effort of the task. She and Rachel had participated in the event for years, usually baking a batch or two of gourmet treats to add to the ample supplies provided by local caterers.

When they'd started, Abby had felt like the baking—her father's favorite creative outlet— was a way for Rachel and her to share a connection with their parents. Through the experience, Rachel's interest in the culinary arts had grown, and so had the Memorial Day tradition. Now the downtown Chicago center, supported by the Montgomery Foundation, hosted dozens of veterans and their families for the annual event.

Last year Abby and Rachel had made just twelve dozen cookies. Hours of creaming butter, sifting flour, melting chocolate, and forming the large dough balls that baked into four-inch cookies made her swear every year that no matter how much her sister protested, they were going to hire the job out next time.

But Harrison had suggested that this year

could provide an opportunity for Rachel to improve her chances of being accepted to the Baldovino competition. When Monsieur Billaud had agreed, their lots had been cast. The energy this undertaking would require would help Abby take her mind off her mounting frustrations at work—and also the haunting sound of Ethan's departing words ringing in her ears.

"All I know is," she finally said, "between him and Harrison, I'm about to pull my hair out."

"Don't," LuAnne quipped. "You'd look crappy in a wig."

LuAnne had called that afternoon and volunteered to help with the baking. The offer, Abby knew, had nothing to do with benevolence and everything to do with the fact that her friend was dying to know what had happened on Tuesday night with Ethan. Abby had artfully managed to avoid answering questions, but her grace period had run out the minute LuAnne walked in the door.

Abby laughed and continued removing ingredients from the refrigerator.

LuAnne twisted her blue ponytail into a simple knot and secured it with a bamboo skewer. "So what I want to know is, did you tell Harrison what he said?"

"Are you kidding?" Abby added several dozen eggs to the growing stack on the counter. "God, talk about a coronary!"

"Myocardial infarction," LuAnne said.

Abby laughed. "Do you even know what that means?"

"No, I just like the way it sounds. One of my clients had one."

"Is he still a client?"

"She is, actually."

"Then whatever it is, it's not as serious as what would have happened if I'd just casually mentioned to Harrison that Ethan said he wants me." Abby groaned. "God, that's a nightmare." She thought about it for a minute, then slammed a package of cream cheese onto the counter. "And just what the hell do you think he meant by that, anyway? I mean, what kind of statement is that?"

"You want an answer?" LuAnne reached for an apron inside the pantry door. "Or are you just blowing off steam?"

Abby added three more packages of cream cheese. "You know what I mean," she replied irritably. "He just said that to annoy me. No one normal runs around saying stuff like that. It sounds ridiculous."

"It sounds sexy as hell to me." LuAnne glanced at the contents of the pantry. "What do you need out of here?"

Abby frowned. "Flour, sugar, salt, baking soda, and baking powder. Oh, and I think she's got the baking chocolate in there too." She leaned one hip against the counter and drummed her fingers on an egg carton. "And don't change the subject."

"I'm not." LuAnne handed her a ten-pound bag of flour. "I just don't think you want to hear what I have to say about this."

"Since when does thinking I don't want to hear something keep you from saying it?" Abby dropped the bag on the table and reached for the sugar.

LuAnne laughed. "I'm mellowing."

"Bull."

LuAnne dumped ten boxes of brown sugar into Abby's waiting arms. "But since you asked," she said, "I think the man wants sex."

"Oh come on, Lu. Get real."

"All men want sex. You haven't learned that by now?"

"You know what I mean. I am not the kind of woman who inspires men to wild sexual passion."

"Abby—"

"Seriously. Men don't make life-changing decisions just to take me to bed."

"Maybe this one will."

"You're making it sound like I could just drive the man crazy with sexual desire."

"Any man can be driven crazy with sexual desire," LuAnne announced.

"By the right woman."

"Maybe *you're* his right woman." LuAnne handed her friend a box of baking soda.

Abby plunked it on the table. "Maybe he just wants to really piss off his father."

That made LuAnne frown. She stepped out of the pantry. "Is that what you think is going on here?"

"I don't know. You should have seen the look on Harrison's face today, Lu. I expected him to be angry—well, miffed maybe. I didn't expect him to look so devastated."

"How long did you say it's been since the two of them talked?"

"A long time. I guess I just thought they were both really stubborn and somebody had to make the first move."

"Do you think Ethan hates him?"

Abby thought that over. "No. It's not like that." She pondered the empty tone in his voice whenever he spoke about his father. "It's not that passionate."

"What do you mean?"

"I can't explain it exactly. He just gets kind of lethal when the subject comes up. Sometimes I can almost see the walls drop into place."

LuAnne groaned. "There is *nothing* sexier than a man with hidden angst."

"Oh, knock it off, Lu," Abby said good-naturedly. "I assure you, this is not a case of the misunderstood rebel looking for solace."

"If you say so."

"I just wish I understood what was going on between the two of them. We've only discussed it a couple of times—and Harrison always made it fairly clear that he didn't want me to bring it up again."

"What *do* you know?" LuAnne handed Abby an apron.

Abby flipped the bib strings over her head and reached for the ties. "Mostly only Ethan's side of the story. And it's not pretty." She wrapped the ties around her waist. "What Ethan says about Harrison—it doesn't fit. I mean, I've known the man for over ten years. He doesn't seem like the type to just write off his own child. Not when he . . ." She shrugged. "It just doesn't fit, is all."

LuAnne nodded. "I can see why you'd think that."

"Don't you think it's weird?"

"I don't know Harrison, except through you," LuAnne said carefully, "and I've never met Ethan Maddux."

"Consider yourself blessed."

"Not to hear Rachel tell it," LuAnne quipped.

"He can be very charming."

"Yeah, well, he pretty much charmed her thirteen-year-old hormones right into a full-blown infatuation. That girl has it bad."

"He gushed over the food. You know how she is."

"She says he's a first-class stud."

Abby's stomach clenched. "I suppose he is."

LuAnne gave her a narrow look. "You *suppose* he is? That's not what you were telling me after you got back from San Francisco."

"I left out a few details."

"A few?"

"Okay, *several* details."

"Like the fact that the man is drop-dead gorgeous."

"He's . . ." Abby searched for the right word. "Charismatic. He just sort of captures a room when he's in it. You should see the way his employees respond to him."

"Sexy as hell, isn't he?"

"Definitely," Abby confessed.

"And he wants you." LuAnne regarded her shrewdly. "And you want him."

Abby frowned. "Lu—"

"Don't bother to deny it. What I want to know is, what's the problem here?"

"The problem is, I can't shake the feeling that he's playing some giant game with me. And I don't like it."

"Honey, there's only one kind of game men play when they say they want a woman. He does not mean he wants to play accountant and business advisor to his father. And he sure as hell doesn't mean he wants to be financially responsible for you for the rest of his life." LuAnne put her hands on her hips and gave Abby a knowing look. "It's like I told you. That man wants sex. And you're going to have to trust me on this. I know more about it than you do."

"You've got this all wrong," Abby insisted. "I think it's more like an I-want-you-so-Harrison-can't-have-you kind of thing, instead of an I-want-YOU remark."

LuAnne snorted. "If you say so."

"I'm serious. He just knows that if I align with him"—at Luanne's raised eyebrow, Abby flipped a dish towel at her—"Harrison will take it really hard. And that's what he wants."

"So he's a complete jerk, is what you're telling me."

"Noooo." Abby pictured him patiently asking Rachel questions about her cooking lessons. "Not a jerk. Just a little clouded, maybe, about what he wants."

"Doesn't sound like it to me."

"You weren't there."

"Good thing, too. If he'd said that to me, I would have jumped his bones."

Abby laughed. "Liar!"

"Probably. But here's what I want to know. What kind of man says something like that and then just waits for you to make a move?"

"Ethan Maddux, evidently."

LuAnne tapped the counter with a red fingernail. "Hmm. What are you going to do about it?"

Abby didn't want to answer that. Truth was, she'd been trying not to answer that particular question since the moment he'd made his preposterous announcement. Nor had she wanted to analyze the source of the clenching sensation she got in her stomach when she pictured him saying it. It was ten times worse than his "I'm doing this for you" statement. Then, at least, there had been a sort of devilish sparkle in his eyes. This time, he'd looked so serious.

Impossibly serious.

Frustrated, Abby ran a hand through her hair. "Beats me," she finally admitted. "I haven't talked to him since, and after my conversation with Harrison this afternoon, I'm not sure I should."

LuAnne considered her words for a minute. "You said he took the financial reports with him?"

"Yes."

"Then he's expecting to talk to you again. Do you think he's waiting for you to call?"

"Who the hell knows what he wants?" Abby replied. She frowned at her reflection in the oven door and was saved from elaborating when Rachel entered the room, tying apron strings around her waist.

"Okay," Rachel announced. "Sorry about that. I called Monsieur Billaud to check on something."

Abby glanced at her sister and stifled a twinge of nostalgia. At thirteen, Rachel was developing their father's easy charm, natural good looks, and social finesse. With her father's gorgeous olive skin and hazel eyes, and an inherent grace that was already drawing attention from her peers, the young woman her sister was becoming bore little resemblance to the angst-ridden child who'd witnessed her parents' death. The scars, Abby knew, still ran deep, and she fervently hoped that when the time came for Rachel to face those demons, she could give her sister everything she needed.

Rachel finished tying the apron and added, "I needed a little expert advice on a couple of recipes."

"We're doing something new?" LuAnne asked.

"Abby talked to the nutritionist at the center last week. He asked us what the possibility was of adding some diabetic-friendly stuff to the mix."

Abby nodded. "I thought it was a great idea."

"We're going to be using some artificial sweeteners and substitute sugars, so I wanted to check on how I should adjust the existing recipes. Since Monsieur Billaud does that entire sugar-free menu thing, I figured he'd know."

"Good answers?" Abby asked.

Rachel produced a piece of notepaper from her apron pocket. "Guess we'll find out." She looked over the piles of ingredients with a knowing eye. "Okay, let's get to work."

Abby reached for the butter. Rachel's strategy for the massive job always entailed preparing large batches of raw ingredients, then mixing as needed. It seemed to make things go faster than working on one recipe at a time. "I'll cream the butter," she said.

Rachel gave her a surprised look. "You hate that part."

"I need the exercise."

LuAnne picked up a package of chocolate. "What do I do with this? Smelling it is starting to make me high."

"Chop it," Rachel said. "Really fine pieces." She brought out a grinder from the pantry. "I'll do nuts."

LuAnne opened the package of imported chocolate and rolled her eyes in exaggerated bliss. "I think I'm gaining weight just handling this. What is it?"

Rachel laughed. "It's Couverture Chocolate."

"Expensive," Abby assured LuAnne.

"Yeah," Rachel concurred. "That bar you're holding is worth more than my allowance for an entire month."

"I'm salivating." LuAnne licked her lips.

Abby shook her head with a slight laugh. "Well, don't try it. I guarantee you'll get addicted."

Five-thirty. Ethan glanced at the clock on his desk. In four hours it would be precisely three days since he'd informed Abby Lee of his terms. And he had nothing to assure him she'd fully under-stood his proposition, except for her startled intake of breath and the wary way she'd watched him pick up the reports on Harrison's company and walk out of her town house.

And the sound of the dead bolt turning in the lock seconds after he'd closed the door behind him.

The dead bolt had given her away.

He had to admit that she'd impressed the hell out of him by not calling him this week. He'd expected either outraged demands for an explanation, a flat refusal, or, at the very least, an indignant request for an apology and the blunt information that he would not be welcome at her home the following Tuesday night. She had responded with a polite and aloof thank-you note for giving her his time.

And neatly put the ball back in his court. Abigail Lee was proving to be every bit as fascinating as he'd hoped.

Ethan drummed his fingers on the desk as he absently listened to the droning voice of a colleague on his speakerphone. Caution was telling him to let things simmer for a while before he made another move. He could let Abby stew until Tuesday. She'd probably blink if he made her wait that long before contacting her. Harrison needed help, and she needed an answer. If he showed his hand too soon, he'd give her an edge. She was in a much stronger bargaining position than she probably realized at the moment. If he were smart, he'd leave it that way.

That was precisely what Pamela had been trying to tell him that morning.

He wasted fifteen more seconds mentally de-
bating the wisdom of what he was about to do. A
wooden pencil on the edge of his desk caught his
eye, and he pictured it wrapped in the coils of
Abby's hair. "Screw it," he muttered.

"Ethan?" came the voice on the speakerphone.

Ethan snatched up the receiver. "Nothing, Bob.
Listen, something just came up, and I've got to cut
this short."

"But I thought—"

"Can't be helped," he told the other man. "Besides, it's Friday. We couldn't get in touch with
Severs now even if we wanted to."

"Didn't you say you wanted concrete numbers
on this by Monday morning?"

Ethan frowned. "Monday's a holiday, Bob."

"A holi—hell, Ethan. What's wrong with you?"

Good question, he thought. He never took holidays. And he sure as hell never spent three days
wondering why some woman hadn't called him.
He felt like a teenager. A cranky, hormone-ridden,
lust-driven teenager. "Nothing," he told Bob. "I
just don't think we can realistically pursue this
until next week."

"Well, according to my source at the Justice Department, there's a very good chance we're going
to be sucked into it."

Ethan already had his pocket PC in his hand

and was clearing his calendar. "And I can't do a damned thing about it until Tuesday, so why are we talking about it now?"

"But, Ethan—"

"Tuesday, Bob. You can go over the numbers with Beverly. In fact, make that Tuesday afternoon. I won't be able to get to them until—" He pictured the homey interior of Abby's house and made yet another quick decision. "Actually, Wednesday morning. I've got to make a trip out of town."

"Ethan—"

"Don't worry about it. Beverly's the best I've got. She can give you whatever you need."

"I know, but don't you think—"

He lost what was left of his patience. "Wednesday morning. That's what I think. I'll be out of the office until then, and if Carlyn needs anything, tell her to contact Edna. I won't be taking calls."

"You won't— Ethan, where the hell are you going? Zimbabwe?"

"Chicago." He hung up, and was about to punch the button for his assistant when the second phone on his desk rang. Ethan looked at it with a fierce frown. He got three kinds of calls on the private line. Calls from Pamela, though she hadn't used it since she'd broken their engagement. Occasionally, someone dialed a wrong number. And from time to time, calls from the few members of the Montgomery clan with whom he'd maintained a semblance of a relationship. He thought about not answering, but couldn't make himself do it. Reaching for the receiver, he was hoping for a wrong number.

"Maddux."

"Ethan? Darling? Is this a bad time?"

At the sound of his aunt Letty's voice, some of his tension eased. Of all Harrison's relatives, Letty was the one Ethan liked the best. She had provided maternal comfort and support during those tense years between his mother's death and his final argument with his father. Letty had been the one to help Ethan with the simple funeral arrangements.

Ethan settled into his chair. "Come on, Letty. When is it ever a bad time with you?"

She laughed. "Charming as usual, I see."

Ethan picked up the pen on his desk and twirled it between his fingers. "But as it happens, I'm on my way out the door. Was there something specific you needed, or could I call you tomorrow?"

"Well . . ." She hesitated.

"Yes?"

"It's just that I heard something, and I was wondering—I mean, not that I—"

"Yes," Ethan said patiently. "I was in Chicago on Tuesday."

"Oh."

"How did you know?"

"I'm not going to tell you," she said. "You'd get mad, and then I might not find out again."

"Well, since everyone is so fascinated by my travel arrangements these days, you might as well know that I'm headed back to Chicago this evening."

"Really?" She sounded way too interested for his peace of mind.

"Yes. Really."

"Ethan, does this mean—"

"I am not going to Chicago to see Harrison."

"Oh." Silence.

Ethan glanced out the window. "I'm going to see Abigail," he admitted for no logical reason.

"I see." The tone in his aunt's voice told him that she saw way more than he wanted her to. "Abby's trying to get you to help Harrison with MDS."

"Shrewd as usual."

"Are you going to?" she asked.

"Depends."

"On?"

"On Abby."

He was certain he heard her smile when she said, "Ah."

"Don't sound smug," Ethan warned her. "It's unbecoming."

"But wickedly satisfying, darling."

Despite himself, he laughed. "Then I'm sure you'll understand why I have a flight to catch."

"Of course. But believe it or not, I did call you for a reason."

"Not just to pry?"

"No. And since you're going to be in Chicago this weekend, you might even give me my way."

Ethan dropped the pen into its holder. "Letty, when have I ever failed to give in to you?"

"Never. It's why I love you."

"Liar," he muttered.

She laughed. "What I called about was that Carlton is graduating this weekend."

Ethan recognized the name of Letty's stepson, the son of her third husband. She'd maintained a very close relationship with the young man even after her divorce from his father. Ethan hadn't been surprised. Letty had never had children of her own, and Carlton had been at a vulnerable age when he'd entered her life. She'd immediately taken to him just as she had to Ethan. Their bond seemed to have strengthened when Carlton lost one of his legs in an automobile accident. Through Letty, Ethan had remained somewhat informed of his cousin's progress through college.

"Is he?" Ethan asked.

"Yes. He's magna cum laude—did I mention that?"

"A few times," he said with a slight smile.

"Well, I was hoping you'd meet with him. Just for a few minutes. He could use some good career advice."

"He can come work for me."

Letty sucked in a breath. "I wasn't asking that."

"I know. But he can."

"Ethan, really, I just wanted you to give him some career advice."

"The best advice I can give him is that he should come work for me. Software development is his thing, isn't that right?"

"Yes."

"Fine. I've got a division for that. I'll give him a decent salary and benefits, and we'll see what he can do."

"Really, I—"

"Letty, I'm glad to do it."

"Not everyone expects you to do them favors, Ethan. You know that, don't you?"

He didn't bother to respond to that. "Tell Carlton he can expect confirmation from me in the mail. I'll have my assistant send him his paperwork."

"Don't you even want an interview?"

"He's related to you," Ethan told her. "That's all I need to know."

"Oh, Ethan, what in the world am I going to do with you?"

"Beats the hell out of me."

"Would you at least like to come to his party on Saturday? You're going to be in town."

He hesitated. "Where is it?"

Letty coughed slightly. "Harrison's yacht."

Ethan glanced at the Rothko painting on the wall of his office and had a mental picture of Abby staring at it while a pencil held her hair in place.

"What time should I be there?" he asked.

"You'd come? You're serious?"

"I'm about to hire my newest software genius. The least I can do is show up at his graduation party."

"You're sure?"

"Have you ever known me to be anything but sure?"

Letty laughed. "It's part of your charm. But, Ethan, the party—"

"I know. Swarming with Montgomerys. What time should I be there?"

Letty paused. "I'm sure Abigail has the information."

"I'm sure she does."

"One piece of advice, Ethan?"

"Only one?" he teased.

"One for now," she clarified. "Everyone loves her—the entire family. Abby is . . . unique."

An understatement at best, he thought. "I can see that."

"Don't hurt her."

"I'll try."

"That's all I ask, darling. I can't wait to see you."

"Bye, Letty."

He hung up with a shake of his head. He had to be losing his mind to even think about getting involved with Abby Lee when the Montgomery clan had obviously claimed her as one of their own. Rather than diminishing the appeal, however, the knowledge that she'd managed to woo and win most of his estranged family held an odd fascination. Charming, gracious, complicated, Abby somehow managed to be both sophisticated and unaffected. If any other woman had neglected to call him after the conversation they'd had on Tuesday, he could have comfortably assumed she was biding her time. With Abby, he was prone to suspect she had probably just forgotten.

The realization made him feel irritable and agitated—two words he hated. In Ethan's life, moods were inconvenient realities of the human condition. And if he had a brain in his head, logic told him, he'd recognize that Abby Lee had an ability to bring out every mood he possessed—including a few he'd never acknowledged.

The only way, he thought, staring at the San Francisco skyline, to regain control was to settle the question of Abigail Lee and just what the hell he was going to do with her. And that question had to be settled in Chicago.

Before he could think better of it, he punched the intercom button on his phone. "Edna?"

"Yes, Ethan?" Edna asked.

"Get Bill for me, will you? I need him on the runway, fueled and ready to leave in half an hour."

"What should he put on his flight plan?"

"Chicago," Ethan said.

"Really?" She sounded disgustingly cheerful.

Ethan didn't try to suppress a wry smile. "Really. And don't sound so damned righteous about it."

"Temper, temper, Ethan. Ladies don't like that."

"Then this one should have called." He replaced the receiver and reached for his briefcase. Sitting inside was a preliminary memo Jack had given him an hour ago about his analysis of the MDS report. It would give Ethan something to read on the plane—something to take his mind off the way Abby had looked in a sweatshirt and jeans, with her color a little high and her lips slightly parted.

A sudden hunger pain reminded him of two things. First, it had been a hell of a long time since he'd actually *craved* a woman. Though he and Pamela had shared a satisfactory sex life, he'd never felt this yearning desire for her. Even toward the end, when he'd tried to let himself go, it hadn't been like a fire eating at his guts. That probably should have alarmed him, but once he'd made the decision to ignore all the warning signs, he hadn't looked back.

And second, with any luck, he could wrangle another meal or two out of Rachel—whom he suspected could easily become his strongest ally in this pursuit. He tossed a few more items into his briefcase, then snapped the locks shut and headed for the door.

As he entered the outer office, Edna gave him a

dry look. "Am I allowed to ask when I can expect you back in the office?"

"Wednesday."

Her eyebrows disappeared into her hairline. "I wonder what in the world could hold your attention in Chicago until Wednesday."

"Dinner."

Six

Abby opened the door of her town house three hours later and regarded Ethan with a sharp look that was seriously diminished by the smudge of flour on her nose. "What are you doing here?"

Not exactly the welcome he'd been hoping for. He braced one shoulder against the doorframe and wiped the smudge from her nose with his thumb. "Hi."

"Hi? It's ten o'clock at night and that's all you have to say for yourself?" She blew a curl off her forehead.

He caught a whiff of the incredible scent coming from the kitchen, as well as peals of laughter. "Actually," he said, "I have a few more things to say, but they can wait." He looked beyond her shoulder. "What's going on?"

She wiped her hands on the front of her flour-streaked apron. "We're baking. Did you want something?"

"I want to come in." He shifted away from the doorframe and took a step toward her, so she was forced to tip her head back to maintain eye contact.

"You can't," she told him. "We're—"

"Abby?" Rachel had pushed open the kitchen door. "Who is— Oh, Ethan. Hi!"

Ethan chuckled. "At least someone here is glad to see me," he told Abby in a quiet voice meant for her alone. "Hello, Rachel."

Rachel hurried toward them. She was wiping her hands on a dish towel she had flung over her shoulder. "What are you doing here?"

"I hope I'm getting to eat whatever that incredible smell is. What *are* you making in there?"

Rachel slid between Abby and the doorframe. "Cookies."

He remembered. "The Baldovino competition."

"Yeah. Making the cookies counts toward the apprentice hours I have to complete to qualify."

"Rachel." Abby put a hand on her sister's arm.

"Come on in," Rachel told Ethan. "I'll show you."

He grinned at Abby. "I can't remember when I've had a better offer." He trailed after Rachel.

Abby muttered something that sounded distinctly unladylike and slammed the door. Rachel was explaining her baking project in extensive detail. They entered the kitchen with Abby trudging behind. "This is LuAnne," Rachel announced. "LuAnne, this is Ethan Maddux."

Ethan didn't miss the looks that passed between the blue-haired woman and Abby. They'd discussed him, and probably discussed his last conversation with Abby as well. He couldn't suppress a knowing smile.

"Nice to meet you," LuAnne said.

"He's not staying," Abby declared.

"Are you kidding?" he said smoothly. He glanced around the kitchen to see piles of baking ingredients filling every open space. "Why would I leave?"

Rachel beamed at him. Abby looked like she wanted to kick his shins. "If you want to stay," Rachel said, "you have to help."

"No one samples unless they help," LuAnne told him. "I gave up trying to get away with it years ago."

Ethan unbuttoned the cuffs of his denim shirt and started rolling back the sleeves. "Fair enough." He looked at Rachel. "What do I do?"

Rachel pointed to a stack of egg cartons. "Separate eggs and yolks."

His expression turned blank. LuAnne shot Abby another look and said smoothly, "Abby'll show you how."

They spent the next two hours elbow-deep in baking ingredients. Ethan couldn't remember the last time he'd enjoyed himself more. Until he'd tried it with Abby, he had no idea baking could be so erotic. She'd glowered at LuAnne, but *had* shown him the trick of separating eggs. He'd taken the opportunity to put his hands over hers where she held the eggshells. She'd given him a slightly chastising glance that reminded him of his third-grade teacher. "I asked you for a favor," she said in a low whisper, "not to invade my life."

"I'm a corporate raider. Invading is what I do best."

She'd rolled her eyes, but he didn't think he'd imagined the way her fingers trembled beneath his.

As the night progressed, he took every opportunity to touch her. He came up behind her while she was layering a sheet of filo dough with butter. He placed one hand on her shoulder and leaned forward in seemingly innocent curiosity. "What is that?" he asked, moving his thumb to her nape.

Abby tensed but didn't move away. "It's filo dough," Rachel told him from across the room. "Abby is buttering it so we can use it for pastry puffs."

He pressed his lips close to Abby's ear. "What do you have to do with it to make it into a pastry puff?"

"You slice it with a very sharp knife into extremely tiny pieces."

He swept his thumb over the bare skin beneath her ponytail. "Is it sweet enough to eat?"

Her color heightened to a delightful shade of deep pink. "Not until it's stuffed."

He touched the shell of her ear. "I'm getting tired of waiting."

LuAnne coughed and pushed him slightly aside. "Er, sorry, I need the eggs."

"No problem." Ethan lowered his hand and rested against the counter.

LuAnne retrieved the mixing bowl full of egg yolks and gave Abby her attention. "You holding up all right, Ab? You look a little flushed."

Abby slapped another slab of butter on the dough. "I'm fine."

Rachel checked the clock on the oven. "We're almost done," she announced to no one in particular. "As soon as we get the ingredients prepped, we'll quit for the night."

"Quit?" Ethan asked.

Rachel nodded. "I always do the ingredients the night before. It saves time with the baking."

LuAnne swiped another cutting board full of chopped chocolate into a bowl. "What time are we starting tomorrow?"

"Not too early," Abby said. "Rachel and I have Carlton's graduation party in the morning."

Rachel groaned. "I told you I don't have time for that. How am I supposed to get all this done by Monday?"

"I'll help," Ethan volunteered. "It'll make it go faster."

Abby looked at him with surprise. "I had no idea you were so domestically inclined."

"You're about to learn several things about me, Abby." He winked at her. "I've got stuff I'm dying to show you."

At 12:30 A.M., Ethan and Abby were the only ones left standing. They'd finished preparing the ingredients a little after midnight. LuAnne had staggered to the guest room, while Rachel had curled up on the sofa and fallen asleep in front of the TV during a rerun of *Iron Chef*. Ethan had the advantage of West Coast time on his side—his internal clock said it was shortly after ten-thirty. Abby had dumped mixing bowls and utensils in the sink and was scrubbing them hard enough to wear down the stainless steel.

With a slight smile, Ethan eased up behind her and put his hands on her shoulders. They tensed. She kept scrubbing, so he started rubbing the knotted muscles. "Tough week?" he asked.

She sighed. "You could say that."

"I was expecting you to call."

She dropped a large spoon into the sudsy water. Her head came up, and she met his gaze in the reflection of the kitchen window. "Why?"

He tipped his head to one side. "Why not?" He

rubbed his hands down her arms. "Are you annoyed with me?"

She shook her head. "I just want to know what you're doing here."

He wasn't sure he knew how to answer that. "My assistant told me I've been acting like a jerk. I gave it some thought, and realized there was some unsettled business between us."

"You said you were coming back Tuesday."

He studied her reflection, trying to decide if she was being sarcastic. "I said certain other things to you that night too. Things that warranted a little more attention."

"I don't think—"

He caught her wrists and pressed his thumbs to her pulse. "I'm starting to think maybe you didn't exactly understand me."

"Why would you think that?"

"Because I got this funny little note from you that sounded like we were colleagues at a dinner party," he said patiently. "Obviously, you missed some of the, ah, undertones of the conversation." He stroked the inside of her wrist with his thumb. "I thought I'd better come and set things straight with you."

Abby pulled her hands free and turned to face him. He should have backed up a step so she wouldn't have to stand so close to the counter, but he was enjoying the sensation of having her pressed against him in such tantalizing proximity. "I know you think I'm some kind of moron, but if I'm supposed to have figured this out, I haven't. I've lost plenty of sleep over it, though."

"I'm glad to hear I wasn't the only one."

Abby searched his gaze. "I'm kind of a plain-speech sort of person, you know. And if you're saying what I think you're saying, then maybe you've got the wrong girl." She blew an errant curl off her forehead.

No, he thought as he watched the curl spring back over her face, definitely the right woman. No question about it. He barely resisted the urge to topple her into his arms. He wasn't going to wait much longer to kiss this woman. "I don't think so," he assured her. "But I haven't quite got you figured out yet."

"And it's driving you crazy, isn't it?" She managed a slight laugh. "Good grief, Ethan, I'm really not that complicated."

"On the surface maybe. But there are layers. I'm very interested in layers."

He thought he saw her color rise. "I don't think—"

"I told my CFO today that I was taking off for the holiday."

"So?"

"So I haven't taken a holiday in eight years. He was a little stunned."

"Did you tell him you're thinking about getting involved in Harrison's life again?"

"Yes. He may never recover."

"I doubt Harrison will either."

He put his other hand on the counter so that he bracketed her hips. "I don't give a damn about Harrison. He's not the reason I'm here, and you know it."

Her eyes widened. "I was really afraid you were going to say that." She scooted several steps away before she slid a chair between them. "And I wish you'd stop."

"Stop what?" He advanced a step.

Abby's fingers tightened on the chairback. "Stop trying to unbalance me."

"Is that what you think I'm doing?"

"Of course it's what you're doing. Did you even look at those reports I gave you?"

"Yes."

"And?"

"I have some people looking into it." He took another step. Abby held her ground.

"Then unless you're prepared to tell me what you can or can't do for MDS, we have nothing to talk about. You said so yourself."

"I did *not* say we have nothing to talk about." He rounded the chair in two quick strides. "That was your line. I remember."

She reached for the chair. "Why couldn't this wait until Tuesday?"

"I'm sick of waiting."

"Are you always this impatient?"

"Definitely." He eased the chair aside with his foot. She didn't look nervous, he noted, or even wary. There was simply an awareness in her eyes, a certain shimmer of energy under her skin that she might excuse away as anxiety, but which looked an awful lot like anticipation. "I don't believe in delayed gratification."

"Oh, crud, Ethan. I—"

It was the look of recognition in her eyes that pushed him over the edge. She might as well have said yes in the same sultry voice she'd used the other night. It gave him the assurance he needed, and the willpower to wait until the time was right. He wasn't prepared to start something with her sister sleeping in the living room. When he finally gave vent to his physical desire for Abby, he wanted her undivided attention.

He thrust his hands into his pockets. If he couldn't accomplish his first goal for the evening, then he might as well settle for the second. "Look, Abby—"

She held out a small hand. "Can you just give me a minute to think? I can't do it when you do that."

"Do what?"

She waved her hand at him. "That. It's that look. It unnerves me. I'm having that gazelle feeling again. No," she said sharply when he would have moved toward her. "Stand right there and don't budge."

Ethan stilled. "You know," he said, "I'm not very good at taking orders."

Her hand dropped to her side. "Are you always such a pain in the ass?"

That made him laugh. "That's what I've heard."

"Look, I came to you with one request, and it seemed pretty simple. I just wanted to know whether or not you were willing to help your father. If you're not, you're not."

"I didn't say I wouldn't do it."

"But you didn't say you would, either."

It was just as he thought, he realized. Abby wasn't the kind of woman to settle for anything less than a total commitment. She'd be that way in her personal life as well, instinct told him. The same depth of loyalty that kept her tied to Harrison would demand a similar commitment in return. If he'd ever entertained the notion that any relationship he might have with Abby could be uncomplicated, he cast it aside in the cluttered confines of her kitchen.

And while that should have scared the hell out of him, he could feel the insistent gnawing hunger driving him toward her. "Tomorrow," he said carefully. "Tomorrow I'm going to Carlton's party too. I had assumed you would be there."

She seemed to process the information. "Carlton's party?"

"Letty invited me."

"Harrison will be there."

"I figured he would."

"You know what will happen if you go."

"There won't be a spectacle. I'm perfectly capable of behaving myself." At her skeptical look, he chuckled. "Despite all appearances to the contrary."

She shook her head. "Harrison is mad as spit that I went to see you." She frowned. "I've never seen him like that."

"That bad?"

"Worse. When he sees you tomorrow, I don't know what he'll do."

"Nothing," Ethan assured her. "The man's a coward."

She flinched, but didn't disagree with him. "Ethan"—she held out one hand—"please don't make this any harder than it already is."

"I won't humiliate him, if that's what you mean."

"I know you won't."

He didn't dare consider why the calm assertion meant so much to him. "But if I'm going to get involved in this, sooner or later he's going to have to face me."

Abby sighed. "I know. I just thought—I mean,

Carlton's party. It seems so public. Are you sure you want to subject yourself to the entire clan?"

"You'll make it worth my while."

"So you say."

He shook his head. "Don't argue, Abby."

"Would it do me any good?"

She sounded so disgruntled that he laughed. "Not really. You had to know when you asked for my help that you'd have to make certain concessions."

"Like always giving you your own way?"

He leaned forward and caught the scent of cinnamon lingering on her skin. "It's a start."

"I just think we should—"

He headed off what he knew was an inevitable objection. "Don't say you think we need to talk." He stepped back against his chair. "I've never had a good conversation that started that way."

"But I can't—"

"Can't what, Abby? Trust me? Is that it?"

"I don't know."

"You trust me," he assured her. At her disgruntled stare, he nodded. "You do. If you didn't, you never would have come to me in the first place. I wouldn't be considering bailing Harrison out of his financial woes, and I sure as hell wouldn't be in your house."

Abby stared at him for what seemed an endless stretch. He was beginning to wonder if she was going to respond. Finally, she reached out a hand and laid it on his sleeve. "It's not you," she said softly—so softly, he had to move closer to hear her over the hum of the dishwasher. "It's just that I—I'm not sure I can trust myself."

He raised an eyebrow. "Why not?"

She raised her extraordinary eyes to his, and the look he saw in them stole his breath. Surrender, desire, hunger, they were all there. Waiting for him. His fingers tightened on the back of the chair. Abby brushed a curl behind her ear. "I've had a week and a half to think about this," she admitted. "And it's nuts. It's certifiable. If I told this to anyone, they'd think I was the craziest person alive."

"And?"

She clutched her fingers together. "And—I don't think I can trust myself not to fall for you."

Peace settled on Ethan like a comfortable blanket. He felt the sudden stillness ease the tension that had been steadily building in him since Tuesday. "That," he said softly as he reached out to cup her face, "is undoubtedly the best news I've had in weeks." With a slight smile, he bent his head and pressed a brief, hard kiss to her lips. "Tomorrow, after the party, we'll go over the numbers. I'll show you what I've come up with."

"I have to help Rachel tomorrow."

"We'll do that too."

"You don't have to—"

"I wouldn't miss it." He swept his thumb over her lips. "Have sweet dreams, Abigail. I'll see you in the morning."

Ethan rested his back against the rail of the *Flying Cloud*, Harrison Montgomery's elegantly appointed yacht, which sat dockside on Lake Michigan. He'd deliberately arrived early, wanting to board the sleek vessel before the Montgomerys, and more pointedly, before Abby. Several members of Harrison's crew remembered him, so he'd had no trouble talking himself aboard. He'd chosen a strategic spot near the starboard bow where he could watch the activity around the gangway and decide when to reveal his presence.

Abby and Rachel arrived soon after, despite their late night. He frowned as he watched them directing the caterers and the crew for the setup. Trust Harrison to invite the woman to his nephew's party only to expect her to coordinate it for him—as she did everything else in his chaotic and crumbling empire.

Abby seemed none the worse for the too-few hours of sleep she'd gotten, which made Ethan feel unaccountably provoked. He'd lain awake in his downtown hotel room replaying the evening in his mind. She, if the sparkle in her eyes and the spring in her step were any indication, had evidently slept like a baby.

She was giving orders with the practiced precision of a field marshal. He'd never had the chance to observe her, he realized, when she hadn't known he was watching. The experience was quite revealing.

Abby moved with a natural grace, like a woman who instinctively knew who she was and what she wanted. The underlying tension he'd seen in her before was gone. Easily in her element as she attended to the details, she exuded a quiet confidence that made him wonder what kind of lover she was. Unless he missed his guess, Abby would be the type of woman he most enjoyed.

He watched in masculine appreciation as she strolled across the deck and checked the caterers' supplies. Ivory shorts hugged her generous hips. He had a recollection of her telling him she'd gained five pounds from Rachel's cheesecake. If that was true, she owed her sister a debt of gratitude.

Her body was a seamless sweep of rounded lines. A navy blue tank top, practical, loose-fitting, and sexy as hell, hugged her breasts. Occasionally, when she reached for something or bent a certain way, he caught the barest glimpse of lace and silk underneath the plain blue cotton. Absolutely fascinating, he decided as he took a sip of his drink. A woman of secrets, just as he'd thought.

She didn't seem to know that her braided hair begged to be mussed or that her tanned limbs asked for his hands. She remained focused on the bustle of activity. Now and then she would pause to wipe a bead of sweat from her forehead or toss her thick braid over her shoulder, but she worked steadily with her sister, supervising the setup for the party.

One of the caterers said something that made her laugh. When Abby tipped her head back, the sun brought out red lights in her hair. Ethan decided he'd been patient long enough. He set his drink down and strode across the deck.

"Need a hand with that?" he asked quietly as she juggled a covered box of canapés.

Startled by his voice, Abby lost her precarious hold on the box. It tumbled into Ethan's arms. She suppressed a twinge of envy. "My God," she muttered, pushing a lock of hair off her damp face. "Where did you come from?"

He nodded toward the shadows. "I was waiting."

She moved to take the box back, but Ethan tightened his grip. "You're up awfully early—considering," she said.

"Couldn't sleep," he told her, and took a step closer.

She pressed her lips together in slight disapproval. "Join the crowd."

She looked so disgruntled, he chuckled. "Bad night?"

She made a charming little squeaking noise

in the back of her throat. "You could say that."
She moved a few inches away from him. "And
stop looking at me like that. I can't think when you
do."

"That's generally the plan. Every time I give you
room to think, you start coming up with excuses."

"And they're good ones," she pointed out. "Like
the fact that Harrison is going to be here soon."

"And you don't want him to see us together?"
He couldn't quite keep the accusation out of his
voice.

"I didn't say that. I just don't want him to get
the wrong idea."

"What idea would that be, Abby?"

She did him the favor of not saying anything
inane. Instead, she shook her head. "I'm not going
to have this discussion with you right now."

He shrugged. "Your choice. It's always been
your choice."

No wonder her nerves felt scraped raw, Abby
thought. The man was relentless. "You could try
to make this a little easier."

"I'll be on my best behavior," he promised. He
shifted the box under one arm. "If the old man
doesn't throw me off the ship, you can consider it
progress."

"I just wish you'd—"

"Try to understand him? See things his way?"
His laugh was humorless. "I stopped being able to
do that the day I had to bury my mother."

"I didn't deserve that," she said softly. "When have I ever said that to you?"

He frowned. "Sorry. He brings out the worst in me."

"I know." Abby studied him in the bright sunlight and felt the familiar tingles along her nerve endings. He wore a hunter-green shirt tucked into khaki trousers, and deck shoes with no socks. The look should have been comfortable, casual. But if she'd learned one thing about him, looks were almost always deceiving. There was nothing casual in the corded strength of his tanned forearm wrapped around the box; nor in the sleek, dark hair lifted slightly by the wind so it framed his angular face and strong jaw. He appeared to be brooding this morning, and the slight edge to his expression made her yearn to comfort him.

She placed a hand on his arm. "For what it's worth, I don't understand everything that's happened between the two of you, but I'm sorry I dragged you into this."

His lips turned into a slight smile that chased away the lingering sadness in his gaze. "There it is again," he said.

"What?"

"When you feel very passionate about something"— he seemed to roll the words off his tongue—"you get this breathy tone in your voice." He leaned close enough for her to catch the scent of his soap. It was masculine and unsubtle—

like him. He touched the end of her braid where it rested on her shoulder. "I think I'm getting addicted to it."

Before she could respond, Rachel bounded up the stairs from the galley. "Abby, I thought—" She stopped when she saw Ethan, then broke into a wide grin. "Ethan! Hi."

He hesitated for the barest of seconds, then dragged his gaze from Abby and gave Rachel a warm smile. "Hey, Rach."

"I didn't know you were coming here today." She took the box of canapés from him.

"Last-minute change of plans," he told her.

Rachel clearly shared none of Abby's trepidation over Ethan's presence. She grabbed his arm and started tugging him forward. "This will be great. I was going to be so totally bored all day, knowing I have all that baking to do at home."

"I told you I'd help you this afternoon."

"Yeah, I know. Still, it's going to take all night."

He shot Abby a wry look. "I do some of my best work late at night."

Abby rolled her eyes. Rachel laughed. "Well, at least this won't be boring, now that you're here."

"Stuffy parties not your style?" he teased.

"As if." Rachel linked her hand through his elbow. "Carlton's okay, though, so it shouldn't be too gruesome."

Ethan slanted another look at Abby. "I hope not. He's coming to work for me next month."

She had no idea how to interpret that comment. The man was turning out to be every bit as perplexing as she'd feared. Rachel, she noted, feeling strangely irritated, displayed no such qualms. "Come on, Ethan," she was saying. "I'll show you around."

Abby watched them go, frowning into the early-morning sunlight. In the days since his startling announcement on Tuesday night, she'd tried hard to persuade herself that she had everything blown completely out of proportion. Ethan was a very attractive, dynamic man, and naturally she found him compelling. She'd come very close to convincing herself that the strange nervousness she felt around him, and the way her skin seemed a little more sensitive and the blood seemed to ring in her ears, were merely symptoms of the stress she felt over Harrison's obvious displeasure with Ethan's involvement in MDS's financial crisis. Anyone in her shoes would feel the pressure.

Anyone, she'd told herself.

And almost believed it. Until she'd heard his deep voice this morning and her heartbeat had tripped into double time—reminding her that she had the worst possible timing and taste. While trying to help one of her oldest and dearest friends face a potentially devastating personal crisis, she was falling for his sworn enemy.

With a groan, Abby dropped into a deck chair.

"Moron," she muttered, and buried her face in her hands. Years ago, she'd stopped worrying that her hormones seemed to be on a permanent sabbatical. After the death of her parents, she'd been plunged headlong into adulthood. No wonder, she'd long ago decided, that she lacked the kind of sit-up-and-pay-attention sex drive her friends had. LuAnne was prone to fall head over heels in love with a different man at least once a month. To Abby, things had always appeared more serious.

Somewhere along the way, she'd even invested money in a psychiatrist, who'd calmly informed her that losing her father at such a young age had understandably cast her into an endless search for a replacement. It had sounded like crap at the time, but Abby had taken the advice and distilled it into her own, more practical view of her general lack of interest in the male species. It wasn't that she didn't like men, exactly; it was just that she didn't particularly need them. She'd gotten on fine without one for most of her life, and neither her heart nor her hormones seemed especially inclined to change that fact.

And then she'd come face-to-face with Ethan Maddux. Though she'd seen him maybe a half-dozen times before, and always at a distance, that day she had realized she'd never really *seen* the man at all. At least, not quite like that.

In a sudden moment of clarity, her sex drive, like Rip Van Winkle, had snapped from its inexplicable slumber and come to complete and arresting attention. Her hormones had gone from zero to full throttle in the space of a heartbeat, and she'd been struggling for equilibrium ever since. Her mind had started to drift during the day. She'd find herself remembering the way he twirled his fountain pen between his fingers, or how his silvery eyes darkened when he was intent on understanding something. Or, more often, she'd hear the shiver-inducing sound of his voice in her dreams. Always saying, "I want you, Abby," in that go-to-hell half whisper that raised the goose bumps on her skin.

When he'd kissed her last night, she'd practically melted like one of Rachel's chocolate desserts. Lord knew, if her sister hadn't been sleeping in the next room, she probably couldn't have found the courage to stop him. She had a sinking sensation that she was rapidly getting in over her head—and the worst part of it was, she didn't feel very inclined to do anything about it.

Of course, it didn't help one damned bit that the man kept turning up in her life looking like some fantasy out of a women's handbook on perfect specimens of the male species. Even today, clad in simple, casual clothes, he exuded a raw sort of power that had her body humming a few degrees above normal.

With a low groan, she sat back in the chair to await the inevitable. Harrison would arrive soon. He'd see Ethan and hell would break loose. Then, maybe, she'd have some peace.

 *Seven*

It was like a scene in a silent-movie melodrama, Ethan mused as he faced his father across the deck of the yacht. Most of the Montgomerys had already arrived. Letty had greeted him warmly. Other reactions had ranged from avidly curious to openly hostile. So far Abby and Letty had managed to keep the peace. But at precisely two minutes to ten o'clock, Harrison strolled up the gangway.

Ethan was surprised by the absolute lack of emotion he felt when he saw his father. Generally, just the thought of the man had the power to infuriate him, but the few times he'd seen him, he'd found himself curiously ambivalent. With measured precision, he set his glass down on the table and stood.

Abby, he noted with some satisfaction, had begun making her way steadily toward him. She wore a look of determination that tempted him to wrap one arm around her waist and pull her against his side. She'd slug him, he figured, if he did that. He saw his aunt Letty shoot him a worried look. He answered with a slight wink that seemed to set her at ease.

Harrison greeted two of his sisters before his gaze fell on Ethan. The older man's shoulders squared and the space between them seemed to stretch like a fathomless divide across the sleek wooden deck. Several seconds of nerve-racking silence cluttered the breezy air. Abby jabbed Ethan in the arm. "Say something," she demanded.

He gave her a censorious look. The fierce expression in her eyes told him she was seriously contemplating kicking him in the shins if he didn't do something to break the tension. With a weary sigh, he faced Harrison again. "I won't say it's nice to see you," he announced. That won him another jab from Abby.

Harrison scowled. "I can always count on you to be honest, at least."

"At least," Ethan concurred.

The collected members of the Montgomery brood watched anxiously as the two men squared off. Letty finally stepped forward and wrapped her hand through the bend of Harrison's arm. "Now, Harrison, don't be difficult. I invited Ethan to come today. He's my guest."

Harrison scowled at his sister. "It's *my* yacht."

Letty was undeterred. "And it's my party. So don't spoil it."

"Damn it, Leticia—"

She laughed. "Now I know you're mad. You never call me Leticia unless you're positively fuming."

Harrison glared at her. "I would have preferred a little notice."

"I didn't know until yesterday." Letty glanced at Abby. "Abby will tell you. Won't you, dear?"

Ethan had actually started to enjoy himself. He looked sideways at Abby, whose expression of discomfort somehow managed to look charming. She replied, "He got into town yesterday."

"And you decided it was a good idea to bring him along?"

Ethan folded his arms over his chest. "Actually, I decided that."

Harrison continued to observe Abby with something close to condemnation. "What the hell were you thinking, Abby?"

She made a disgusted sound in the back of her throat. "For the love of—" Giving Ethan a hard look, she continued. "You're acting like ten-year-olds."

"You can't possibly understand," Harrison said tightly.

"And obviously, neither can you. What do you

think is going on here—that I just figured I'd find a way to really piss you off today? Is that it?"

Ethan swallowed a chuckle. Harrison's eyebrows drew together in a fierce frown. "Abigail, *really!*"

She glared back at him. "For crying out loud, Harrison, you knew this was going to happen sooner or later. We talked about it yesterday."

"I would have preferred something more private."

"He's family," she said. The collective gasp of the Montgomery clan was so strong, Ethan was surprised it didn't ruffle the sail. Abby seemed undeterred. "He's got a right to be here."

Harrison's face had turned red. "I'm not going to explain myself to you."

"No," she said. "You aren't. You never would."

"I don't have to."

The verbal dart hit a nerve. Abby took a slight step back. "I don't suppose you do."

Visibly frustrated, Harrison focused his angry stare on Ethan. It had little effect. He'd become immune to it years ago. "I should have known—"

Abby held up a hand to interrupt him. "You could try acting like a grown-up." She looked at Ethan. "And so could you. If the testosterone gets any thicker up here, we'll need respirators."

That remark won another muttered reaction from the Montgomerys. Ethan stifled a laugh and reached for Abby's hand. "Thanks for the tip,

Miss Manners." He ignored her tug on his hand and tucked it close to his side. Giving her a beatific smile that amplified the fierceness in her gaze, he lowered his voice for her ears only. "I promised you I'd behave myself, didn't I?"

"Then do it," she urged him through clenched teeth.

From the corner of his eye Ethan saw Harrison staring at them, his jaw tightened to form a look Ethan remembered. Displeasure and anger were warring with his self-control. He had been on the receiving end of that look too many times. Letty gave her brother's arm a slight squeeze. Harrison stared hard at Ethan, then finally relented. Sending a silent, waved signal to his skipper to set sail, he turned his back on Ethan. The small crowd aboard the boat let out a collective gasp of relief.

Abby finally managed to free her hand from Ethan's grip. "Ugh," she muttered beneath her breath.

Ethan looked at Harrison's turned shoulder and fought a silent war with restraint. The tone in Abby's voice kicked his temper up another notch, but he couldn't disguise the anger in his eyes. "What did you say?"

"I said, ugh."

"You had to expect—"

She held up her hand. "That's not what I meant. I meant, 'Ugh, why does he have to be so damned stubborn?' " She brushed her braid over her shoulder, and Ethan felt his equilibrium start to return.

"He enjoys confrontation," Ethan said. "No matter *what* he says."

"I know that."

Would she ever stop surprising him? he wondered as he contemplated the idea that he couldn't remember the last time someone had defended him.

A slight smile played at the corners of her mouth. "I'm blond, but that doesn't mean I'm dumb." She leaned a little closer to him. "And actually, by the strictest definition of the term, I'm not really blond either."

He laughed, surprising himself. In a thousand years he wouldn't have believed he could walk away from a confrontation with his father and find something to laugh about. "Your stylist deserves a commendation, then."

"My stylist has blue hair," she reminded him. There was a look of camaraderie and gratitude in her eyes. "In case I forget to tell you later, thank you for being so generous."

He raised his eyebrows.

"That could have been a lot uglier. Harrison probably would have liked an excuse to throw you off the yacht."

"You can count on it."

"Thanks for rising to the occasion."

"Don't get your hopes up. The party's just starting."

"But don't worry." She patted his arm. "I got you into this, and I'll get you out. Just follow my lead."

The yacht pulled away from the dock while Harrison's family continued to feel their way gingerly through the emotional minefield on board. Ethan stood his ground, talking casually to anyone who approached him, but making no move toward his father. Abby upheld her end of the bargain by not leaving his side. Harrison finally meandered across the deck and stood directly in front of them. "I'll see you below in the lounge, Ethan," he said, his tone grim. "If you can spare the time." His gaze flicked to Abby. "Alone, I think, would be best."

Abby frowned. "I don't think that's a good idea."

"We aren't going to kill each other, Abigail," Harrison said.

She gave Ethan a look that said she didn't quite trust that remark. He kept his expression deliberately impassive. Abby shook her head. "I just think I should be there."

Harrison didn't relent. "Some things are better discussed without an audience."

Irritation again flared in her eyes. "Think of it this way. It's like eastern Europe. The Russians"—she poked Harrison's chest—"were determined to annex the entire eastern bloc. The Balkans"—she indicated Ethan with her thumb—"were the wild card. They could have bolted at any time."

"And where do you fit into this charming metaphor?" Harrison asked her.

Abby nodded. "I'm Poland. I'm the buffer state that keeps everyone from killing each other."

"Well, then, if the peace talks spin out of control, I'll send for you." He looked at Ethan. "Are you coming?"

Ethan felt Abby tense beside him. She'd probably kill him for it later, but he couldn't resist the urge to touch her a final time. He cupped her face in one hand and bent his head to press a swift kiss to her lips. "Wait for me," he whispered.

Abby glanced from him to Harrison and back again, then nodded. Ethan didn't miss the bitter stare she received from Harrison moments before the older man headed for the stairs.

Harrison poured himself a bourbon as he watched Ethan across the heavily decorated room. The dark paneling and overstuffed furniture looked formal and outdated—like the owner, Ethan mused. "Drink?" his father asked.

"No. I don't."

Harrison regarded him with a raised eyebrow, then replaced the stopper in the decanter. "Charming display up there."

Ethan crossed his arms over his chest. "Wasn't it? Reminded me of old times."

Harrison slammed his tumbler down on the

desk with such force, the amber liquid sloshed over the rim. "All right, Ethan, care to tell me what this is about?"

"Letty invited me to come to Carlton's party," he said with deliberate calm. "It seemed like the best opportunity for you and me to set a few things straight."

"Why? So you could ruin the event for my nephew?"

Ethan shook his head and sat in one of the burgundy leather chairs. "No. I did it because I was relatively certain you wouldn't want to embarrass the poor guy by having me thrown overboard."

Harrison stared at him for several seconds before he sat down behind the desk. "And Abby?" he asked.

"Is old enough to make her own decisions."

"And you think she'll decide on you?" Harrison's eyebrows drew together in a fierce frown.

Ethan shrugged. "I don't know yet."

"But you hope so?"

"What's between Abby and me isn't really any of your business, Harrison."

At the sharp rebuke, the older man straightened in his chair and regarded Ethan with a censorious frown. "Abigail doesn't deserve to be used."

"Maybe I'm not using her."

Harrison snorted. "You can't expect me to believe that the possibility of visiting revenge on me through Abby has escaped your attention."

Ethan narrowed his gaze. "Why don't you tell me about that?" he probed. "Where did you find her, anyway?"

Harrison swirled the drink in his glass. "Did your private investigator leave out some details? I know you've had someone doing an investigation."

"I wasn't trying to keep it a secret."

"Does Abby know?"

"That's between me and Abby."

Harrison scowled. "Damn you, Ethan. Why does it always have to be about winning and losing with you?"

Ethan's laugh was humorless. "Because that's the pattern you established for me."

"I never meant—" Harrison broke off with a shake of his head. "It's too late now. If you're hell-bent on destroying me . . ."

"If I was hell-bent on destroying you, I'd let your company go down in flames."

"I'm not talking about MDS. Abby isn't part of that equation."

"When did you become so softhearted toward your employees, Harrison? I remember a time when you wouldn't give them the time of day." Ethan pinned him with a harsh look. "No matter who they were."

Harrison sucked in a sharp breath. "I'm not going to get into a discussion about your mother."

"Of course not. You never would."

"You don't understand."

"No," Ethan said between clenched teeth. "I certainly don't."

Harrison sagged in his chair, as if the weight of the conversation had become too much for him. He buried his face in his hands. "If I thought I could make you—" He paused and shook his head. "Abigail shouldn't be dragged into the middle of this. What's between you and me isn't her problem."

"I don't plan to make it her problem."

A few minutes of silence passed between them. Finally, Harrison placed his hands on the desk. "Tell me why you're really here, Ethan."

"Abby asked me to look into your financial problems."

"And you agreed. Why?"

"Actually"—Ethan crossed his long legs in front of him—"I haven't agreed yet."

"Bullshit. You wouldn't be sitting here if you weren't going to do it."

"Maybe not." Ethan rubbed his fingers on the burled wood arm of his chair. "There are—considerations."

"Do they have to do with Abigail?"

"Some of them."

"You're a real bastard, you know that?"

At the irony of the statement, Ethan shrugged. "You don't have to tell me that."

Harrison ignored his sarcasm. "Abby's a good

friend and an innocent bystander. She doesn't deserve to get hurt."

"Why is everyone convinced that I'm going to hurt her?"

"Aren't you?"

"Not if I can help it."

Harrison glared at him. "Get real, Ethan. What are you prepared to offer her?"

"Good God, Harrison, are you asking me what my intentions are?"

"I'm asking you to be decent."

"Like you were?"

Harrison's lips pressed into a thin line. "I deserved that, I suppose."

Damned right he did, Ethan thought. "I'm willing to discuss MDS with you, but what's between Abby and me—" He waved a hand in the air. "That's off limits. It's a bit late in the day, don't you think, for a father-and-son chat on the importance of honor and decency?" The words hit their mark. Harrison glowered at him, but Ethan didn't back down. "Tell me how you got yourself into this mess," he insisted.

Harrison rubbed a hand over his face in frustration. "I don't owe you any explanations."

"You damned well do if I'm going to get sucked into saving this company of yours."

"You have no idea what you're dealing with. Neither does Abby." He shook his head. "If I have to sell, it's not the end of the world."

"It's the end of the Montgomery fortune." At Harrison's raised eyebrows, Ethan nodded. "I've seen the statements. The hit will wipe out most of your assets."

"You can't necessarily believe what you see on paper," Harrison replied carefully. "Numbers can be deceiving."

"I'm starting to get a picture. And I'm starting not to like it." Ethan gazed deeply into the pale blue eyes of his father. They looked weary, and they'd lost some of their fire. "Do you want to tell me what's been going on, or do you want me to figure it out on my own?"

"I have no idea what you're talking about."

"No?" Ethan rose from his chair to pace the confines of the small space. "You don't know that your accounts have been leaking for the past eighteen months?"

"Financial oversight—"

"Or that you're draining off your assets at rates that should have you out of business in less than a year?"

"We were undercapitalized."

"You don't know that inexplicably large investments have been made in risk ventures?"

"The global market—"

"Or that low-end stock trade-offs have your balance sheets in the gutter?"

"I needed to increase our reserves."

Ethan pinned him with a hard stare. "Where's the money going, Harrison?"

The old man seemed to hesitate for a few moments. Something in his expression told Ethan he knew more than he had let on, but then the look was gone. Harrison shook his head. "I don't know what you're talking about."

"I have some of my people checking into it. I'm starting to hear words I don't like—like 'collusion' and 'insider trading.' "

"You should be familiar with how to handle that, then. I understand you have a client under investigation for racketeering."

"I guess I'm not the only one who's been investigating."

"I watch the news."

"And pay Atkison Bates," he said, naming the firm Harrison employed to track Maddux Consulting's business ventures, "to give you quarterly reports." When Harrison didn't respond, Ethan told him, "I've known for years."

"Whether you believe it or not," his father said, "I wanted to know how you were doing."

"You'll forgive my skepticism?"

Harrison shrugged his broad shoulders. "It doesn't bear discussing, I suppose." He traced his fingers over the smooth surface of his desk. "For what it's worth, Ethan, I regret that things turned out the way they did." He met Ethan's gaze. "I never wanted anyone to get hurt."

Ethan frowned. "Is that how Abby ended up working for you?"

"Can't a man regret the decisions he once made and try to make good on them later in life? Is there anything wrong with that?"

Ethan didn't respond. Harrison shook his head and asked abruptly, "Are you sleeping with her?"

The door to the vault rattled. Ethan had to clamp down hard to suppress his rage. "Are you?" he shot back.

That had Harrison on his feet. "Damn you—"

"You damned me a long time ago, Harrison. But unfortunately for you, I just won't go away, will I?"

Harrison took a step back. "That's not what I meant."

"I imagine that whole childhood-and-youth phase I went through was really tough on you. I mean, it had to be a nightmare having me right under your nose to remind you that you never could stand up to your father. The stakes were always too high, weren't they?"

"It wasn't like that," Harrison replied through gritted teeth.

"Either way," Ethan said, unwilling and unable to keep the bitterness from his voice, "you finally got what you wanted. I walked out of your life."

"And now you're back."

"The prodigal has returned. What a joyous occasion."

"And you want Abby, don't you?"

Ethan hesitated, then nodded. "Yes."

"She's out of your league."

"Probably," he admitted.

"But it isn't going to stop you from pursuing her."

"Why does that bother you?" Ethan asked. "If you were going to seduce the woman, you'd have done it years ago."

"You don't think I have?"

"Hell, no. Abby's got too much class for that."

Something softened Harrison's expression. "So you aren't after her because you think she's my lover?"

"No," Ethan said tightly. "Believe it or not, the thought of bedding your conquests leaves me a little cold. That's your style, not mine."

Harrison sat down again. "Why do you always have to be so difficult, Ethan?"

Ethan watched him warily, but didn't try to answer. "What's going on in that brain of yours, old man?"

"I'm not entirely sure yet. I have to think about it for a while. When it comes to Abby, though, I wish you'd trust me and leave her alone."

"It's too late for that." Ethan studied his father closely.

The look Harrison gave him had a definite sadness to it. "It's too late for many things, Ethan. Far too many things."

This was the closest to an apology he was likely to get, Ethan supposed. He shook his head. "I'm not your enemy, you know."

"Not yet you aren't."

"Care to explain that?"

Harrison shrugged. "Suffice it to say that you're wading into some very deep water if you decide to get involved in the MDS buyout. If you're as smart as people say you are, you'll go back to San Francisco and forget everything about this. In a few months it'll all be over."

"Over?"

Harrison picked up his bourbon. "Watch your back, Ethan. And whatever you do, don't let Abby get hurt."

"You think she will?"

"I think she could." Harrison looked him in the eye. "You've got a right to hate me, but you don't have a right to destroy her. She never did anything to deserve that from you."

"I'll bear that in mind."

"And for what it's worth," his father told him, "I appreciate your willingness to do this. If you manage to bail us out of this mess, I'll take back every rotten thing I ever said about you."

Ethan shook his head in frustration and reached for the door. "That's something to live for."

He found Abby near a secluded area of the deck. On the opposite end of the yacht, Carlton's party was in full swing, but Abby had pulled away from the crowd to watch the waves lap the hull as the sleek craft cut through the water. She had wrapped her arms around herself to guard against the spray and the slight chill of the wind. Ethan walked up behind her and wrapped his arm around her waist. "We both survived," he said into her ear. "No blood was drawn."

She didn't move. "What did you tell him?"

"I told him I had some people looking into things, and that I hadn't fully decided whether or not I wanted to get involved in this."

She turned then and stood with her back to the rail. "Why?"

"Why haven't I decided?"

She shook her head. "Why didn't you just tell him what you told me? That I'm part of the bargain?"

He wasn't sure if he heard hurt in the question or not. He was starting to have a bad feeling that he was seriously screwing this up. He almost wished Pamela were here to set him straight. What he wanted from Abby was too important for him to blunder with his usual lack of tact. He gave her a shrewd look. "Why did you defend me earlier?"

"I wasn't defending you," she said absently. "I was keeping the balance sheet even. It was you and all those Montgomerys. It didn't seem fair."

Ethan played with a tendril of her hair as a

smile lifted the corners of his mouth. "Like the avenging angel against the class bully?"

"I'd hardly say you were outmatched *or* outwitted. I just didn't think you should have to take that verbal barrage from Harrison just because you're doing the man a favor."

"It's like I told you, he's not the one I'm doing the favor for."

Abby glanced at the water. Several moments of silence elapsed. When she spoke, her voice was so low, he could barely hear her over the hum of the engine and the slap of the water. "Ethan, are you telling me that if I don't agree to have sex with you, you won't try to bail out MDS?" She looked sad, he observed, as if the question had hurt her to ask it. She didn't want to believe he was capable of something like that.

Relieved by the revelation, Ethan realized this was where he had misstepped. He'd momentarily forgotten that Abby was eons removed from the Pamelas of the world. The sophisticated repartee he could expect from his ex-fiancée wasn't part of Abby's vocabulary. She was honest and straightforward, in a classic, elegant kind of way. He'd expected her to return his verbal volleys with coy remarks and practiced phrases, but she was a woman who simply said what she meant. And the thought was having a profound effect on him. "No," he said finally. "I'm not saying that."

Confusion clouded her eyes. "But . . ."

He reached for one of her hands and guided it around his neck. "I'm saying," he told her, "that I won't agree to get involved in Harrison's life without certain promises from you."

"What kind of promises?"

"That when the time comes, you'll trust me to tell you the truth. That no matter what he says or who tells you I'm lying, when it comes right down to it, I'm the only one you can trust."

"I barely know you," she protested.

He traced the line of her jaw with his thumb. "Don't you?"

"Harrison is my friend—"

"And I have no idea where this is going. But I'm not willing to pursue it unless you tell me you trust me."

She searched his gaze, her own anguished and uncertain. "And all the rest?" she asked.

Ethan nodded and pressed the pad of his thumb to the corner of her mouth. "All the rest we'll settle when the time comes. I want you, Abby. I'd be lying if I said that didn't include wanting you in my bed. But it's more, believe me. I want to know that if you end up having to choose sides, you're going to be on mine."

She glanced along the rail of the ship to where Harrison's family was gathered. "They've taken care of me for a long time."

He knew exactly who she was talking about. "Have they?" he probed.

Her eyes drifted shut. "It's the only family Rachel and I have left."

"I understand that."

"You're asking me if I can turn my back on them."

"I'm asking you if you can trust me enough to believe me, even if it means accepting something you don't want to about Harrison Montgomery."

"Before this is over—" She hesitated. "You think I'll have to, don't you?"

As much as he would like to spare her, he knew it was better to lay it out now. "Yes."

"Can you tell me why?"

"I will when I have something concrete to show you. Right now, I just have hunches."

"And isn't it possible that you're wrong?"

"Anything is possible."

She glanced toward Harrison's family again. Laughter carried along the deck, in stark contrast to her noticeably melancholy mood. "What if I can't?"

"Then tell me now, and I'll go back to California."

Abby worried her lower lip with her teeth. "I'm not sure."

"I have to have it all," he told her. "It's the only way."

She watched as her sister made her way around the buffet table, delicately sampling each of the various dishes. She seemed to find strength in that. When she looked at Ethan again, her eyes showed determination and a subtle will that made him ache to kiss her. "Can I ask one thing in return?"

"The moon," he replied.

She shook her head, and the wind lifted one of her curls and danced with it. "Nothing that complicated." She placed both hands flat on his chest. "Promise you'll never try so hard to protect me from the truth that you refuse to give it to me."

He frowned. "Have other people done that to you, Abby?"

A host of conflicting emotions moved across the planes of her face. Her fingers curled into his shirtfront, and she laid her cheek against his chest. "I don't know yet," she said so softly he had to bend his head to hear her. "But I have a feeling I'm about to find out."

Eight

Abby closed her eyes. "I had no idea it was that bad."

Ethan gathered the stack of reports he'd been showing her for the last half hour. He and Abby sat on the couch in her living room. From the kitchen, they heard LuAnne and Rachel laughing as they worked on the baking project. The house had the delightful scent of chocolate and cinnamon.

"It'll take a miracle," he concurred.

She opened her eyes and looked at him. "But can you do it?"

At the hope in her gaze, he felt his stomach knot. "Maybe. I'm not sure."

The sound of clanging baking sheets in the kitchen momentarily drew her attention. Then she said, "When you were looking at the reports, did you come up with any idea how Harrison got into this mess?"

She was going to extract the answer from him. He should have expected it. He knew her well enough to realize that she would have examined these reports dozens of times, probing for anything that might provide a way out of the mess Harrison had created. Abby might not be a financial expert, but she was not a fool either. She was bound to have seen the inconsistencies.

If Ethan had spotted the truth from his rather cursory examination of the numbers, then Abby surely would have seen it too. For reasons he didn't begin to understand, he didn't want to tell her what he suspected—what was gradually being confirmed by the investigation in his office. He didn't want to be the one to shatter the illusions she held about Harrison Montgomery.

"Did you?" she asked again.

"It appears," he said, "that either someone is embezzling Harrison's company into ruin, or else he's gotten himself blackmailed."

Abby let out a long breath and rested her head in her hands. "I knew it."

He rubbed one hand up her spine. "And you wanted me to confirm it for you?"

"No, no, it wasn't like that." At his skeptical look, she nodded. "Really, it wasn't. When I came to see you the first time, I had no idea. It wasn't until after—while you were in Prague. Things started to get really bad. Several of Harrison's business associates called, looking for answers. And the family—" She shrugged. "They started getting hysterical when funds began to get tight. People were calling me, asking questions. I didn't know what to say. That's when I really started to go over the reports."

"But you weren't sure?"

"No. I'm not an expert, and there was every chance I was reading something wrong." She rubbed her eyes with her thumbs and forefingers. "I really wanted to be wrong."

Ethan kneaded a knot in her shoulder. "For what it's worth, I'm sorry. And I'm sorry you had to find out like this."

"Me too." She drew a fortifying breath. "But you still don't know exactly what's happening, do you?"

"Some of my top people are on this. At best, you've got an embezzler on your hands. If we find the culprit, then we might be able to repair some of the damage."

"And at worst?"

"At worst, Harrison has been bleeding the profits himself. Maybe he got over his head somewhere."

"Or it could be blackmail?"

"It could be," he concurred.

"And then what?"

"There are stockholders involved," he said slowly.

"I know."

"Other people's money."

"I know."

He hesitated. She still seemed to be waiting for an answer. Ethan forged ahead. "He might be in violation of federal trade laws."

She shuddered. "Oh, God."

"Which means he could go to jail."

Abby shivered. "I don't understand this," she said, and he heard the hurt in her voice. "How could he have let this happen?"

Ethan didn't answer. Abby seemed to make a decision then. She wiped her hands on the legs of her jeans and said quietly, "I can't change it."

"Not today," he agreed. And silently added, *And probably not ever.*

She appeared to process what he said for several seconds before she stood and extended a hand to him. "Then we might as well get back to work. If we don't help Rachel with the baking, we won't be able to taste."

Ethan took her hand, but made no move to rise from the sofa. "For what it's worth, Abby," he said quietly, "I may not like the man, but I didn't want to see you get hurt."

"I know." She folded her hand in his. "But there's no evidence yet, and you said yourself you could be wrong."

"I could be." He hoped she wasn't holding too tightly to the idea.

"Then I'll believe it when I see it."

And ignore it in the meantime, evidently. She'd probably hate him for it when he had to show her the truth, he mused. The thought made him want to strangle Harrison. Would the man ever lose the power he had to destroy people? The thought that he might not annoyed him. Abby seemed to have made a conscious decision to put the grim afternoon behind her. She was actively tugging on his hand. "Come on. We've got more than a thousand cookies to make before Monday."

Ethan didn't say another word about Harrison, MDS, or their conversation on the yacht that morning. Apparently he'd shifted his focus from Abby to the intricate and detailed process of baking. She wished she had his willpower. Her mind spun a mad dance from topic to topic, leaving her feeling distracted and dizzy.

As if he sensed Abby's need to retreat, Ethan maintained a lively conversation with LuAnne and Rachel. He asked Rachel enough questions to write his own cookbook. Rachel interacted with him in an easy banter, while Ethan seemed content to hand her ingredients and let her have command.

By noon they had twenty different batches of

cookie dough waiting to be shaped and baked. Ethan suggested dinner. Abby dropped into a chair with a weary groan and shook her head. "There's stuff in the refrigerator. There's no way I'm going out. I think I have enough flour in my hair to look like I survived a grain-elevator explosion."

Ethan was watching her closely. Too closely. So closely, she could feel her heart racing. When they'd returned from Carlton's party, he'd donned a pair of glasses to go over the reports with her. He still wore them. Though they should have made him look slightly bookish, they seemed to accentuate the carved lines of his face and the intensity of his silver eyes.

LuAnne reached for her purse. "I'm not for cooking, even if it's just the microwave. Why don't I go pick us up something?" She glanced at Rachel. "Chinese okay?"

"Bobby Chan's is pretty good," Rachel conceded. The popular take-out place specialized in lighter cuisine.

LuAnne nodded. "I could go for that." She gave Rachel a gentle shove toward the door. "You can come with me and help me carry it."

Rachel threw a glance at Ethan. "Oh, but—"

LuAnne gave her a not-so-subtle shove. "You need to get some daylight, girlfriend. You're coming with me."

Rachel's gaze passed from Ethan to Abby and

back again. She untied her apron without further comment. "All right. Would you guys watch the timers while we're gone?"

"Gladly," Ethan said.

The kitchen door swung shut behind them. Abby looked at Ethan with a slight shake of her head. "I can always count on LuAnne to be so subtle."

"I don't have much patience for subtlety."

"I hadn't noticed," she quipped. The front door clicked shut.

With a slight smile, he spun a chair around so he could straddle it. He propped his muscular forearms on the back and gave her a beatific smile. "I think that's the first compliment you've paid me."

"Don't let it go to your head," she grumbled.

With a slight chuckle, he took off his glasses and placed them on the table. "I've been wanting to know what you've been thinking since this morning," he said.

Abby shook her head as awareness crowded in and told her that the next few seconds would be potentially life-changing. With his face close to hers, and the clean scent of his soap mingling with the smells of baking cookies, he looked as tempting as the fruit of a forbidden tree. Over and over, his challenge from that morning kept running through her mind. When they were the only ones standing, would she still be on his side? There was something inexpressibly sad about that remark, as if he'd spent too many days alone and fought too many battles by himself. He couldn't have known how irrevocably that realization would bind her to him. He couldn't possibly be aware that nothing could wrap itself tighter around her heart than the sure knowledge that he'd been too long without someone to trust.

She'd sat in that same dark place for too many nights. She'd wondered too many times how God could have left her alone. She could no more turn her back on Ethan than she could rip her own heart out.

In the end, she knew, she was probably going to get burned by this. The day she'd seen him in San Francisco, she'd set them on an unalterable path. If he hadn't known it too, he wouldn't have given her that speech about trust and choosing sides. She could ignore it for a little while, but sooner or later she'd fall prey.

That alone should have scared her. Abby had spent a lot of time trying not to get hurt. Her parents' death, she'd decided ages ago, had been a big enough emotional hit for one lifetime. But sometime between last night and this morning, another, even more depressing reality had overcome her. She'd spent so much time protecting her life and her heart that she'd never really felt the intoxicating rush of adrenaline that came with risk. She'd managed to avoid disappointment and pain, but in doing so, she'd also managed to deprive herself of the keen knife-edge of pleasure that bordered on being too much to bear.

This newfound awareness had awakened a sharp craving, unlike any she'd ever experienced. The craving was strong enough to drown out the loud voice in her head that insisted she should know better. It beat into submission the feeling that Ethan Maddux was out of her league. It made her blood flow a little faster and her heart beat a little quicker. And it had all but demolished her usually reliable voice of reason.

Belatedly, she realized he was still awaiting an answer. "You're going to kiss me," she said, "aren't you?"

Ethan reached for her hand. "I'm seriously considering it."

"I'm pretty sure it's a bad idea," she told him. "All day I've been trying to figure out why."

"Come to any conclusions?"

"No, but I can't shake the feeling."

He smoothed his thumb over her knuckles. "Me either."

That made her smile. "Different feeling."

"You think so?"

"Definitely." Her head dropped back slightly. "You're making my ears ring," she said.

He lifted his other hand and cupped her face. "You might have to trust me on this."

"Why should I?"

"Because I keep having visions of what it'll be like when I have you next to me in bed. And I can't shake the feeling that the reality is going to beat the hell out of the fantasy."

The shiver that raced through her was more like a shudder. It started at the base of her spine and spread to her scalp and toes. "Ethan—"

"And you'll say my name," he said softly, dipping his head slightly. "Just like that."

He released her fingers so he could cradle her face in both of his hands. "Aren't you dying to know what it's going to feel like?"

She shut her eyes. "Ethan . . ."

He trailed his fingers along the curve of her jaw and slid them into her hair. "I've been wanting to touch your hair since that day in my office."

"It's out of control." She thought her voice was remarkably calm, considering that the blood was ringing in her ears.

"It's incredible." He twined a curl around his index finger. "Unique. Like you."

"Why are you doing this?" She curled her fingers around his hand.

"To get that breathless reaction out of you," he confessed. "I'm starting to get addicted to the way you say my name when you're a little off balance."

"Ethan—"

"Like that." He leaned closer to her.

"I don't think we should—"

He didn't let her finish. "Ah, Abby," he said softly. "Stop fighting me."

Her hands curled tensely onto his forearms. "Please . . ."

"Please, yes," he said, and put his hands on her shoulders to ease her toward him. "Or please, no?"

She met his gaze squarely, her hazel eyes clear and undaunted. Her lips parted. Ethan slid one hand onto her nape to cradle the back of her head. "Just say yes, Abby," he urged.

She could feel the incredible heat of his fingers against her flesh. "I . . ."

"Just say yes," he prompted again.

There was something a little vulnerable about him, something that touched her and crumbled what was left of her resistance. So she wished for luck, resigned herself to the consequences of the fall, and took the plunge. She placed both hands on his shoulders and leaned forward in her chair. "Are you ever going to kiss me? I've been waiting forev—"

He didn't let her finish. With a slight growl, he covered her mouth with his and guided her arms around his neck.

Positively worth the wait, he decided as he claimed her lips. He trailed one hand along the underside of her bare arm, down her rib cage, and around her waist. She froze for an instant, then made that intoxicating little noise again. He smiled against her lips and pressed his hands to the small of her back. The stiffness flowed out of her as she leaned into him. Ethan savored the kiss, and soon grew annoyed with the hindrance the chairback presented. He stood, bringing Abby with him.

She tilted her head back and threaded her fingers through his hair. "Oh, God, Ethan."

This time there was nothing hesitant in the way she said his name. It was more of a demand, and he gladly kicked the chair out of the way and pulled her firmly against him.

The contact was electrifying. He shifted one hand to her hips and aligned her body with his, then inched his lips down her throat.

Abby made an enticing little sound in the back of her throat. "I never—"

He kissed her again before she could finish the statement. He wanted to leave it at that so he could fill in the rest with his imagination. She'd never had it like this? He hoped so, he thought as he drank from her mouth again, because he hadn't either. She'd never burned quite this hot? He skimmed his hands down her body. He felt caught in a conflagration. She'd never wanted a person this much? He couldn't remember the last time he'd craved something until he hurt from it.

He maneuvered her two steps backward until she bumped into the kitchen table. His fingers found the hem of her tank top and he pulled it up so he could slide his hand over the bare skin of her midriff. Rose-petal soft, he thought. He felt her shiver as his fingertips danced over her spine. One of her hands glided into his hair as she rocked against him.

He lifted her onto the table, pushed her knees apart, and stepped between them. Abby sighed and draped her arms over his shoulders. He tore his mouth from hers to plant a line of kisses down her throat to her butter-soft neck. She tasted like cookies, he decided. Brown sugar, cinnamon, and cocoa blended on her skin and intoxicated him. "Ah, baby . . ."

Abby gasped when he gently bit her collarbone. "What are you doing?"

He trailed his mouth up her neck. "Tasting you. It's incredible."

"I can't—"

"Don't fight me." He slid his hand over her rib cage. "Enjoy me." He kissed the corner of her mouth. "Let me enjoy you."

"You're—"

He kissed her hard to keep her from finishing. Abby moaned against his lips and tipped her head back so he could plunder the depths of her mouth. He drank so deeply he could feel heaviness gathering in his lower body. Abby whispered something to him, then pushed him away. "Please. Please stop."

He blinked. "Abby—"

"Please," she whispered again and pressed her

flushed face to his chest. "A minute. Just a minute."

Ethan gathered her to him and took long, calming breaths. He had to mentally remind himself that he wouldn't die if he couldn't have her right then, and the thought shocked him. He wasn't used to this fierce wanting; it felt dangerously close to that place in his soul where passion could control him.

Abby finally broke the embrace and moved a step backward, then another. Her lips were swollen and red from the kiss. She held one hand to her chest and closed her eyes. "Rachel," she said softly. "They'll be back soon."

She was right. Self-recrimination flooded Ethan as he realized he'd broken his own promise to himself by starting something he couldn't finish. If Abby hadn't taken control . . . His gaze flicked to the table. He had to shake his head to clear it. Her skin was flushed, and he could see the rapid beat of her heart where the pulse pounded in her throat. He scrubbed a hand over his face. "You're right."

Abby's fingers twisted into the fabric of his shirt. "This is moving so fast."

Not fast enough to suit him. "I have tomorrow and Tuesday," he said. "Then I've got to go back to California."

"It'll give us some time."

The last thing he wanted was time. "I want

you to come with me." He pressed his lips to her temple.

She laughed. "Are you kidding?"

"Not at all."

Abby shook her head. "I can't possibly go running off to California with you!"

"Because of Rachel?"

"Because it's idiotic. I've got a fund-raiser to plan, three major events coming up, and a life to run." She covered her eyes with her palms. "Not to mention the fact that I barely know you."

Frustrated, Ethan stuffed his hands in his pockets. "I could try to make it back before the end of next week, but it's doubtful."

"You don't have to. I'm sure you can do most of the work for MDS from your California office."

He wanted her to feel as crazy as he did, he realized. He wanted her to be going nuts trying to figure out how much longer she'd have to wait before she could have him. He shouldn't be the only one in that boat. "Sure I can," he concurred, "but I can't try to seduce you from California."

"Make a bet," she muttered.

He grinned at her. "Okay, not as *effectively* I can't."

Abby pressed her fingers to her temples. "This is crazy."

Ethan shrugged. "Maybe, but I think I have a right to know just how long you want me to wait."

"It's not like I can check my PDA and tell you I

have an opening for sex a week from tomorrow," she quipped.

A search of her clear hazel eyes showed nothing but lingering desire and honest intent. "Don't get me wrong. I'll wait. Anticipation can be—nice."

"This from the man who said he doesn't believe in delayed gratification?"

"I said it was nice. I didn't say it was nicer than other things."

"Lord, Ethan."

"I'm not trying to railroad you."

Her eyes widened. "You're kidding."

"All right," he conceded, and stroked his thumb over the corner of her mouth. "Maybe a little."

"Or completely."

He shrugged. "I'm not going to promise that I won't do everything in my power to accelerate the, ah, timetable. I happen to be a strategic genius."

"There's more?" she said incredulously.

"Baby, I'm just getting started." He cupped her face in his hand. "I want you. Sooner rather than later. I've been nothing but honest about that."

"Brutally," she aknowledged.

"And you're overwhelmed?" he asked, cautious.

"No," She tipped her head and pursed her lips. "No," she said again. "At least, not in a bad way."

"There's a good way to be overwhelmed?"

"Well, yes. I"—she hesitated—"I can't say I've ever inspired a person to do something really reckless before."

A warning bell went off in his head. There was that word—that slight accusation which could so easily turn to condemnation. "Reckless?"

Her eyes sparkled with mirth. "I mean, would you really have tried to ravish me on a table full of sugar and flour if you'd had time to think about it first?"

If he hadn't known better, he'd have sworn she sounded flattered, and not the least bit intimidated. "Depends," he replied.

Abby was brushing flour dust off his shirt. "Oh?"

"Yes." He caught a strand of her hair between his fingers and brought it to his face so he could inhale the scent of her shampoo mixed with the baking ingredients. "You can do a lot of really interesting things with flour and sugar."

Abby's color heightened, and her hands stilled on his shirt. "You're impossible."

He rubbed the curl over his lips, then laid it back on her shoulder. "So I've heard."

She was saved a reply by the buzz of the oven timer.

Ethan frowned as he listened to the voice on the other end of the phone. "What are you saying, Charlie?"

The private investigator Ethan had hired to look into Abby's relationship with Harrison had called him in his Chicago hotel room to deliver an update. "It's weird, Ethan. It's like she didn't exist before her father was killed."

"That's not possible. You have to be missing something."

"I'm looking. I've called everyone I know, and pulled a hell of a lot of strings. I'm getting nothing."

Ethan stared at his reflection in the rain-streaked window. It was late Sunday evening. Rachel had finally finished the baking, and Ethan had left Abby's house feeling a little off balance and unaccountably agitated. The call from Charlie didn't help.

"All right. Here's what I want you to do." He issued several instructions to Charlie, then hung up and immediately dialed his CFO.

Jack answered his cell phone on the second ring. "Hey, Ethan. How's things in Chicago?"

"Edna told you?"

"Gleefully."

"That woman is way too interested in my personal life."

Jack laughed. "Who are you kidding? Edna practically *is* your social life."

Ethan let the comment pass. "Jack, listen. I don't want to impinge on your weekend, I just want you to do something for me if you have time."

"Sure."

"Do you remember that deal we struck with Maddigan and Cullen a couple of years ago?"

"The defense contractors? Sure, I remember."

"There was a key player in that negotiation. A guy by the name of Hansen Wells."

"Yeah, you tried to hire him."

"That's the one. Can you run down a current phone number for me? I have something I want to talk to him about."

"Do we have an opening?" Jack quipped.

Ethan laughed. "Don't worry, Jack. Your job's secure. I just need to ask Hansen a couple of questions."

"I'll see what I can do."

"Thanks. Oh, and leave Edna out of the loop, if you don't mind."

"Ethan—"

"Don't sound so worried," his boss assured him. "It's not a big deal. Edna would just take unnecessary interest in this, and it's a personal matter. I'd like to keep it that way."

"All right. Whatever you want."

"Thanks, Jack. You can reach me on my cell phone for the rest of the weekend."

"Will do. Listen, have you had a chance to look over that stuff I gave you on MDS before you left?"

"Yeah. Looks grim."

"Are you still thinking we're going to wade into this?"

Ethan had a mental picture of Abby, seated on her kitchen table, looking at him with bright eyes and kiss-swollen lips. "I'm already in, Jack."

"Seriously?"

"I'd say very seriously."

"Does Montgomery know it yet?"

"More or less. Why?"

"Because my source says on Tuesday he plans to announce he's splitting the company and putting it on the block."

"Damned fool."

"It's probably too late for you to do anything for him."

"I'm not in this for him," Ethan explained. "It's a long story. I'll fill you in when I get back to San Francisco."

"Wednesday morning, Edna said?"

"Yes. I'll probably fly in late Tuesday night."

"Okay, then, but we'll need to meet. You've got to spend some time listening to Lewis about the Kinsey matter."

"Wednesday," Ethan promised. "You can have my undivided attention."

Jack chuckled. "If you say so. I'll get back to you as soon as I have that number for Wells."

"Thanks, Jack. I appreciate it." Ethan hung up and tossed the cordless phone onto the bed.

Thrusting his hands in his pockets, he stood with his back to the room and stared out at the Chicago skyline. He replayed his conversation with Charlie in his mind and his frown deepened. Instinct told him that whatever answers he could get from Charlie or, with any luck, from Hansen Wells weren't going to be simple—and probably weren't going to be pleasant.

And he'd have to be the one to break the news to Abby.

Nine

"Well, hello there, gorgeous."

Abby smiled into the well-wrinkled face of General John Standen. "John, you've got to stop flattering me like that. It'll go straight to my head."

General Standen, who was in his nineties, still had a bright twinkle in his eyes. "I live in fear that some young fellow is going to come along and snatch you away from me," he said. His sharp gaze darted to the edge of the room where Ethan and Rachel were unpacking the gift boxes full of cookies. "Like that one," he said, tipping his head in Ethan's direction. "With the long hair."

Abby laughed and patted the old man on the shoulder. "I'm sure he'd be thrilled to learn you think his hair is too long."

The general scoffed. "He couldn't care less. I

can tell by looking at him. He's one of those self-made hooligan types you girls go for."

Abby smiled, as much at the description as at the gentlemanly way it was delivered. "Would it do me a bit of good to tell you it's none of your business?"

"No way. I've got to look after my girl, you know."

She dropped a kiss on his weathered cheek. "I'll let you know if I get myself into trouble." She started to make the rounds of the gaily decorated room. This was probably her favorite part of her job at the foundation. As much satisfaction as she got from administering the organization's myriad programs, nothing compared with the personal fulfillment of spending time with the men and women the foundation supported. It made her feel connected to the memory of her father and to the friends who had helped her survive the sorrow of her parents' death.

In honor of the holiday, the staff of the Chicago Metropolitan Veterans Center had hung flags and garlands, but despite the festive atmosphere, Abby was aware of the undercurrent of sadness that flowed among the residents. Few outsiders understood how difficult Memorial Day was for them.

In her experience, people often made the mistake of believing that veterans were united by their shared experiences of war, but Abby knew better. What bound them together was their shared grief at the loss of so many close friends. They seemed to have a resilience that inspired her, and in the years since her parents' death, she'd made sure that Rachel had the benefit of their experience. Though each veteran in this room had suffered unimaginable losses, and many had overcome hardships and trauma that she could only begin to imagine, they all had found the courage to rebuild their lives and their friendships.

And Abby loved them for it.

She greeted several friends as she slowly made her way toward the corner where Colonel Archie Jameson sat by himself, clutching a small American flag. He greeted her with his usual sad smile. Abby took his hand and gave it a tight squeeze. The colonel had been one of her personal projects for the past two years. "Hi, Colonel. Happy Memorial Day."

He turned his wheelchair toward her. "Hello, Abby."

"How are you doing today?" She sat in the chair next to him.

His eyes looked misty to her. "A little worse than usual," he admitted. "This holiday is almost the toughest. Christmas is worse, though."

Abby nodded. "I know." Archie Jameson's story had struck a certain chord in her, one that had wrapped tighter and tighter around her heart the longer she knew him. "Thinking about Miss Jo?"

Josephine Wyler had been Archie Jameson's high school sweetheart and, as far as Abby knew, his only love. He'd gone off to fight with the Allied forces in France while Josephine had stayed behind. Archie had lost both his legs on the beaches of Normandy. Josephine had written him after hearing the news, telling him he'd better come home to her and that at least she'd always know he couldn't stray from her side. Archie had clutched that letter during the long days of recuperation in the hospital, the difficult days of recovery, and his subsequent ship's voyage back to the United States. He'd arrived in New York and been greeted with the tragic news that his beloved Josephine had died waiting for him to return. Archie's spirit had never recovered.

"I'm always thinking about Miss Jo," Archie answered, and his voice sounded a little thready.

Abby wove her fingers through his trembling ones. They had almost ten minutes, she knew, before the program started. "Why don't you tell me your favorite thing about her, Archie?"

He clutched the flag a little tighter. "Did I ever tell you about Jo's hair?" he asked softly.

At least half a dozen times, Abby thought with a slight smile. "What was it like?" she prodded. "Pretty, I'll bet."

"The most beautiful hair I've ever seen."

She felt two strong hands settle on her shoulders. Ethan dropped a kiss on top of her hair. "I know just how that feels," he said, his voice close to her ear.

Abby drew a sharp breath. Since their conversation on Saturday night, Ethan had made good on his promise to try to accelerate the timetable of their relationship. He was constantly finding excuses to touch her. She'd never imagined that baking could turn so quickly into foreplay, but he would come up behind her and pin her to the counter so he could look over her shoulder; or lift her dough-covered fingers to his mouth to taste them, and she'd break into shivers.

Though he'd remained circumspect in front of Rachel and LuAnne, he'd somehow managed to corner her alone several times. In the past two days she'd learned what she imagined were all the ways a woman could be kissed. Softly, hungrily, hard, gentle, demanding, begging, Ethan seemed to know them all—and he was a great communicator. Her lips tingled just thinking about how he'd caught her in the hallway that morning while Rachel and LuAnne were loading the car. Before she had time to think, Ethan had pressed her up against the linen-closet door with her hands pinned near her shoulders. He'd covered her mouth in an intense kiss that tasted like toothpaste and something else, something wildly forbidden. "I missed you last night," he'd whispered against her mouth, and sent shivers skittering down her spine.

Abby coughed and met his gaze. "Hi."

Archie gave him a once-over. "You a friend of Abby's?"

"Yes." Ethan took the chair next to Abby.

"A good friend?" the colonel asked, looking at Abby.

Ethan reached for her free hand. "I like to think so."

Archie stared at him for several seconds, sizing him up. Finally, he nodded. "You got a good one. You treat her right."

"I'm trying." Ethan gave her hand a squeeze, then released it. "Everything's unpacked," he told her.

She nodded. "Where's Rachel?"

"Charming the crowd." He draped his arm across the back of her chair. "She's a natural."

"Abby," Archie prompted, "aren't you going to tell me the man's name? I got a right to know."

She laughed. "Subtle as usual, Colonel." She squeezed his hand. "This is Ethan Maddux. Ethan, Colonel Archie Jameson."

Ethan extended his hand to the colonel. "Nice to meet you."

Archie hesitated, then shook Ethan's hand. "I guess you'll do," he said, "although you're going to have your hands full fighting off some of these guys for Abby's attention. She's got 'em all under her thumb."

"I'm starting to gather that," Ethan drawled.

A slight commotion at the front of the room signaled that the program was about to begin. On cue, the lights dimmed as a young man from one of the local high schools began playing "God Bless America" on the slightly beat-up piano in the corner. Ethan moved his hand to Abby's shoulder and began to rub it in a slow, mesmerizing circle. "All right, Colonel," he said over her head. "No trying to make time with my girl after the lights go out."

Archie's soft laugh lightened Abby's heart. With a slight shake of her head, she admitted to herself that she'd actually gone and done the one thing she'd sworn she wouldn't: she had fallen for Ethan Maddux. Hard. Extremely, irrevocably hard.

The realization, she supposed, should at least have made her nervous. If she really sat down and thought about it, it probably would. But at the moment, it caused a warm feeling to flow through her blood. A feeling so tantalizing, she wanted to wallow in it.

With Abby's head tipped against his shoulder and a middle school choir singing the armed services medley, Ethan wondered why it had taken him his entire life to discover how incredible simple pleasures could be. He'd seen operas at La Scala. He'd sat in concert halls and listened to performances by the world's most renowned musicians. He had attended movie premieres, sponsored plays by leading dramatists, and gone to more galas and media events than he cared to count.

And he couldn't remember the last time he'd enjoyed himself more.

As the program unfolded, some hidden spring inside Abby seemed to gradually unwind. The dark smudges under her eyes hadn't disappeared, and he knew that the time spent in the kitchen wasn't the sole cause of her fatigue. He was suffering the same affliction. Lying alone in his hotel room, he'd resorted to everything from cold showers to midnight swims in the hotel pool to burn off the excess energy of his growing desire for Abby.

It hadn't helped.

To make matters worse, the only sign he had that Abby was showing any ill effects from the strain of too-close proximity and unfulfilled sexual desire was the incriminating circles under her eyes. Even those were barely noticeable, and if Rachel hadn't let slip that Abby had resorted to using frozen cucumber slices that morning, he might not have known.

So he'd kissed her in the hallway of her house

just to be sure. And she'd melted against him like clarified butter. Her arms had wended around his neck and his world had righted itself on its axis. She wasn't pushing him away, and the depth of his hunger didn't intimidate her. As long as he played it easy, he could have her.

Abby's guard had definitely dropped, he decided the instant he felt her head tip against his shoulder. He stole a quick glance and saw her eyes were shut. She seemed to have slipped into lassitude. He took the opportunity to study the interesting features of her face. In stark contrast to Pamela's classic beauty, Abby looked fresh. He'd been pretty pleased with himself when he'd decided on this word late last night. He'd been lying in bed, fighting a war with his libido, trying to figure out just what it was about Abby's face that he found so irresistible.

It was round, with a smattering of freckles across the bridge of her slightly upturned nose, and she had none of the tired look he'd seen so often. When she smiled, he could see the tiny gap between two of her bottom teeth. He found that gap utterly infectious—it was like a flaw in an otherwise seamless piece of marble. The gap gave her smile dimension and character.

Abby was all about character. Perhaps that explained why he knew he could trust her. Abby respected and cared for Harrison Montgomery, but she wasn't blind to his flaws. If and when the time came for Ethan to expose those flaws, she'd trust him. She'd given him her word on that.

And if he hadn't believed it for any other reason, he'd been sold the moment she'd risen to his defense on Harrison's yacht. When he walked into MDS tomorrow and informed Harrison that he'd made his decision, Abby would be irrevocably caught in the middle. He couldn't spare her that. The best he could do was struggle to contain the anger he'd suppressed for all these years.

That was getting tougher to do.

Being back in Chicago and spending time with the Montgomerys had begun to awaken a sleeping giant. It had been years since he'd allowed himself to revisit the seething rage he'd felt the day he'd hurled two house keys and three thousand dollars in cash at Harrison and announced he was leaving. The house keys opened the door to Harrison's downtown apartment, where Ethan had lived since his mother's death. The cash, which Ethan had earned through a series of odd jobs, covered his mother's funeral expenses.

He'd spent years after that episode feeling like a victim of that rage. Only his self-control had helped him conquer the anger, but it simmered just below the surface. It was one of the facets of that same deep passion that had destroyed his mother—the same recklessness that had driven her into the arms of Harrison Montgomery and ultimately ruined her life. At all costs, Ethan knew, he had to control his emotions or lose everything.

Abby stirred against his shoulder and released him from his melancholy thoughts. She blinked, and the confusion cleared from her eyes. "Sorry," she muttered, sitting up. Her hand automatically went to her hair.

"Don't be." He nodded in the direction of the stage. A student was reading a poem about Pearl Harbor. "I was enjoying the program."

A smile played across her lips. "Not your usual style of entertainment, I'm sure."

He shrugged. "A man can take only so much opera. Besides"—he reached for her hand—"I hear this place serves really great refreshments."

"What makes you think we'll get any? I've seen these people eat."

"I've got connections with the chef." He planted a kiss on the back of her hand. "I conned her out of a tray of lemon bars. They're hidden in the back."

She smiled a sleepy smile and leaned against him again. "I happen to love Rachel's lemon bars," she murmured.

"Well, Abby, I trust you enjoyed your weekend." Deirdre strode forcefully into Abby's office.

Abby glanced up from her computer. "Actually, yes."

"That little scene at Carlton's party on Saturday was particularly charming."

"Everyone seemed to enjoy it." She swiveled to face Deirdre. "What can I do for you today?"

Dressed in a lipstick-pink silk suit with matching ostrich skin pumps, Harrison's sister sank dramatically into the chair across from Abby's desk. "Come on, Abigail. You've got to know everyone's dying for the story."

"What story?"

Deirdre's perfectly plucked eyebrows rose. "The Ethan Maddux and Abigail Lee story."

"Then they'll have to perish waiting," Abby said patiently.

"You really aren't going to tell me, are you?"

"I'm really not."

Deirdre clucked her tongue. "I thought we'd developed something of a rapport lately, Abby."

"I feel the same way." As annoying as Deirdre could be at times, Abby usually found the woman's candor refreshing. Most of the Montgomerys had an annoying habit of coyness and false humility. With Deirdre, what you saw was what you got.

"But you don't trust me?" the older woman pressed.

"It has nothing to do with trust."

Deirdre gazed at her fingernails in speculation. "I happen to know that Ethan Maddux has a team looking into this right now."

"Do you?"

"He's here to bail out MDS from its financial woes."

And maybe save Harrison from personal ruin, Abby thought. There was something irrepressibly sad about Harrison's having to turn to his estranged son for help while the rest of his family watched in horrified fascination. "Let's hope it works, then."

Deirdre looked up, and some of the artifice was gone from her expression. "How bad is it, Abby?"

Abby shrugged. "I think that's a question you should ask your brother."

"Is he going to lose everything?"

"Hard to say." She leaned back in her chair. "I hope not."

"But he could?"

"It's a possibility."

Deirdre shook her head. "I can't believe—God, the man is insufferable sometimes!"

"I'm hearing that a lot lately." Abby's gaze drifted to the shaft of light near her window. Dust mites danced on the beam.

"You can't understand what it was like," Deirdre continued. "Father was—well, it's no wonder Harrison is like he is. He was the only son, and Father had enormous expectations for him."

"How did Ethan's mother fit into those expectations?"

Deirdre's snort was inelegant. "I don't suppose you've ever discussed that with Harrison?"

"Only once. He didn't tell me much." Abby looked back at Deirdre. "I'm not trying to pry."

"You've got a right to know. Especially if you're involved with Ethan."

"Deirdre—"

She held up a hand. "Abigail, I may not be the sharpest tack in the box, but I know a lot about men. I should," she added with a slight smile. "I've married five of them."

"What exactly is it about the Montgomerys that none of you can manage to stay married?"

Deirdre laughed, and the sound lacked its usual brittle quality. "It's a relentless taste for adventure. Believe it or not, Ethan has it too. He'll never settle in one place—I think you should know that."

Abby reached for a pencil and twirled it between her fingers. The site of the chewed eraser brought a smile to her lips. "You don't think so?"

"No, dear. He's a Montgomery. He's got the curse."

"The curse?"

"Oh, yes. It's genetic."

"Deirdre, I've known this family for ten years. No one has ever told me anything as interesting as a family curse."

"We don't discuss it often, but trust me, dear, it's real. There's not a Montgomery alive who is capable of stability."

"Is that why Harrison never married Ethan's mother?"

"No." Deirdre tapped one finger on her knee.

"He would have married her, I think. I don't know how long they could have stayed married, but Harrison wanted to marry Lina."

"But he didn't."

"Father wouldn't allow it." Deirdre pursed her lips at the memory. "You never met him, Abby. You can't possibly understand what the man was like."

"Harrison hardly ever talks about him, but I've heard things."

"I imagine you have. There were plenty of Father's board members who were determined not to let Harrison have control of the company."

"Your father left it to him?"

Deirdre's laugh was harsh. "Oh, good Lord, no. First of all, Father had no intention of dying at all, much less making Harrison his heir at the company."

"The will—"

"There wasn't one."

"My God, you're kidding!"

"No." Deirdre drummed her fingers on the arm of her chair. "Father seemed in good enough health when he died. Nothing could have prepared us for his heart attack."

"What about your mother?"

"Oh, he'd killed her years ago."

"Deirdre!"

The other woman waved a hand in dismissal. "Sorry. That sounded grim. What I mean is, Father had the same curse as the rest of us. He wasn't about to settle himself on one woman. But his generation did its wandering more privately, if you know what I mean."

"Yes."

"Father went through a string of lovers. It broke Mother's heart. I think she really loved the old bastard, though I can't for the life of me figure why." She shrugged. "I suppose that's why she had five children with him. It felt like a way to keep him bound to her."

"How did she die?"

"She was weak, really. I never remember her being well. Mother spent most of her time in bed after Letty was born. I don't think she died as much as she just stopped living one day."

"And that left the five of you alone with your father."

"And the nannies. Yes. Although he did remarry briefly."

"Constance?"

"Harrison told you?"

"Once."

"Hmm. Harrison liked Connie. She was young, nearly Harrison's age then. I'm not really sure why she married Father, to tell you the truth. She never seemed particularly interested in his money."

"Harrison still sends her a stipend."

"Well, yes, but when Father died, she inherited everything because there was no will."

"I've heard the gossip, but Harrison and I never talked about it."

"Harrison doesn't like to discuss it. He and Connie struck some sort of deal. For reasons I've never been told, she was perfectly content to disappear to the house Father owned in Palm Beach, and to surrender control of the entire fortune and the company to Harrison. She signed over all her stock to him, which gave him control of MDS."

Abby couldn't shake the feeling that something about the conversation was eluding her. It danced at the edge of her conscience like the dust mites bobbing on the periphery of her vision. "Where did Ethan's mother fit into all of this?"

"She worked here." Deirdre narrowed her gaze. "You really don't know any of this, do you?"

"It was Harrison's personal business. I didn't feel right about discussing it with anyone but him—and the topic has always been off limits."

"But you want to talk about it now?"

Since Ethan, Abby admitted to herself. Since she'd spent most of the weekend trying to figure him out. "Things are different."

"Because of Ethan?"

"Yes."

Deirdre nodded. "I thought so. Just be careful."

"Now you sound like Harrison."

"With good reason. Lina entered the picture a couple of years before Harrison graduated from college. Father and Connie were separated by then, and she was living in Palm Beach. Harrison worked summers and holidays at MDS. That's where he met Lina. She was a secretary for someone down in Accounting, I think—or maybe it was Development. Whatever. She and Harrison met and it was one of those summer-sizzle kind of things."

"I've heard this part of the story," Abby said. "They were practically inseparable."

"That's one way of putting it," Deirdre drawled. "In less delicate moments, my sisters and I agreed that the two were screwing like minks."

Abby laughed. "I'm sure Harrison appreciated that."

"Harrison was too distracted by Lina's, er, assets to bother with the four of us."

"And Lina was distracted by Harrison's money?"

"That's what Father thought."

"What about you?"

"Well, at first, yes, that seemed logical. She was a little trashy, you know. Dressed a little wild and had the behavior to match. A far cry from the debutantes Father had picked out for Harrison's attention."

"Maybe that's what Harrison liked about her."

"No doubt. Lina had a reputation for being fast, easy, and cheap. She didn't really demand much of Harrison as far as we could tell. And in reality, he didn't have that much to give her. Father didn't hand us money. All we had was what we earned. Harrison was as cash-poor as any normal student— he just had a name that opened doors for him, and enough clout to get himself in trouble."

"Or to get Lina in trouble?"

"Or that. Lina was pregnant—not surprisingly— within a month. I knew about it first. Harrison and I were always close."

"When did your father find out?"

"A month later. Harrison announced that he was going to marry Lina."

Abby's eyebrows rose. "So he did plan to marry her?"

"Oh, yes. I'm not sure whether he thought he wanted the child, or if he just wanted to really piss Father off. But either way, he was going to marry her. I've always been sure of that."

"Ethan thinks differently."

"I can see why Ethan would. I doubt he ever took Harrison's word for anything."

"Your father wouldn't allow the marriage?"

Deirdre chortled. "You could say that. You should have heard the argument. Father was livid. First, that Harrison had done something as asinine as get Lina pregnant. And second, that he actually wanted to make the stupidity permanent by marrying her." Deirdre shrugged. "Personally, I think it would have been good for Harrison. He might have learned that standing up to Father wasn't the end of the world."

The thought depressed Abby. "Wasn't it possible that Harrison actually cared for the woman?"

"In his way, I suppose he did." Deirdre gave Abby a shrewd look. "But Harrison is . . . *different* from the rest of us in that regard. He's not prone to passion. Only the rest of us have that affliction. Harrison is perfectly controlled all the time. How he ever managed to lose himself enough to get Lina pregnant, I'll never know." She stopped and thought that idea over. "I suppose that's why Father always believed the baby wasn't really his."

"Did you believe it?"

"No. Harrison was different with Lina. He seemed more relaxed. The façade was gone."

"Less cold?"

"You have to understand, Abby. Harrison could be positively *arctic* when he wanted to."

"Like his son," Abby muttered.

"What?"

"Nothing. So your father said no."

"My father *bellowed* no. He did everything but scream no. He told Harrison he'd cut him off if he married Lina, that he'd never recognize the child, and that he'd have Lina investigated and prosecuted on charges of extortion if he could prove that she'd slept with anyone other than Harrison in the past two months."

Abby nodded. "So Harrison backed down."

"In a way. To be honest, Abby, I think he didn't want to know that Lina could have cheated on him. That probably played as big a role in the entire mess as his fear of Father."

"What happened when Ethan was born?"

"I don't know. I'm not sure Harrison does either. Lina disappeared for a while. She didn't come back until Ethan was three."

"Ethan says she was ill by then."

"Cancer," Deirdre confirmed. "She didn't want Ethan to live his life in foster care when Harrison could give him everything money could buy."

But not the love he'd needed, Abby thought sadly. In contrast, her own life had been so much richer. "Harrison took them in that time?"

"He did stand up to Father, much to everyone's surprise."

"Surely your father wouldn't have—"

"Yes, he would have," Deirdre said without hesitation. "I'm relatively certain Connie had something to do with it, but no one knows for sure. Harrison and Father had a ripping argument, and the next thing we knew, Lina and Ethan were living in the downtown apartment."

"Harrison never lived with them?"

"No. That's when things turned strange. Even by Montgomery standards." Deirdre's tone was dry. "Lina would come to the house sometimes for family events. I think she enjoyed making my father angry. She resented the hell out of him, and from what I could tell, she didn't like Harrison much either."

"Would you have if you'd been in her shoes?"

Deirdre shrugged. "Hard to say. I suppose it depends on what the woman's goals were. Either way, she didn't live long after that."

"And after her death, Ethan lived with Harrison."

"Well, not actually *with* him. Ethan stayed at the apartment with a nanny. He rarely saw Harrison. Father died shortly after. I doubt Ethan remembers much about him."

That, at least, was a blessing, Abby thought. The more she heard of the story, the more confusing and disconcerting it became. How could the Harrison Montgomery who'd gone to such great lengths to provide her and her sister with desperately needed stability be the same man who'd cast aside his own child? Something didn't fit. "Things never got any better, did they?" she asked.

"No. The gulf grew steadily wider between Ethan and Harrison, and by the time Ethan reached adolescence"—Deirdre shook her head—"well, it was already beyond redemption. Harrison had no idea how to relate to him. Ethan was very angry."

"And hurting," Abby pointed out. "He must have taken his mother's death very hard."

"I imagine he did." Deirdre noticed Abby's frown. "Try to understand. I know you were close to your parents, but things weren't like that for any of us. I was closer to my nannies than I ever was to my father."

"He was lonely, Deirdre. You have to understand that."

"Of course I do. And thank God for Letty. She's the only one of us with a maternal bone in her body."

"Ethan is still quite close to her."

"She mothered him as best she could, but the older Ethan got, the more bitter the feud between him and Harrison became. It wasn't long before it became obvious to all of us that to side with Ethan was to side against Harrison."

Abby knew that feeling all too well. "So he was left alone." Again, she added silently.

"As long as Harrison controlled the fortune—" Deirdre held out her hands in a helpless gesture. "Let's just say that no one had the nerve to cross him."

Abby thought that over. It seemed irrepressibly sad, somehow, that Harrison's vast and sprawling family was held together by fear and avarice, while she would have given anything for just one more day with her parents. It took her less than a heartbeat to recognize why she found Ethan so irresistible. That hollow look she sometimes saw in his eyes mirrored the one she'd once seen in her own. He was still the hurting, abandoned child who'd lost his mother and experienced no love from his father, and he was desperately yearning for someone to understand him. She could no more turn away from that than she could tear her own heart out.

The fate that had flung her into his path was the same fate that was going to break her heart, she was almost certain. Because now that she knew most of Ethan's story, she was virtually powerless to turn him away. He might hurt her in the long run, but she couldn't push him away until she'd helped him fill that hollow place.

If she had a brain in her head, she thought wryly, she should feel some angst because she was about to topple headlong into love with a man she barely knew, a man who gave her every reason to believe he wasn't the least interested in anything other than a passing affair. Since she'd waited long enough to fall this hard for a man, she should at least have had the sense to pick one more wisely.

But strangely, the realization brought a certain kind of freedom. Seeing her inevitable tumble into heartache made it easier to accept.

He really was making her crazy, Abby thought as she reached for the folder on her desk. The next time she discussed Harrison or Ethan, or the history of their relationship, she wanted the dialogue to be with them. Her fierce sense of loyalty demanded it. She flipped open the folder. "Whatever's going to happen," she told Deirdre, neatly dismissing the topic, "is between Harrison and Ethan now."

"And you're stuck right in the middle."

Abby handed her a report from the folder. "Only if I want to be." She smiled slightly. "And believe it or not, I have other things to do today than to keep discussing the two of them. This event is three weeks away."

Deirdre accepted the report. "I've been thinking through the options of themes," she said.

Abby stifled a groan. It was going to be a very long day indeed.

Ten

"How long have you known her?" Ethan asked General John Standen that afternoon at the Chicago Metropolitan Veterans Center.

The general stroked his chin. "Well, let's see. I think I first met Abby a couple of years after her parents died." He looked at the playing cards in his hand and tossed two onto the table. "Give me two."

Ethan handed him the cards. The man next to the general nodded. "Yeah, that's right. Abby started coming in here real regular right after they were murdered."

"Anybody know her father?" Ethan probed, and handed the man the three cards he'd requested. Ethan had talked to his investigator that morning. Charlie had run into more roadblocks as he tried to get to the bottom of Abby's past. Frustrated, Ethan had spent a grueling morning in the hotel pool, swimming three miles of laps to clear his head and think through the puzzling information. Finally, when his body was demanding a break from the pace of his workout, he'd remembered Charlie's mention that Abby's father had fought in the Vietnam War.

He hadn't been able to shake that thought, nor the conviction that answers lay somewhere in that piece of information. So he'd come to the Veterans Center, where he knew Abby and Rachel were both heavily invested with the residents. If anyone would have answers, it would be these men who treated her like one of their own.

The general frowned. "Seems like everyone knew of him, but it's been a while." He gave Ethan a dry look. "Once we get here, we don't always last so much longer."

The other two men at the table nodded their agreement. "I've been here for almost ten years," one of them said as he tossed two pennies into the kitty. "And that's longer than most."

Ethan tapped his own cards in frustration. Though he had no reason to believe Abby was lying to him, he was sure something was missing. Instinct told him she had carefully avoided telling him the entire truth of her relationship with Harrison. He tried to gauge whether or not his suspicion about Harrison's motives for being so generous to her and to Rachel was influencing his judgment, but he didn't think so. He'd built a career out of following hunches. And this one told him that Harrison at least had knowledge of the mysterious circumstances surrounding her parents' death.

"I knew him," said a voice from behind Ethan's shoulder.

Ethan glanced around to see Carter Jameson sitting to his left. He'd wheeled his chair over and was regarding Ethan with a piercing gaze. "I knew Abby's father."

The general disagreed. "You couldn't have, Carter. You haven't been here that long."

One of the other men nodded. "He died over ten years ago."

Carter Jameson shook his head. "Before. I knew him before."

Ethan studied him for a second, then tossed his cards onto the table. "I'll have to fold, gentlemen. The colonel and I have something to discuss." He rose.

"Wheel me outside," the colonel suggested, "and I'll tell you what I know."

It was after 2:00 A.M. when his cell phone rang. Ethan was lying in the bed of his Chicago hotel room, mentally replaying his conversation with Carter Jameson. He'd seen Abby and Rachel for dinner that night, and though the tone of the conversation had been light, he'd sensed an underlying tension in Abby. When he'd questioned her, she'd given him a vague explanation of her meeting with Harrison that afternoon. Ethan suspected that Harrison had thrown some of the same warnings at her that he'd hurled at Ethan on Saturday. The day had obviously taken a toll on her.

When he'd kissed her good night, she'd practically clung to him, and he'd known something was seriously troubling her. Abby was definitely not a clinger. Whatever was bothering her had her uncharacteristically on edge. Against his better judgment, he hadn't pressed her for information.

He had, however, been unable to sleep. So the jarring ring of his cellular phone made him instantly alert. He sat up and snatched it from the bedside table. Abby's number flashed on the ID screen. Frowning, he punched the Receive button. "What's wrong?"

"Someone was here." Her voice sounded breathless.

Ethan gripped the phone. "What?"

"Someone tried to get into the house. He broke the window."

He was already out of bed and reaching for his pants. "Did you call the police?"

"Yes." She sounded terrified.

He managed to pull his pants on and step into his shoes. "Is Rachel with you?"

"Yes."

"Abby, are you all right? Is Rachel all right?"

"If I hadn't—he was coming through the window."

"Are you all right?" he asked again.

"I hit him in the face—he was wearing a mask."

"Did he hurt you?"

"No." He heard her struggle for breath. "No. I used an umbrella and I hit him. I think he ran off."

Ethan hoped the bastard was lying under her window with a broken nose. He dropped his keys into his pocket. "Abby, listen to me."

"He would have come in."

"I know, honey." He had to struggle to keep his voice calm. The last thing she needed right now was to sense how angry he was at the thought of someone trying to hurt her. "Did you reset the alarm?"

"Yes."

"Check it now while I'm on the phone."

He heard her move across the room and punch the buttons. "It's armed."

"Okay. I'll be there in fifteen minutes."

"Please hurry," she said. "God, please hurry."

Ethan jammed the cell phone into his pocket and grabbed his shirt on his way out the door. The terror in her voice had his adrenaline flowing fast and furious. She wasn't the type to scare easily or cower quickly, but she'd sounded damned near hysterical on the phone.

Considering the violence of her parents' death,

he could only imagine what she must have felt when she realized someone was breaking into her home. He'd noticed that Abby was extremely security-conscious the first time he'd set foot in her house. Despite the secluded residential neighborhood, there were double locks on all her doors and windows and a state-of-the-art security system on the house itself.

Any professional thief would have seen the signs and wiring from a cursory glance at the perimeter and wouldn't have attempted the break-in. So this was either some neighborhood kid playing a badly executed prank, or the break-in had been designed to terrify her. Ethan's money was on the latter. And from the sound of her phone call, it had been extremely effective.

If someone was trying to scare her, there was a reason for it. He'd stake his life that the reason lay somewhere beneath the sketchy evidence he'd obtained that afternoon from Carter Jameson. Harrison had told him on Saturday that he had no idea what he was getting himself into. Ethan was starting to believe it.

He bit off a curse as he turned into Abby's driveway. Every light in the house was on, and he could see the broken shards of glass covering the porch. "Bastard," he muttered.

He hurried up the front steps and was reaching for the bell when Abby tore open the door and flew into his arms. He had a brief glimpse of the dark blue satin nightgown and robe she wore before she buried herself against him. "Thank God," she said, clinging to him. "Thank God you're here."

Ethan wrapped his arms tightly around her. The anxiety he'd felt since that afternoon was slowly beginning to ease. He could solve whatever problems arose, and he was confident he could protect her, even from Harrison. The fact that she'd turned to him and not to his father when she'd needed help convinced him of it. Abby needed him. He could work with that. For a while, he'd worried that he'd pushed her too hard—that she'd seen the passion in him and had started to draw away. But she needed him. And for the moment, that was all that mattered.

She broke the embrace before he was ready, but he saw her reach out a trembling hand to Rachel. Rachel stood in the shadows looking confused and exhausted. "Hi, Ethan."

He eased Abby to one side. She couldn't possibly imagine the impact she was having on him. The blue nightgown skimmed her body and outlined her full breasts. It dipped low enough to tantalize him with shadows and curves. He put one arm around her waist just so he could continue touching the soft fabric and the softer woman underneath. He entered the house. "Hey, Rach. You doing okay?"

Rachel shrugged. She wore cotton pajamas and

Tweety-Bird slippers. "It was kind of creepy, you know? He woke me up when he started messing with the window."

Ethan glanced at Abby. Her face was as color-less as an icicle. The dark blue satin accentuated the circles under her eyes. Her hair was unbound and untidy, another sign of her general distress. She looked considerably more shaken than her sister. "Let's sit down," he suggested.

Abby followed his lead. Rachel trailed behind them and flopped into the armchair. "We called the police. They should be here soon."

Ethan guided Abby to the sofa. He took the seat next to her and reached for her hand. "Tell me what happened."

"I was on the sofa," she said, shoving a way-ward curl behind her ear. "I fell asleep reading."

His gaze flicked to the coffee table. A novel and a half-empty glass of milk sat near the edge.

"I was upstairs," Rachel added. "I went to bed right after you left."

Ethan nodded. "Around ten."

"Yeah." Rachel slung her legs over the arm of the chair. "I woke up when I heard the glass break."

Beside him, Abby shuddered. "I saw his hands. He was reaching for the lock."

"I heard Abby yell at him."

"And Rachel ran downstairs."

"I didn't know what was going on."

Abby's fingers had tightened on his hand. "I grabbed the umbrella from the coat rack and hit him across the face."

"You should have seen it," Rachel said. "She whacked him right across the nose. He started howling."

Abby gave Ethan a hollow look. "He would have come in. If I'd been upstairs—"

"You weren't," he reminded her gently. "And he didn't."

She shivered. "God. How could this happen?"

The mirror above her mantel reflected the flashing blue lights of a squad car. Rachel jumped up from the chair. "I'll get it."

Ethan took the opportunity to wrap an arm around Abby's shoulders. She leaned heavily against his side. "It's going to be all right," he told her. He dropped a kiss onto the top of her head. "I promise it's going to be all right."

"Thank you for coming," she whispered.

He brushed her hair away from her face and gently traced his fingers along her cheek. "Abby, honey, listen to me a minute."

"I don't know why I got so scared," she continued. "It's just that I always felt so safe here."

"I know."

"I didn't think something like this could happen."

"I know," he said again.

She shivered. He could hear Rachel talking to

the police officers in the foyer. "I know I'm being silly."

"No, you're not. Baby, listen to me."

"I'm sorry I'm being so hysterical."

He cupped her face to get her attention. "I need to know if he said anything—anything at all."

Abby shook her head. "No." She frowned. "Not until I hit him with the umbrella. He called me a bitch because he cut his hand on the glass trying to go back out through the window. So I hit him again."

Ethan suppressed a smile and stroked her cheek with his thumb. "That's all he said?"

She was still very shaky. "Yes."

He pulled her to him again. "Okay." He didn't like the way she was shivering. "I think you should have some tea now."

"I'm all right."

"Honey, you're shaking like a leaf."

"It's just aftereffects."

Two policemen entered the living room with Rachel. Ethan glanced at them over Abby's head. "Thanks for coming. I'm Ethan Maddux."

"No problem." The taller of the two nodded. "I'm Detective Nick Krestyanov. This is my partner, Detective Garrison. We need to ask some questions."

"I told them what *I* know," Rachel announced.

"Ms. Lee," Detective Garrison said to Abby, "can you talk to us for a few minutes?"

She pulled away from Ethan's embrace with a slight shudder. "Yes. Yes, I'm all right."

Ethan looked at Rachel and mouthed, "Tea." She stared at him for a minute, then seemed to understand the silent question. With a nod, she padded toward the kitchen. The two detectives sat in the chairs opposite the sofa. Ethan used the opportunity to get up and walk casually toward the broken window. Shards of glass crunched beneath his feet. He picked up a cotton throw rug and tossed it over the pile of glass beneath the sill.

"Were you in the house, Mr. Maddux?" he heard Detective Krestyanov ask.

Ethan glanced back over his shoulder. "No. I came when Abby called."

Abby waved a hand in his direction. "Ethan is from out of town. He's a—friend."

That seemed to satisfy the detective. Ethan stared at the window, studying the jagged shape of the hole and fighting another surge of rage. A streak of blood smeared the glass where the intruder had cut himself. At a sudden break in the clouds, moonlight spilled onto the porch and reflected off shards that littered the weathered boards. Ethan saw a flash of white and frowned.

He glanced at Abby and saw her telling Detective Garrison her story. The other detective was watching Ethan. Ethan made a subtle gesture with his head, and the policeman excused himself to join Ethan at the window. Ethan pointed to where a small envelope lay amid the broken glass on the porch. The detective frowned and pulled a flashlight from his pocket. He shone it on the envelope. "Bill?" he called his partner.

"Yeah, Nick?"

"Come take a look at this."

Garrison and Abby hurried to the window. Abby was barefoot, so Ethan took a step toward her to halt her progress. "Glass," he explained when she frowned at him.

She looked down in consternation. Ethan wrapped his arm around her waist and lifted her easily onto the cotton rug he'd placed over the mess. Detective Krestyanov indicated the envelope with a flick of the flashlight. "Looks like we have a calling card."

Garrison took a latex glove from his jacket pocket. "I'll get it."

Abby looked at Ethan. "Do you think—"

"I think it wasn't a routine break-in," he told her.

Krestyanov nodded. "That would be my guess." He pointed to the window. "This isn't the work of a pro, and amateurs usually work during the day. Whoever did this was coming to tell you something."

Garrison returned with the envelope. Abby reached for it, but the detective shook his head. "It's evidence, Ms. Lee. If it's got fingerprints, I don't want to muddy them."

"What's in it?" Abby asked.

He gingerly opened the envelope and withdrew a flat playing card from inside. He frowned. "A jack of spades." He turned it over. "No writing."

Detective Krestyanov said, "Do you have any idea what this means, Ms. Lee?"

Abby stared at the card. Her face, Ethan noted, was even whiter than when he'd arrived, but she shook her head and replied, in a voice so calm it made him shiver, "I have no idea, Detective."

Ethan studied her through narrowed eyes. Detective Garrison glanced at him. "Anything, Mr. Maddux?"

"No," he said slowly. "Not that I can think of."

"All right." The policeman shrugged and dropped the card and the envelope into a plastic bag, which he slid into the pocket of his jacket. "We'll take it to the lab and see what they come up with."

Detective Krestyanov pulled two business cards from his wallet. "We'll do what we can, Ms. Lee, but to be honest, nothing was stolen and nobody got hurt." He handed Abby a card.

She accepted it with a nod. "I know. We're not a high priority when your resources are already overextended."

"It's not a matter of priorities," he said, handing the other card to Ethan, "it's practical. If you can come up with something, anything that might help us, we can investigate this more seriously. But unless we turn up fingerprints on that card—"

"You aren't going to dust the rest of the window?" Ethan asked.

The detective shook his head. "No point." He took the flashlight out of his pocket again and directed its beam at the blood smear on the broken glass. Snagged on the sharpest edge of the glass was a piece of dark wool. He pointed to the fiber. "Gloves," he said. "And sure, if this were a murder, we'd collect that."

His partner's smile was affable. "People watch a lot of television," he explained. "They have an interesting concept of what we do."

"Mostly what we do," Krestyanov added, "is arrest the people victims help us catch. But what we have here is an attempted break-in."

"We're not making light of this, Ms. Lee," the other detective said. "But unless you can give us something more . . ."

"I understand." Abby was clutching the business card so tightly it had crumpled between her fingers.

"If you need anything else," Krestyanov told her, "please call us."

Ethan stepped away from the window and swung Abby free of the glass. She walked with the two detectives toward the door. Ethan used the opportunity to shut the storm window against the elements.

Garrison shook Abby's hand. "And if you can think of anything else, it would be a big help."

"I'll remember. Thank you, Detective."

"Any time, Ms. Lee."

Krestyanov gave Ethan a final glance, then nodded to Abby. "If we discover anything from that envelope, we'll let you know."

She shut the door behind them and momentarily leaned her head against it. Rachel came through the swinging door of the kitchen with a tray on which stood a pot of tea and three mugs. "Are they gone?"

"Yes," Ethan told her. "Have you been hiding in there?"

She put the tray on the coffee table with a slight shrug. "My hair looks crappy. And that tall one was really cute." She glanced at Abby. "I figure we'll be seeing a lot of them later. I can make a better impression."

Abby reset the alarm, then turned to look at Rachel. "We'll probably never see them again, Rach."

Rachel frowned. "But last time—"

Ethan's eyebrows rose. "Last time?"

Abby swept the fall of her hair behind her shoulder and padded across the living room. "The murder," she explained. "The police came and went for days." To Rachel she said, "Honey, I had no idea you remembered that."

Rachel poured tea into one of the mugs. She

wouldn't meet Abby's gaze. "It went on for a really long time."

"Yes." Abby waited while Ethan took the seat across from her. "Several months."

Rachel handed her a mug. "It seemed longer."

"You were practically a baby. I can see why it would."

Ethan reached for his mug while Rachel filled the third. "It's not a big deal, Abby," she said. She picked up her mug and tumbled next to her sister on the couch. "I just don't remember any of them being really cute."

Abby tenderly brushed Rachel's hair away from her face. "They weren't," she assured her. "You didn't miss anything."

Ethan watched the exchange between the two sisters and realized that the impact of the evening had been harder on Rachel than he'd previously thought. She was curled against Abby while Abby gently untangled strands of her hair. In his association with them, he'd never seen Rachel allow, much less seek, physical comfort from her sister. For her part, Abby looked lost in a world of her own.

"Won't they have to come back," Rachel asked after several minutes, "to tell us what they found in that envelope?"

Abby tensed. "Did you hear that?"

"I was listening through the kitchen door," Rachel confessed.

"They'll probably just call," Abby said.

Rachel leaned back and regarded her curiously. "But it was the jack of spades, Abby. Why didn't you tell them it had something to do with Mama and Dad's murder?"

Eleven

Abby's heart skipped a beat. She felt her breath catch as several flashbacks played through her mind. "Rachel," she said carefully, "what do you remember about that?"

Rachel's eyebrows drew together in concentration. "I told you before, I don't really remember anything. I only know about the jack of spades because you told me about it."

"When?"

"You know—that time I was doing the report for school on Dad's military service. You told me it was kind of a thing with him and his buddies. They called him a jack-of-all-trades, which got shortened to 'Jack Spades' when they started playing poker together."

Abby sagged against the couch in relief. "Oh."

She wasn't ready to get into a discussion with her sister, or with Ethan, about the night her parents were killed, or about her interpretation of the playing card's significance.

Jack Lee's nickname had been one of those silly, almost unaccountable things that came about in times of duress and togetherness. He'd picked it up somewhere in Vietnam during a late-night poker game that took place amid mortar fire and shelling. The stories had varied slightly regarding who had first pinned him with it, but it had stuck. The nickname had become so common, it wasn't unusual for people not to have known Jack's real last name.

Rachel hugged her knees to her chest. "So do you think the card meant anything?" she asked.

Abby could feel Ethan's eyes watching her, probing her. She had to struggle not to look at him. She shook her head. "I don't know, sweetie. But the police are handling it now. There's nothing to worry about."

That answer seemed to satisfy her sister. Abby wished she could convince herself as easily. Rachel tipped her head against the couch. "Do you think they'll find anything this time?"

"I don't know. I hope so."

"Are you worried?" her sister persisted.

"I'm just worn out," Abby said evasively. "It's been a long night."

Rachel nodded. "Can I stay home from school tomorrow?"

"You can at least go in late," Abby promised. "We'll see how it goes from there."

"Okay." Rachel looked at Ethan. "Are you staying the night?"

Abby heard the slightly wistful note in her sister's voice and moved to head off the conversation. "He can't. He's supposed to go back to California in the morning."

"Actually," Ethan said, "I was supposed to leave tonight. Those thunderstorms we had earlier changed my plans."

"Are you leaving tomorrow?" Rachel asked. "Really?"

"I was considering it," he replied.

"But you might stay?" she persisted.

Abby glared at him. "There's no need."

He gave her a knowing look. "I'm not so sure."

She bit back her frustration. What she needed was time to think about what had happened tonight and what it meant. Ethan was too shrewd and too persistent to let her off as easily as Rachel had. No way would he accept a simple explanation about the significance of the jack of spades in that envelope. Rachel might have dismissed the entire business, but Ethan would hound her until he got the truth. "The alarm is set. I'm sure he's not coming back. We're perfectly safe."

Ethan steepled his fingers beneath his chin. She saw absolute determination in his gaze. "Still," he said softly, "I'd feel better if I stayed."

"So would I," Rachel said.

Abby pressed her lips together in a tight line. "I don't think—"

"Come on, Abby." Rachel nudged her with her toes. "It couldn't hurt. Ethan can sleep in the guest room." She gave him a winning smile. "I'll make blueberry waffles in the morning."

"Why would I turn down an offer like that?"

Abby felt herself losing control of the situation. She made one more play for the upper hand. "If you have to catch an early flight in the morning, don't you have to go back to your hotel and check out?"

"I think we should talk about that." His voice held a hint of steely determination she knew spelled trouble. "If I'm going back to San Francisco tomorrow, then I want you to consider coming with me."

Abby's mouth dropped open. Rachel sat up on the couch with a cry of delight. "Oh, wow! Could we?"

Ethan nodded. "Considering what happened tonight, I think it's an excellent idea."

Abby shook her head. "I can't. You know I can't."

He glanced at the window. "Abby, I know you're not going to like this, but I don't think this is the last you'll hear from this guy."

"It's impossible," Abby insisted.

"Why?" Rachel asked. She was already firmly

on his side. "I only have two weeks of school left. And I finished exams. It's no big deal if I skip."

Abby sighed in frustration. "It's not just school, Rach."

"I can reschedule my lesson with Monsieur Billaud."

"There are other considerations." Considerations like the time Abby needed to figure out what to do about the playing card in that envelope. And the time she needed to sort out the facts. And because she couldn't imagine herself running off to California with Ethan Maddux. "There's everything going on at the office right now. I have the fund-raiser—"

Ethan cut in smoothly. "I'll give you an office to work out of."

She gritted her teeth. "And my files? My staff?"

"We've got teleconferencing capabilities. And I'll provide you with an assistant."

Abby pressed her fingers to her temples. "What about Deirdre?"

Rachel groaned. "Now *there's* an incentive to get out of town."

Ethan chuckled. "She's got a point, Abby."

Abby set her mug down on the table. "We're not going," she declared with careful precision. "I'm not running away." She couldn't possibly hope to make him understand this—not without telling him things she wasn't ready to reveal. She looked at her sister. "I think you should go to bed,

Rachel. It's late, and we aren't going to settle this tonight."

Rachel frowned. "Why can't I—"

"I don't want to talk about it now."

Rachel glared at her and surged to her feet. "Like always, you mean. When do you ever want to talk about anything I want?"

Abby recoiled. "Don't talk to me like that."

"Why not? You're not my mother, you know."

The charge cut deep. Abby nodded. "I know."

"You can't run my life forever."

"I can right now," she shot back.

"Oh!" Rachel slammed her mug down on the table. "I'm not a baby!"

"Then stop acting like one."

Her sister rolled her eyes. "Oh, just forget it. Like I have any say in anything anyway." She tossed her hair over her shoulder and looked at Ethan. "Thanks for coming over."

He nodded. "Of course."

Abby was already regretting losing her temper. "Rachel, I didn't mean—"

"Yeah. Whatever." She stalked toward the stairs.

When she was out of earshot, Abby winced and looked at Ethan. "Sorry for the scene."

"Are you kidding?" he asked, his eyes devilish. "I'm related to the Montgomerys. I live for scenes."

She shook her head. "I'm sure this is more than you bargained for."

He reached across the table and took her hand in both of his. "In more ways than you can imagine." Stroking her wrist where the sleeve of her robe ended, he added, "Are you going to tell me now what all this is about?"

"Am I allowed to say no?"

"I could torture it out of you."

She searched his features. "Would you?" she asked quietly.

"Are you ready to tell me?"

Abby shivered. "It's not that I'm not ready. It's—I can't."

"I'm going to find out, Abby."

"Can't you just give me a little time?"

"I could, but I'm not going to leave you here alone if you're in trouble."

"We're not," she assured him.

"How can you know that?"

"There was a reason that man left that playing card," she admitted. "But he didn't do it to scare us. He did it to warn us."

Ethan rose from his chair and moved the short distance between them. When he cupped her face in both his hands, the warmth of his fingers sent goose bumps skittering along her skin. His eyes showed a host of conflicting emotions, and she sensed the struggle in him to keep them in check.

"Abby." He kissed her gently, then pulled her

to her feet so he could embrace her. "Whatever is going on . . ." He touched her temple with his lips. "You can trust me. I swear you can trust me."

Did he know how desperately she wanted to? Could he imagine what it had been like to carry these secrets for the past ten years and have no one to share them with? For a few moments she fought a silent war with herself. Ethan placed one hand at the small of her back, his warmth radiating up her spine. He cupped the back of her head with his other hand and lifted her chin so he could meet her gaze.

He let her look into his eyes for long, silent seconds. It was a shockingly intimate sensation. With her body nestled against his, and his gaze open and revealing, she felt simultaneously protected and exposed. "Ethan—"

"Not now," he whispered as he lowered his head. "When you're ready." He covered her lips in a kiss rife with meaning and intent. As his mouth glided over hers, Abby sensed that the emotion she'd seen shimmering just beneath his surface had poured out and rushed into her. This was not a practiced seduction or even a moment of sexual hunger; this was a demand to be heeded and answered. Fervor was spiking inside him, and she could almost feel the internal battle he waged. For reasons she didn't fully understand, he kept that side of himself rigidly controlled. The calm, implacable façade he showed the world was stripped away in the heat of his kiss. In its place was a breathtaking fervor, and in the tremors of his hands, the depth of his kiss, the sheer intensity of the moment, she could feel him wrestling with it, struggling to tame it.

The realization surprised her, as did the knowledge that she felt in the middle of the storm. With a flash of insight, Abby understood that Ethan needed to feel safe there too. The boy who'd lost his mother and struggled with a bitter and distant father needed to know that intense emotion didn't pave the way to his destruction—it alone could set him free. Abby wrapped her hand around his nape and pressed him closer. She could show him that.

Ethan groaned low in his throat and toppled them onto the couch. "Abby . . ." He tore his mouth from hers and glided it along the curve of her jaw. "God, Abby."

She stroked the back of his head, gasping slightly when he nipped her earlobe. She had to stop him soon, her brain warned. Soon, or she wouldn't be able to. Ethan's hand slid inside her robe to caress her through the navy satin of her nightgown. A shudder raced through him when his fingers found the hammering pulse in the hollow of her throat.

Abby summoned the shreds of her willpower

and covered his hand with her own. "Rachel," she whispered.

He stilled. His head dropped to the curve of her neck and he sucked in great breaths of air. Every one of her senses seemed to be on fire. She could feel each individual silken hair on his head splayed against the flesh of her shoulder. She heard the clock on the mantel ticking, and smelled the uniquely masculine combination of shampoo and soap.

He placed a soft kiss on her throat. "Sorry," he muttered.

"Don't be."

Ethan raised his head. The stark emotion was gone from his gaze. In its place was a chiding humor. "I shouldn't have started something I can't finish." He swept her hair back from her face. "You'll think I'm a tease."

That made her laugh. "I'm sure all the girls say that about you."

A sensuous smile curved his lips. "Actually, I've been told that I'm quite good at fulfilling."

A spark of heat ricocheted off her nerve endings. "I can imagine."

He nuzzled her nose. "You won't have to much longer, Abby." He gave her another brief kiss, then sat up straight. He pulled her up with him. "Now, where can I find a pillow and a blanket? We both need some rest."

"You don't have to stay the night."

His frown was censorious. "No arguments, Abby. You couldn't throw me out of here if you tried."

"But your flight—"

"I own the plane, and the pilot's on my payroll. He's not going to take off without me, I assure you."

Abby hesitated for a moment longer. Ethan squeezed her shoulder. "Humor me," he urged her. "I'd never sleep if I had to go back to my hotel."

"Me either," she admitted.

"How are you doing today, Carter?" Abby asked Colonel Jameson the following afternoon. With the Memorial Day event behind them, Abby had stopped for a follow-up meeting with the center's administrator. Carter's eyes looked a little brighter than usual, she observed with envy. She imagined she looked like a wrung-out dishrag.

He reached for her hand. "I'm doing fine," he said with almost uncharacteristic energy. "What about you?"

"Good." Abby gave him a bright smile and took the seat next to him. Unable to sleep even after Ethan had settled in the guest room, she'd spent the small hours of the morning reviewing the events of the night.

The jack of spades in that envelope had continued to taunt her long after the dark shadows had passed. Someone knew something that had never been revealed about her parents' murder. She'd never doubted that. Because Jack Lee's poker buddies had routinely called him Jack Spades, her father's restaurant had been cluttered with the playing-card motif. Friends had frequently given him things that featured his signature playing card in the design.

It had seemed odd to no one, then, that a jack of spades was found near Jack's body when he died. It could easily have been knocked off the wall, or dropped when the thief made his escape. No one, that is, except Abby. Though the police had eventually decided that her parents had been victims of a random robbery gone horribly wrong, Abby knew better. She'd tried to persuade the police, but the colder the trail had gotten, the less success she'd had.

But someone had left the jack of spades at the scene of the crime for a reason. Someone knew the truth. And, for reasons she couldn't begin to understand, was warning her now not to pursue it. Abby shook off the grim thought and concentrated on Carter. "Something going on I should know about, Colonel? You've got that twinkle in your eye that says you're up to no good."

His expression was pure mischief. She couldn't remember ever seeing him look so animated. "I'm up to something, all right," he confessed. "But there's plenty of good in it."

General Standen spotted them from across the

room and waved at Abby with his cane. He made his way toward them with a steady gait and, she noted, a slightly taller posture. Was it her imagination, or was there a renewed energy about the place today? Maybe Rachel's cookies were having some miraculous medicinal effect.

"Abigail," he said. "Good to see you, darling."

"You too, General. What's the news?"

He chuckled and placed both hands on his cane. Leaning toward her, he said, "Well, nothing mobilizes a bunch of old soldiers like a new mission."

"A new mission?" She saw the glances that passed between the general and Carter. "Somebody want to tell me what's going on around here?"

"Can't say right now," Carter answered. "We've got orders."

"Orders?"

The general nodded. "Just something we're looking into. Nothing for you to worry about."

Abby raised an eyebrow. "Is that so?"

"Yep," he assured her. "And you couldn't beat it out of us anyway."

"If you say so."

Carter squeezed her hand. "You look a little tired today, Abby. You been sleeping all right?"

Abby managed a slight laugh. "Now, Carter, since when did you start interrogating me? It's usually the other way around."

"I was just wondering if something, or someone, was maybe keeping you up late." His expression turned knowing.

"Are you trying to pry into my personal life?"

General Standen sat on the opposite side of her. " 'Course we are. What else do you think we do for fun around here?"

"Checkers gets old," Carter told her.

"And we got to sneak around to play poker," the general added.

"So we mostly just fight over who's going to ask you out," Carter said.

The general snorted. "Only we can't go out—so we just fight over it."

Abby held up her hands with a chuckle. "All right, all right. I surrender. I don't know what's gotten into the two of you, but I'm no match for it."

"Then you'll tell us all about this Ethan fellow?" Carter asked. "We got bets riding on how long you're going to string him along."

"I'm not stringing him along."

"Abigail," Carter said patiently, "one thing men our age know a lot about is the wiles of women."

"I don't have wiles."

"Hah." He folded his hands over his chest. "All women have wiles. Isn't that right, General?"

John Standen nodded. "Definitely right."

"And all women know how to use 'em," Carter continued. "Whether they admit it or not." His eyes twinkled. "Are you chasing this fellow or is he chasing you?"

The general grunted. "Now come on, Carter. What kind of question is that? You and I both know that man is footing it after Abby."

"That's what my money's on," Carter assured her.

"Thanks for the vote of confidence," she said dryly.

"But what I want to know is," he continued, undaunted, "when are you going to let him catch you?"

"I'd like to know when he plans to get his hair cut," General Standen added.

Carter pinned her with a shrewd look. "And when's he coming back to Chicago?"

"Do you think I need a haircut?" Ethan asked Jack Iverson. He was in his San Francisco office, awaiting a phone call from Hansen Wells, the man he'd asked Jack to find and who he hoped could give him some crucial information about Jack Lee. He'd come straight to the office from the airport and had just finished changing his shirt when he asked Edna to summon Jack. Ethan was standing in the private bathroom off his office suite, tying his tie.

Jack was seated across from Ethan's desk. "I'm not in the habit of studying your hair," he pointed out.

Ethan frowned at his reflection. The dark waves had started to look shaggy. He'd forgotten that during the two years he'd dated Pamela, she'd taken care of things like his personal appointments. He cinched the knot to his throat, then joined Jack in the office. "Who's your barber?" he asked him as he sat at his desk.

Jack's eyebrows rose. "I have a stylist," he replied. "It's considered more chic."

Ethan snorted and hit a button on his telephone. "I want a haircut, not a lifestyle."

"Yes?" Edna's voice came through the intercom.

"Edna, can you make me an appointment to get my hair cut this afternoon?"

"Sure. Any particular place?"

Ethan thought about the glass-and-neon shop Pamela had frequented and dismissed it. "Where does your husband get his hair cut?" he asked his secretary.

"Joe's Barber Shop on Geary. I don't think it's your kind of place."

"It's fine. See if they can take me at three."

"Ethan"—her tone was pure amusement—"Joe's Barber Shop doesn't make appointments. It's a first-come, first-served type of place."

"Does Joe do shaves too?"

"Yes. That takes longer."

His gaze flicked to the calendar open on his computer screen. "Fine. Have a car ready for me at two-thirty. I'll go over there and wait."

"If you say so."

He punched the button to end the call. Jack was

watching him curiously. "You're acting weird," he announced.

Ethan shrugged. "Didn't get much sleep over the weekend."

"Really? Anything to do with Abby Lee?"

That made Ethan frown. "Not the way you think." He took out a piece of paper from his briefcase and handed it to Jack. It was the e-mail he'd received that morning from Charlie Blevins about his investigation of Abby Lee. "Tell me what you make of this."

Jack glanced at the address line on the e-mail. "You're having her investigated?"

"No. I'm having the situation investigated. I'm starting to believe that Harrison knows something about Jack Lee's murder."

Jack scanned the contents of the report. "He can't find anything other than birth records for Abby or her sister prior to the murder?"

"That's what he says."

"Didn't her father run a successful business in the downtown area?"

"A restaurant."

"Hmm." Jack continued to read. "Must have been fairly fanatical about his privacy. No Chamber of Commerce memberships, civic organizations. Nothing." He tapped the report with his finger. "The police determined that the murder was a random robbery."

"Yes."

"But you don't think so?"

"I'm not sure."

"What do you think Harrison knows about it?"

"I'm not sure about that either, but I find it odd that Charlie interviewed half a dozen people who supposedly knew the Lees very well and none of them remember him having daughters."

"What do you make of that?"

"I'm wondering if they knew the Lees at all, or if someone had an interest in creating a new circle of friends for Abby's parents after the murder."

Jack set the e-mail message aside and frowned at Ethan. "Who'd possibly have the motivation to do something like that?"

"Someone who wanted to keep anyone who knew a lot about Jack Lee and his past from talking to the police—or to anyone else."

"You think Lee was hiding something?"

"I think when a man runs a public business and has no public life, there's a reason." Ethan reached for a file folder, sifted the contents, and produced another piece of paper for Jack. "Look at this."

Jack studied the sheet. "This is the deed of sale for the building where Lee ran his restaurant."

"He bought it. Paid cash for it."

"Quarter of a million bucks."

"Where does an army corporal get that kind of money?"

Jack pondered the question. "Maybe his wife inherited."

Ethan shook his head. "I checked. There's no trail."

"Did Charlie check the financial records?"

"In the early sixties, Jack and Lucinda Lee started investing two to three thousand dollars a month in stocks and bonds. They were very lucky. Got in on the ground floor of some aeronautic stocks. Always in when stocks were low and out when stocks peaked."

"Pretty damned good for a couple of amateurs."

"Too good," Ethan concurred. "In seven years, they had enough to buy that building and, according to Charlie, to pay cash for the house they lived in outside the city."

Jack let out a low whistle. "Sounds like Jack was wasting his time in the restaurant business. He could have made millions as a broker."

"But he was also a lousy businessman. His IRS statements show consistent losses for the restaurant. There's no way he could have stayed in business without an independent bankroll."

"And you think Montgomery's got something to do with this?"

"I think it's too damned convenient that Harrison materialized with a job for Abby just a few weeks after Jack's murder. I also find it suspicious that the circle of close friends the police interviewed didn't include any of his restaurant regulars. Jack had a group of poker buddies. They met

in the back room of the restaurant every other
Thursday night."

"The police didn't talk to them either?"

"The only place their names show up in the
case file is in the initial interview Abby had with
the police. She was nineteen at the time, and in
shock the night they interviewed her."

Jack swore. "What about the sister?"

"Three years old. Her mother had hidden her
in the closet when the killer came into the restaurant."

"Abby found the bodies?"

"When her parents didn't come home that
night, she drove into the city to check the restaurant. That's all in the report. The police had already been called to the scene by one of the
neighbors. They interviewed her that night, and
she gave them the names of Jack's poker buddies."

"But no one followed up."

"They also canvassed the neighborhood, which
is how they turned up the names of the people
they did talk to. When they went looking for the
poker players, all five were either out of town in-
definitely or too difficult to locate. With a host of
other witnesses at their disposal, and nothing to
suggest the murder was anything more than a
fouled robbery, the police didn't see the need to
continue investigating."

Jack stroked his chin. "You're right. It's weird."

"Three weeks later, Abby went to work for Harrison. He hired her straight off the street, with no references and no training."

"Maybe he just felt sorry for her."

"That's her side of the story."

"You don't believe it?" Jack asked.

"Harrison never felt sorry for a person in his life. Whatever he did, he did for a reason."

"But you can't link him to the murder."

"No. Right now, I can't even link him to Jack Lee." Ethan leaned back in his chair and folded his hands behind his head. "But even more interesting than Lee's success in the stock market is the fact that those poker buddies all had similar portfolios. Jack was giving free investment advice in that back room."

"That would explain why his friends were hesitant to talk to the police."

"It could," Ethan mused. "But what I want to know is, how was he getting that information and why was somebody giving it to him?"

"Hell, Ethan, the trail is over ten years old."

"I'm willing to lay bad odds that it leads right back to Harrison. I just have to figure out why."

"And that's where Hansen Wells fits into this?"

"Yes. MDS was heavily involved with the Defense Department during that time. If Hansen can give me a couple of contacts, I might make a trip to Washington this week."

"Good. You can take Lewis with you and put the fear of God into Edward Kinsey."

At the mention of his embattled client, Ethan groaned. "What's the status of that?"

"Lewis wants to—" The ring of Ethan's intercom interrupted the CFO.

Ethan held up a hand and hit the button. "Yes, Edna?"

"Hansen Wells for you."

"Great. I'll take it."

Edna put the call through to Ethan's private line.

"You want me to leave?" Jack asked.

Ethan shook his head. "I might need you. Your memory's better than mine." He picked up the receiver on the second ring. "Hansen," he said cordially. "Thanks for getting back to me."

"I think I've found what you need," Hansen told him.

Satisfied, Ethan propped his feet on the desk. He gave Jack a slight nod. "Go on," he told his caller. "I'm listening."

Twelve

Trying to pin the man down, Abby decided two days later, was worse than trying to bottle a cloud. She sat in the cluttered confines of Detective Nick Krestyanov's office and waited patiently while he barked orders to some hapless clerk on the other end of the phone. He slammed down the receiver with a grunt of frustration. "Sorry, Ms. Lee. You were saying?"

Abby took a fortifying breath. "About the break-in. I—I just wondered if anything had turned up about that envelope."

The detective jerked open the bottom drawer of his desk and pulled out a pair of worn loafers. "I don't think we got a report on that yet." He propped one sneakered foot on the drawer and tugged at the laces. "Do you mind?" he said, giving her a quick glance and indicating the shoes. "I have to be in court in thirty minutes."

By the time Abby had shaken her head, he'd already pulled off the first shoe and jammed his foot into the loafer. "So you don't have anything else?"

The detective confirmed her question with a short nod. "I can double-check with Detective Garrison. He might have heard something and forgot to mention it." Krestyanov swore as the laces on his other shoe knotted beneath his blunt fingers. "I doubt it, though. We'll have to follow up, and we just haven't gotten to it."

"I understand," she said.

His hand stilled on the shoe. "Ms. Lee, is there something you want to tell me?"

Abby hesitated. More than she wanted to breathe at the moment, she wanted to unload the worries she'd been carrying for the past three days and hand them over to someone who'd take care of them for her. Ethan called her two or three times a day and continued to press her for information. She'd resisted thus far, but her determination was waning. If only she hadn't promised, she thought glumly. And if only she didn't fear that whatever she told him would create even bigger problems for her and for him.

He'd told her this morning that he was headed back to Chicago today. She was supposed to meet him for dinner at a downtown restaurant. He had something important to tell her, he'd said, and he'd sounded grim. When she'd asked him for details, he'd revealed only that he didn't want to talk about it on the phone.

She'd hung up feeling anxious and dreary.

Finally, she'd decided to see Detective Krestyanov today, hoping that somehow the police would have discovered something about that card. She desperately wanted answers. But he'd confirmed her worst fears. She was buried again in a sea of bureaucracy, and if anything were to be done, she'd have to do it herself.

"Ms. Lee?" he prompted.

Abby flinched. "Oh. Sorry. I was—thinking about something."

He lowered his foot to the floor. His expression turned utterly serious. "I can't help you if you don't level with me," he said. "If there's something you're not telling us—"

She shook her head. "No, there's not. I just wanted to know if any progress had been made."

He studied her for a few moments, then shook his head. "We'll call you if we find anything."

With a short nod, Abby rose to go. "Thank you, Detective. I . . ." She wavered, assailed by memories of the last time she'd sat in a place like this and told her story. Suppressing a shudder, Abby scooped up her purse from the chair. "I'd appreciate that," she said. She felt crowded suddenly, compelled by a strong urge to flee his office and the oppressive atmosphere that went with it. After hurrying from the precinct and out onto the busy sidewalk, she leaned wearily against the brick wall.

The summer sky had turned gray with impending rain. A thunderstorm was probably blowing in off the lake. Abby stared at the dismal clouds and thought they mirrored her mood. Why? she wondered. Why now, and why this? Why, when she'd waited ten years for answers, did they have to present themselves in a way that left her feeling frustrated and confounded?

She briefly closed her eyes. An image of Ethan, his expression concerned and probing, popped into her mind. Fool that she was, she had tumbled for a man who held himself so firmly in check, she barely knew what he was thinking half the time.

In stark contrast to Ethan, her own father had had a very different approach—an ever-present laugh, a winning smile, a generous affection. Jack Lee had been a born entertainer. Abby's mother had watched her husband's gregariousness with an indulgent smile. Abby was sure she had never needed to study the man she loved in a vain effort to read his mind.

"You're a fool, Abby," she muttered to herself as loneliness assailed her. She felt a deep need to talk things over with her parents—even if they couldn't provide her with answers. On impulse, she stepped forward to hail a cab.

* * *

Ethan heard her fiddling with the key in the lock and he strode across Abby's living room to jerk the door open. A rumble of thunder punctuated the steady pounding of his heart.

It was after midnight, and he'd been pacing the floor for the past five hours, growing steadily more panicked. When he'd arrived in Chicago that afternoon, he'd been unable to reach her by phone. Her assistant had informed him that Abby had left the office shortly after lunch and had not returned for the day.

When she failed to show for dinner, he'd known something was drastically wrong. He'd called her house and received no answer. He still had LuAnne's business card in his wallet, and tried that number next. The stylist hadn't heard from Abby that day, but said that Rachel was spending the weekend at a friend's lake house. LuAnne had assured him that she knew where Abby had probably gone. Given the break-in on Tuesday night and the stress of reliving the memory of her parents' death, Abby would likely have taken the time to pay a visit to their graves.

LuAnne didn't know the name or the location of the cemetery. Ethan had called his investigator, who was also unable to supply him with the information. Frustrated at his own helplessness, Ethan had talked again to LuAnne. She'd agreed to let him into Abby's house with her key, but had chastened him not to worry. Abby frequently made visits there, LuAnne had explained. She'd obviously needed the space.

The lecture hadn't helped. The later the hour became, and the harder it rained outside, the more his anxiety had increased. He'd called Detective Krestyanov and discovered that Abby had paid him a visit that afternoon. She'd seemed tense, the detective told him, but not unusually upset.

By the time her key rattled in the lock, Ethan's usually calm nerves were shot to hell. He jerked open the door and found Abby standing there, soaked to the skin. "Where the hell have you been?" he demanded as he struggled with a simultaneous desire to rage at her and to hold her so tightly she could never scare him like that again.

Abby blinked. "Ethan, what are you doing here?" She looked exhausted. She shook her head and drops of water splashed onto his shirt.

"God, you're soaked." He reached for her arm. "Come on, get inside." He pulled her through the door. "Do you have any idea how late it is?" He rubbed his hands on her upper arms to ward off the chill. "Why the hell didn't you call me?" He couldn't seem to rein in the terror and frustration that had been clawing at him all night.

"I don't know."

She sounded hoarse. His hands had grown cold from touching the sodden sleeves of her jacket. "Have you been out in the rain since this afternoon?" he asked as he kicked the door shut with his foot. "I need to call LuAnne and tell her you're all right."

She coughed. "You told LuAnne?"

Ethan reached for her jacket. "Here, take this off." He shoved the jacket off her shoulders and it dropped to the tiled floor with a wet plop. Abby swayed toward him. He steadied her with a hand on her shoulder. "You probably made yourself sick," he said, and touched her forehead. "You're burning up. I think you have a fever."

She shook her head. "No, I'm just cold." She shivered and placed a hand on his chest. "Ethan, please don't—"

"You need to lie down." He led her to the living room and guided her onto the couch, then reached for the phone and punched the redial. Lu-Anne answered it on the first ring. Abby snatched the receiver from his hand with a frown.

"Lu? Yeah, I'm fine." She listened to LuAnne's question while she wiped the dripping rainwater from her forehead. Ethan used the rest of the brief conversation to wring some of the water out of her hair. She finished with LuAnne and handed him the receiver. He slammed it back into its cradle.

Abby sniffed. "She was going to come over if I'm going to be here alone tonight," she told him noncommittally.

"You won't." He tugged her shoes off. "You've got to get out of those wet clothes. I'm going to find a robe and a thermometer." He moved toward the stairs, but she made an inarticulate sound in her throat that stopped him dead.

"Ethan—"

"It's going to be all right," he promised her, and kissed her forehead. "I just need to get some things."

"How did you get in here?"

He brushed her wet hair off her forehead. Now that she was here and apparently in one piece, some of his terror was beginning to ebb. He still felt too emotionally raw, however, to trust himself with anything other than the barest of facts. Tomorrow, reason might return, but now all the horrible visions he'd had during his extended wait were looming over him like specters from a best-forgotten nightmare.

"LuAnne let me in with her keys," he replied. "When you didn't show for dinner—"

She frowned. "Sorry. Oh, God, I'm sorry. I forgot."

He shook his head. "I was worried. I talked to Krestyanov. He said you came to see him this afternoon."

"Yes." She shook her head. She was so cold, her lips looked blue. "He didn't know anything."

"That's what he said." Ethan stroked her face. Abby had begun to shiver again, so he jerked a cotton throw off the back of the couch and wrapped it around her shoulders. "Honey, have you been at the cemetery all this time?"

"I walked to the restaurant." She clutched the edges of the coverlet. "I just wanted to see it again. It had been a long time."

Ethan remembered his investigator giving him the location of the waterfront restaurant. It was at least a mile from the nearest cemetery. Abby sniffed. "I just sort of lost track of time. My car was at the office, and I had to go back to get it to come home."

He nodded. "No wonder." He touched her forehead again. "I still think you've got a fever."

"I don't."

"Baby, this is not the time to argue with me." She had no idea, he thought, of the internal war he was waging. "It's going to get you nowhere." He pressed a fierce kiss to her forehead. "Later you can be annoyed with me. Right now, I'm going to get you dry and warm."

"You don't have to do this."

He ignored her remark as he studied the pale color of her face. "Maybe I should call a doctor."

"No, really, Ethan, I'm fine."

The distress in her voice made his temperature rise. She was hurting, deeply. If she'd gone from the cemetery to the restaurant as she'd said, she'd spent the past several hours reliving the most horrifying experience of her life. The powerlessness he felt made him angry. There was nothing he could do to ease the desolate look in her eyes—a look he remembered seeing in a mirror the day his mother had died and Letty had taken him to her funeral.

What was worse, he was beginning to think he could have spared Abby all this if he'd simply told Harrison to go to hell the day he'd challenged him at Carlton's party. She didn't deserve any of it. At the thought, he felt the door of the vault slam open. He had to take several controlled breaths while he struggled for balance.

Abby drew his hand to her lips and placed a soft kiss on the palm. "I'm okay now. I'm sorry I worried you."

Could she know? he wondered. Something went still inside him. Could she understand? His fingers captured hers. "Honey, you're sick," he said, and now *his* voice sounded hoarse.

Her hand tightened on his. "No." She shook her head. "I'm not sick."

"You look sick," he protested.

She buried her wet face against his forearm. "I'm not."

"You feel feverish."

"I am," she said quietly and met his gaze. The haunted look still shadowed her eyes, but her expression had subtly shifted. "I've been waiting for you."

His world tipped off its axis. Dear God, he thought. Not now. Not when he'd waited so long and his emotions were so removed from his control. "Honey, you don't—"

"I miss them so much," she whispered. "Mother and Dad. It's been so hard for a long time." Her voice sounded hollow. "Don't you remember what it feels like—to think you have no one in the world?"

He felt her shudder all the way to his scalp. His heart beat a maddened rhythm and this time the internal dam burst. He remembered. Some days, it seemed, he did nothing but remember. "God, Abby," he said. "You don't understand. I don't want to hurt you." He threaded his fingers into her damp hair.

"You couldn't," she assured him.

"Now is not the time." Not when she'd hate him for it later.

Abby shook her head. "It's the perfect time. I'm here. You're here. We're here alone. Make love to me, Ethan."

He tilted his head back and fought for control. "I can't," he told her gently. "Not now."

The hurt in her eyes clamped around his heart in a tight band. He deliberately ignored it and eased her backward until she lay stretched out on the couch. "You're exhausted, emotionally and physically. How much have you slept since Tuesday?"

She shrugged. He nodded. "Get some rest. I'll be here when you wake up."

Abby fought her way through a few hours of sleep to find herself curled up on her sofa. Her head ached. The splatter of rain on glass drew her gaze to the window. Pale light revealed streaks of rain sluicing down the glass. Even the weak morning sun made her eyes burn. She dropped her head back with a low groan as she remembered the events of the previous night. She'd gone to the cemetery, where she'd stayed too long and wept too hard.

Melancholy and a need for answers had driven her to the waterfront address that used to house her father's restaurant. A new bar was open there now. Trendy, with an Art Deco interior, it bore no resemblance to the battered but homey place of her childhood. She'd turned and walked through the rain all the way back to her office building, where her car sat in the garage. She barely remembered the drive home.

Ethan had been there. Concerned, maybe even a little angry, he'd greeted her at the door and promptly refused her offer to make love. Abby squeezed her eyes shut and shuddered.

"Feeling better?" his rough voice asked.

Startled, she saw him standing near the kitchen. She struggled to sit up. "What time is it?"

He held two mugs of coffee. "Early. Not quite five." He crossed the room and gave her one of the mugs.

She accepted it with a look of gratitude. "Did you sleep at all?"

"Off and on," he said. "I was worried about you."

"Don't be. I'm not cracking up or anything." She took a fortifying sip of the coffee.

He studied her for a minute, then sat down next to her. He propped his bare feet on the coffee table. "I didn't think you were."

"Yes, you did," she told him with a slight smile. "I'm really sorry I worried you."

He raised his eyebrows over the rim of his mug. "You do seem to be feeling better."

Abby put her mug down on the table, then tucked her feet underneath her. "Sometimes I forget how much it all hurt. I need to revisit it on occasion, just to find my center again." Her gaze turned contemplative. "It's one of the ways I keep them close to me—by forcing myself to remember."

He didn't respond. She watched him curiously. "Don't you do that with your own mother?"

He shook his head. "No."

Somehow, his response didn't surprise her. That formidable calm she'd first noticed gave him the strength not to look back. "Never?" she probed.

"Not if I can help it."

"What if you can't?"

He was starting to look uncomfortable. "Then I deal with it. I don't let it consume me."

"Oh." She thought about that for a moment. "Is that why you're always so controlled?"

"Controlled?" He set his mug down.

"You know what I mean. You don't have emotional outbursts." She gave him a little half smile. "You're the only Montgomery who doesn't."

"I had one last night."

She frowned. "What are you talking about?"

"When you came in. Don't you remember me yelling at you?"

For a moment she thought he was kidding. She actually started to laugh before she realized he was completely serious. "Yelling? Good grief, Ethan. You probably thought I'd been hit by a bus or something. I stood you up for dinner. I didn't come in until after midnight, and when I did, I looked like I'd taken a swim in the lake. No wonder you were keyed up."

He visibly winced. "I shouldn't have lost my temper."

Poor man, she thought. There was such depth there. He had a well of untapped feeling just waiting to spring free, and no one had ever given him permission. What, she wondered, would it take to really send him over the edge? "If I'd been you, I would have been screaming like a banshee."

He gave her a small smile for that comment. "No, you wouldn't. You're not a shrieker."

Abby shrugged. "Shows what you know. Just ask Rachel."

"Teenage girls tend to overdramatize."

"That's an understatement. But I guarantee I

wouldn't have been nearly so calm if the roles were reversed. You'd have been peeling me off the ceiling."

"I'll remember that."

He seemed slightly off-kilter, as if he didn't quite know what to do with himself. Abby decided to forge ahead. "And thank you for what you did last night." At his puzzled look, she felt her skin flush. "About turning me down, I mean. I don't think I was in a good place to make that offer."

His expression was unflinchingly intense. "It wouldn't have been fair."

"I guess not," she said, wishing he'd said more. Wishing he'd gushed out an explanation about how he'd wanted to, really wanted to, but he'd forced himself to walk away and then paid for it all night by pacing the floor and fighting a Herculean battle with his self-control. With a slight smile, she took a few more sips of her coffee. She really had it bad.

Ethan turned his head to gaze out the window. Abby studied the fine lines of his chiseled profile. He reminded her more than ever of a Roman gladiator, alone and stoically brave in the face of his own personal tragedy.

Her heart ached for him, practically overwhelmed by her love of him in that moment. What would she have done all these years if she hadn't had the freedom to rage at fate while she grieved over the loss of her parents? Why had no one ever loved Ethan enough to set him free? Her heart raced as she acknowledged how much she yearned to be the one who'd hand him the key. An inner voice cautioned that the inevitable storm that would follow had the potential to break her heart. But a stronger voice insisted that her heart was a small price to pay when his life seemed to be at stake.

With that realization, a calm assurance and a clear sense of purpose settled on her. She'd proved to herself in the past ten years that the pain of loss didn't outweigh the joys of living—and that she was strong enough to take risks. She would reach this enigmatic, unapproachable man and show him all the riches of life. If she got hurt in the process, she'd always have the memories to sustain her. "Ethan?"

"Hmm?" He didn't look at her.

"I'm feeling much better."

"I'm glad."

"I'm in my right mind."

He still didn't look at her. "I can see that."

"So would it be fair now?"

He didn't move. She wasn't certain why she sensed a sudden stillness about him. The black panther, she mused, was poised to strike. And, God help her, she wasn't even worried about being the slowest and fattest gazelle. "What did you say?"

She touched his arm. "I said, would it be fair now?"

When he turned his face to her, the look in his eyes took her breath away. "Be absolutely certain, Abby," he said slowly. "I'm not going to say no a second time." His voice sounded stark with need.

A good sign, she thought. She eased carefully away from him, keeping her gaze trained on his face. He held out a hand to her. It trembled, she noticed, and found it odd that he would be the one with tremors. She smiled at him softly and placed her hand in his. "I'm sure," she said.

His fingers closed on hers in a crushing grip. He raised her hand to his mouth and kissed her palm. "I won't hurt you," he promised. "You won't regret this."

He obviously had no idea how deep her feelings ran for him, she realized, or he wouldn't have needed to make that promise. She could never imagine regretting something as profound as what she knew she'd share with Ethan. "I know," she assured him, and reached for the buttons of his shirt. "You wouldn't let me."

A violent tremor raced through him. Like a pre-volcanic eruption, she mused. "Upstairs," he said, his voice slightly hoarse, "there's a bed."

Abby placed a hand on each of his shoulders and brought him slowly against her. "Maybe we'll get to it later today."

Something seemed to galvanize him then. He collapsed back on the couch, pulling her with him. Abby felt the amazing sensation of his strong, rough hands as they skimmed her flesh. She began flicking open the buttons of his shirt. He kissed her deeply, intently, as if he couldn't get enough of her taste. "God, Abby, can you imagine how much I want you?"

She worked his shirt open—no easy task while the button, clung to the wet fabric. Little frissons of pleasure were raising the goose bumps on her skin. His chest felt as hot as the rest of him. "I think I've waited forever."

He thrust a hand beneath her shirt and cupped her breast. "You set me on fire."

She hoped so. Lord, how she hoped so. "It's the same for me," she said, feeling a sense of wonder.

Ethan kissed her again. He showed her the entire repertoire of emotions he could put into a kiss. She felt his hunger and answered it with her own, pressing herself tighter to him. When he groaned her name against her mouth, she nipped his lower lip with her teeth.

He dragged his mouth from hers. "Let me slow down," he told her. "There's plenty of time."

She yanked his shirt free of his jeans. "No. Don't. Please don't."

He kissed her once more, but soon broke the delicious contact. His hand traveled down her rib cage and over her hip. "It's too much. Too fast."

"Not enough," she corrected him, and sank her teeth into his earlobe. Ethan released a harsh breath, then abruptly flipped her beneath him.

"Lord, Abby, you're driving me crazy."

She wedged her thigh between his. "Then don't stop. Please don't ever stop."

His hands and his mouth were everywhere at once. He unbuttoned her shirt and peeled it back, gazing at her with a look that stole her breath. "Spectacular," he murmured and dipped his head to kiss the hollow of her throat. His tongue found the wildly beating pulse at the juncture of her collarbone.

Abby gasped as he overwhelmed her with a spiking passion that made her skin burn. She believed she could feel her blood pressure climb. Her heart was beating a mad rhythm. She'd never felt like this. Vaguely, she remembered thinking that she was supposed to be overwhelming him, stripping away his restraint. She hadn't counted on the tables being reversed. She hadn't imagined experiencing this relentless sense of need that drove her to unparalleled heights. She reached for the button of his jeans. His hand closed over hers and held it to his bare chest. "Not yet," he said gently.

"Now," she said, beginning to feel frantic. "Oh, Ethan, please, *now*."

He jerked his mouth from hers and rolled away from her. She felt swamped and overcome by the sudden rush of cold air. He placed one hand on her belly and ripped open the button of his jeans with the other. He made quick work of the zipper before he peeled off the denims. He stopped to place a kiss where his finger rested on her stomach. "I need something," he explained, and grabbed his wallet from the back pocket of his jeans.

Abby reached for the cool, damp leather billfold and opened it for him. Ethan produced a foil packet, which she snatched from his hand and tore open. He finished the job. He kissed her, hard. "Are you—"

She grasped his hips with her hands. "Oh, yes."

Ethan covered her mouth and claimed her in a move of seamless grace that took her all the way to paradise.

His throat felt raw, he realized as he shifted gingerly on the sofa and nestled a sleeping Abby against him. The scratchy feeling owed itself to the hoarse shout that had erupted from his chest the moment Abby had given him unimaginable bliss.

For perhaps the first time in his life, Ethan understood how passion had driven his mother to desperation, and why she'd allowed it. The turmoil of the previous night had still kept him off balance when Abby had awakened this morning. She would probably never know what it had cost him to walk away from her when she'd been so very willing and so very vulnerable.

At least he had that for comfort. He'd managed to cling to his self-control long enough not to take advantage of her. This morning, however, she'd been fully aware of what she was doing. Honor hadn't demanded that he turn her down. Had he known, however, that she was about to send him hurtling over a cliff, stark fear might have sent him running.

He'd never experienced the mind-numbing release he'd had with Abby. Like a match to kerosene, her gentle touch had set off a conflagration. He'd lost control of it almost immediately. He'd rushed to the end with little or no thought for her pleasure. Thank God, he thought with bitter self-condemnation, that he'd had the presence of mind to protect her. He'd demanded everything, taking whatever he wanted and dragging her along with him. While Abby, the most generous woman he knew, had given it all to him.

He'd known the minute he'd joined with her that whatever experience she'd had was limited at best. She'd been exquisite, and innocent, simultaneously soft and strong. She'd welcomed him with a soft cry that had ricocheted off his nerve endings and carried him to new heights. How could he have known that the fierce embrace of an unpracticed but giving woman would have quantum power compared with the practiced seduction of the sophisticated women of his past?

He closed his eyes and softly caressed her shoulder with his fingertip. Like the bastard he was, he'd taken everything she'd offered with no consideration of her needs. There had been no slow, building passion. He'd given her no chance to stop him—or even to slow him down, for that matter. He'd muttered a few obligatory phrases, but he'd known, even then, that the words were empty. He could no more have halted the roar of passion in his blood than he could have kept the sun from rising.

He'd overwhelmed her, and while she might be resting against him now, with her fingers curled gently on his chest, soon she would resent the hell out of him.

That idea left him feeling unaccountably morose. Ethan dropped his head back against the sofa arm with a low groan.

"Ethan?" Her voice was soft, like the rest of her.

"Um?"

"Are you all right?"

Hell, no, he thought glumly. "Why?"

"You groaned." She shifted so her chin rested on his chest. "I thought maybe I was making you uncomfortable."

"You're not." If, he added silently, you don't count the fact that my damned body is already starting to respond to you. He was supposed to be too old for that.

"I had no idea," she said quietly, and a soft blush spread over her face. "I mean—it's never been like that."

Recriminations flooded him. He accepted them as his due and prepared himself for the worst. He smoothed a hand down her bare arm. "I'm sorry, Abby," he told her.

Her eyes widened in momentary confusion. "You're sorry?"

In the morning light, with her hair tumbled around her shoulders, she looked better than any fantasy he'd ever had. He gently touched one of the golden curls on her shoulder. "I didn't give you enough time."

Abby frowned then and struggled to sit up. She pulled the cotton throw around her shoulders. "I see."

"I should have paid more attention."

"You weren't paying attention?"

She wasn't going to make this easy for him, he realized. He should have known she wouldn't be the type to back down—not when he'd seen her ready to do battle with Harrison on his behalf. Guilt roiled around in his gut and started to eat away at him. "I wasn't paying enough attention to you," he clarified.

"Oh." Her eyebrows drew together. "What

were you thinking about, then?" She glanced at the ceiling. "I mean, if I need a coat of paint, I guess I could hire someone."

My God, he thought, was she actually teasing him? "That's not—"

She placed a hand on his chest. "You weren't doing something like analyzing your stock portfolio, were you? Because I could probably get over something like—oh, I don't know—your glancing around the room and seeing the crack in the wall near my door and thinking, Gee, she really ought to get that fixed. But I'm pretty sure I'd have to be *really* offended if you were concentrating on pork futures or something."

He stared at her. She drummed her fingers on his chest. "I mean, geez, Ethan, I've never even *seen* a pork future, but I'm pretty sure I'm more entertaining."

The teasing note in her voice felt like a hammer in his brain. "You are," he choked out. "I should have given you more."

Her lips curved into a sultry smile. "Oh, Ethan. Are you seriously trying to apologize to me?" He didn't respond. She placed a soft kiss on his lips. "In case you didn't notice, I wasn't exactly complaining."

Ethan twined a curl around his index finger. "I could have made it better for you."

Her sultry laugh twisted around his gut tighter

than the curl twisted on his finger. "Really?" There was nothing but wonder in the question. "Is that a promise?"

Slowly, he began to absorb the incredible truth that not only had he not overwhelmed her, but, by some miracle, he'd actually managed to avoid screwing up this relationship. He rubbed his curl-wrapped finger over the smooth skin of her shoulder. "There's so much more," he explained. "I wanted to take my time with you."

She glanced at the clock on the mantel. "Um, Rachel isn't coming home until tomorrow afternoon. You could always take your time now." She was staring at the clock when she said that. Her lower lip trembled slightly.

He felt like he'd barely escaped with his life. Never again, he promised himself. He would never let things get so out of control again. She'd scared him last night, and he'd had trouble recovering, but he could master himself. The stakes were simply too high for him not to. Determined to demonstrate just how inspiring extra attention could be, he rolled onto his feet and extended a hand to her. "I need a shower," he said. "And then I have some things to show you."

"Things?"

"Lots of things." He dipped his head and kissed her softly. "You'll like them."

She laughed in that sultry way that made him

feel a little intoxicated. He nipped her lower lip. "Anything you don't like," he continued, sweeping a hand down her back to clasp her closer to him, "let me know. I'll keep trying until I get it right."

Thirteen

Rain pelted the windshield of Abby's late-model sports car as she navigated the Kennedy Expressway. Ethan winced and clamped his hand on the door handle when she darted between two cars. She was humming an off-key tune and tapping her fingers on the steering wheel in rhythm with the windshield wipers. He was trying not to panic, as she obviously suffered under the delusion that she was flying a fighter jet and not a too-small car that looked like it had come from a blister pack at a toy store.

Another driver merged into their lane, and Abby laid on the horn with a dark curse. Ethan closed his eyes.

"What a creep," she muttered, and jerked her car into the adjacent lane. "Where did you get your license?" she yelled at the offending driver. "A convenience store?"

Ethan's grip on the door handle tightened even more. "Do you always drive like this?"

She glanced at him in surprise. "Like what?"

He resisted the urge to put his hand on the steering wheel and ease the car back into the center of the lane. "Like you have a death wish," he mumbled.

Abby laughed gaily and looked at the road again while he made a mental note not to ask any more questions. "I had no idea you were such a nervous passenger," she said.

He gritted his teeth when she sped up to keep a car in the merge lane from getting in front of her. "I had no idea you aspired to be a stock-car driver."

"Oh, come on," she chided. "You drive in California. It has to be worse than this."

"The operative word is 'drive.' I *drive* in California. I do not use the highway as an excuse to practice counterterrorist driving techniques." A tractor-trailer bore down on them, and Ethan shuddered. "And my car isn't made out of plastic and aluminum."

Abby gave him a reproving look as she dashed across two lanes of traffic toward her exit. "And here I had you pegged for an enlightened male." She shook her head. "Who knew?"

Ethan closed his eyes with a groan and leaned

back against the headrest. He couldn't bear to watch her maneuver through the crowded streets of the Loop, so he tried to tune out the sounds of blaring horns and Abby's muttered curses. She'd already scheduled this meeting with Deirdre and her volunteer committee for today, otherwise they could have spent the rest of the afternoon watching the rain fall—an idea that he'd found oddly appealing.

Ethan rarely afforded himself the luxury of sitting still. It wasn't in his nature. He drove himself in his personal life as hard as he did in his business life. This trait was one more thing Pamela hadn't been able to deal with. Today, however, the idea of simply lying around Abby's house had tempted him. A smile tugged at the corners of his mouth as he considered all the implications of that scenario. He could have spent the rest of the rainy afternoon exploring her secrets.

What he'd learned so far had him itching for more. He spread his hands over his thighs and thought about the way he could make her shiver when he nestled his lips on—

"Damn moron!" Abby yelled beside him and jerked her car hard to the left.

Ethan's eyes flew open. He felt himself anticipating the inevitable crunch of metal on metal. "What—"

She glared at the car next to her. "He pulled out

of that parking deck without ever looking to see if anything was coming."

Ethan drew a calming breath. "I don't suppose there was any chance you were driving too fast?"

She scowled at him. "People shouldn't drive in the city if they don't know how."

Or they shouldn't drive in the city, period, he thought. He shook his head and deliberately changed the subject. "Tell me about this meeting today."

She rolled her eyes. "I can't believe you agreed to subject yourself to it. You know how Deirdre is."

"Tedious?"

"Demanding. I mean, I actually kind of like the woman most of the time, but she's driving my staff insane."

"I can understand that." He couldn't resist the urge to brush one of Abby's curls over her shoulder. She wore a green cotton sweater that made her eyes look like wet leaves. "Is that why you agreed to see her on a Saturday?"

"No." Abby headed for Grant Park. The MDS office building overlooked the park and the harbor. "I did that for the volunteers. I knew Rachel would be gone today—" She shot him a sheepish look. "I didn't know I'd be preoccupied."

He placed his hand on her thigh. "I could preoccupy some more."

"Promises, promises," she teased and pulled into the parking garage. "And I have to get through this meeting first. I still can't believe you're willing to be part of it."

He shrugged. How was he supposed to explain that he wasn't yet willing to let her out of his sight—not after the scare she'd given him the night before. "I don't mind."

She found her parking space, turned into it, and killed the engine. "After we get past this, I'm all yours," she told him.

God, he hoped so. He still had the information in his briefcase that he'd planned to give her last night at dinner. He still had the unpleasant task of telling her that the only hope for Harrison's financial future was to split his company into pieces and sell them to the highest bidder. He still had to let her know that he couldn't give her the miracle she'd requested. He remembered his conversation with Hansen Wells. And he still had to tell her that the man who'd tried to break into her house had felt the need to do it because Ethan had begun asking questions—and finding answers.

Unable to resist, he closed the small distance between them and kissed her deeply. The depth of her response gave him a glimmer of hope. "I'm counting on that," he murmured.

Abby led him through the routine security doors, up the elevator, and into her office. His continued silence worried her. Before they'd left her house, he'd made her promise that tonight she'd tell him what had driven her yesterday to the police station, then to the cemetery. There was no way, she knew, that he'd let her off the hook before she told him everything. The look in his eyes had registered more than a general concern—it held determination.

There was a sort of stoic quality about him, as if he dreaded whatever lay ahead but felt that the burden was his alone to bear. Abby had even sensed a certain edginess to his lovemaking that morning. Something told her that he was waging an internal battle, and that he'd already accepted defeat.

She tried to shake off the glum thought and unlocked the door to her office. "Here it is," she announced. "Home sweet home."

He glanced around with an approving eye. "It looks like you."

"Not nearly as big as yours," she said. "And the art on *my* walls is reproduction."

He had wandered across the room to her desk, where he was idly playing with her nameplate. "If you want the Rothko," he said absently, "you can have it."

That made her laugh. She walked up behind him and wrapped her arms around his waist. "It was just a joke, Ethan. You were supposed to laugh."

"Some people say I have no sense of humor."

Before she could respond to that, Deirdre arrived to break the intimate moment. "Well, I see you two are getting along nicely," she remarked from the doorway.

Abby stepped away from Ethan. "Hello, Deirdre. You're early." The older woman was dressed flamboyantly, as usual, in an orange silk pantsuit with hot-pink trim and the shoes and hat to match.

Deirdre laughed. "On time, you mean. I thought I'd surprise you." She glanced at her nephew. "Still in town, Ethan?"

"Back in town," he said, and set the nameplate on Abby's desk.

"I'd ask you if it was business or personal, but the answer seems obvious." Her comment might have sounded waspish if Deirdre hadn't had a slightly devilish twinkle in her eye. "Actually, I'm very glad you're here."

Ethan leaned against the edge of the desk, crossing his arms over his chest. "In the mood to flay someone alive today, Aunt Deirdre?"

She laughed. "No, nothing like that. I was thinking—"

"Deirdre, where did you say—" Harrison came to an abrupt halt in the doorway of Abby's office. The car keys in his left hand rattled to a stop against his thigh.

Abby let out a low whistle. "I see," she said to Deirdre.

"Don't you just?" Deirdre entered the office and sat on the tweed sofa.

Harrison and Ethan continued to watch each other warily—like beasts of prey squaring off over territory, Abby thought irritably. She wouldn't be surprised if they started sniffing each other. She took a step closer to Ethan. "Hello, Harrison."

"Abby." He gave his sister a hurt look. "Did you know about this?"

"No, I didn't." Deirdre crossed her long legs and settled herself more comfortably on the couch. "I really did think we were going to discuss the plans for the fund-raiser today."

"That was my plan," Abby told her. "You were supposed to be bringing your volunteer committee."

"And I brought Harrison instead." Deirdre folded her hands in her lap. "How fortuitous."

Harrison's expression was pinched. "I suppose," he said to Ethan, "that you're here because you've decided to get involved in my financial affairs."

"No," Ethan replied. Abby stole a quick glance at his profile. The implacable façade was firmly back in place. "I'm here to see Abby."

Deirdre chuckled. "This is almost better than Shakespeare."

Abby shot her a warning glance.

The older woman patted the cushion next to her. "I'm sorry, dear," she said. "I'm not trying to be insensitive. Come here and let's talk business. The two of them have been handling their own feud for years."

Harrison ignored her. "Damn it, Ethan, I warned you—"

"Which never got you very far, did it?"

Abby squelched the urge to bring her heel down on the arch of Ethan's foot. He wasn't going to budge an inch, even if it made Harrison crawl. "It's not what you think," she started to tell Harrison.

Ethan turned his head to capture her gaze. "Yes, it is."

She frowned at him. "Will you stop?" She looked at Harrison again. He seemed to have aged ten years in the past few weeks. "Can we please just sit down and discuss this?"

"There's nothing to discuss," Harrison told her. "I've already decided to sell off the divisions of MDS."

"But—"

Harrison shook his head. "It's too late, Abby. I let the board know yesterday."

Ethan's nod was short. "It's true. The market will open to the news on Monday morning."

Harrison jammed his hands into the pockets of his navy trousers. "I would have told you, but Marcie said you'd left the office early."

Abby nodded, stunned. Harrison continued. "It probably won't affect things for quite a while. It'll take some time to organize the breakup, and more time to negotiate the sale. As far as the foundation is concerned, I'm not sure yet where we're going with that."

"The foundation is self-sufficient," Deirdre pointed out.

Abby stared at Harrison. "You're selling?"

"Yes."

"Everything?"

Ethan placed his hand at the small of her back. "It's the only way, Abby. I was going to tell you last night, but I wanted to do it in person."

She felt a little dizzy, so she walked across the room and sat in the overstuffed chair across from Deirdre. "But I thought—"

Harrison interrupted her. "I didn't want to do it, Abby. If there'd been a way out, I'd have taken it."

Ethan, she noted, was watching him closely. "The assets were too low."

The two exchanged looks rife with meaning. Harrison finally glanced away. He sat down next to Deirdre on the sofa. "Abby, I know you had the best of intentions—"

She shook her head. "I just wanted to help you. The same way you once helped me."

His expression became unspeakably sad. "Ethan will be happy to tell you that you've always had an unreasonably high opinion of me."

Deirdre gave her brother a benevolent look. "It's not nearly as high as your opinion of yourself, Harrison, darling."

He smiled slightly but continued to study Abby. "So there's no need to worry about any of this anymore. It's settled now."

"I still have some questions," Ethan said. He crossed the room to stand behind Abby's chair. "And I'd still like some answers."

Harrison frowned at him. "I can discuss all that with you in private, Ethan."

"I think Abby would like some answers too." He put his hands on her shoulders.

Harrison looked distinctly uncomfortable. "This isn't the time or the place for that."

Ethan rounded her chair to sit on the arm, and draped his arm across the back. "Actually, I think this is an excellent time—especially since Abby would like to know why someone tried to break into her house late Tuesday night."

Visibly startled, Harrison flinched. "What?"

Abby nodded. "It's true. Someone tried to come in through the window. He didn't get in, though." Harrison, she saw, was beginning to look a little pale. Deirdre was watching him through narrowed eyes.

Ethan alone seemed undaunted by the conversation. "You wouldn't happen to know anything about that, would you?" he asked Harrison.

Rage registered on Harrison's face. "No, damn you."

"Ethan." Abby put a hand on his knee.

He covered it with a bruising grip. "The perpetrator left something at the scene," he said with icy calm. "A jack-of-spades playing card in an envelope."

Harrison swore sharply. "The bastard."

Ethan continued. "Is there anything you'd like to add now?"

Harrison lowered his head into his hands. "Oh, God. I never meant—it wasn't supposed to come to this."

"What's going on?" Abby asked. She looked at Ethan. His gaze remained steadily on his father.

Deidre held out a hand to her. "Abby, dear—"

"No," Harrison said, and lifted his head. "I'll tell her." He looked shaken. Abby had never seen him when he didn't look perfectly polished and poised, but the man who faced her now looked like a shell. "Abigail, whatever you believe, you have to know I would never have done anything to hurt you."

Abby frowned. "Of course I know that."

He nodded. "Ethan is right about a number of things. I'm sure you know by now that MDS got into this mess because I was being blackmailed."

That drew a startled gasp from Deirdre. "Harrison!"

He covered her hand with his. "It's all right, Deirdre. It's not as dire as you think."

"My God," she said. "Blackmail. Did you call the police?"

"No." He exhaled a long sigh. "At first I thought I could make it go away—just like before."

"Before?" she asked.

Abby felt Ethan's fingers tighten on hers. She stole a glance at him. Though his features were composed in an expressionless mask, his jaw was set in a hard line that betrayed an inner tension.

Harrison continued. "I've made some pretty horrific mistakes in my life, and until now, maybe I was too much of a coward to face them." He sounded beaten.

Abby felt the pain in his words. She could see what the confession was costing him, and had she not had an incontrovertible conviction that they'd reached the point of no return, she would have stopped him.

He wiped a hand over his face. "But I'd lived with that long enough," he added.

When he looked at Abby again, his eyes were clear. She'd never noticed how much they resembled Ethan's. "Abby," he said, "you'll never know how much I regret that you got dragged into this. If I could have changed—" He shook his head. "I had no idea this was going to happen."

Deirdre turned toward him. "For God's sake, Harrison, what *are* you talking about?"

"When I was a young man"—his voice had a hollow tone—"I met a woman I fell in love with." He glanced at Ethan. "For all my faults, Ethan, I did love your mother." Clouds gathered in his expression. "Lina was the most alive and fascinating person I'd ever know."

Beside her, Abby felt Ethan tense. She shifted her hand in his to twine their fingers together. He gave no other sign of his reaction to the story. "You couldn't marry her," Abby said to Harrison.

His gaze became teary. "I could have. If I'd had the courage to stand up to Father, I could have."

Deirdre shook her head. "Harrison, you know what would have happened."

"He would have cut me off," Harrison aknowledged, and glanced at his sister. "But I never told you that he threatened to cut the rest of you off as well. He knew I didn't care. I was young and reckless, and I didn't think it would matter if I couldn't have his money. So he told me it was time I learned what it meant to have responsibility for a family like ours. If I wanted to support Lina on my own, then I could also support the rest of you."

Deirdre gasped and raised a hand to her throat. "My God! You never told us that!"

Harrison nodded. "I couldn't. I was afraid you'd all think I was a spineless coward for not throwing it back in his face." He looked at Ethan again. "Then your mother got pregnant. And when she told me we were going to have you, that was probably the single happiest day of my life. I felt certain Father would succumb when he realized we were talking about his grandchild."

"But he didn't." Ethan's voice was hard and immobile.

"He was furious," Harrison said. "He threatened your mother into getting an abortion, and she told him to go to hell." A little half smile tugged at his lips. "I wish you had known her longer. She was pure fire, that woman."

"So instead of marrying her anyway," Ethan said, "you let your father send her away."

"No." Harrison shook his head. "God, no. Lina left. I couldn't find her anywhere. I hired investigators to track her down, but nothing turned up. I had no idea what had happened to either of you for six years."

Deirdre nodded emphatically. "It's true, Ethan. Harrison and I talked about it frequently. He had—what was it?" She looked at her brother. "Six different investigators trying to find her."

"Eight," Harrison replied. "Lina disappeared. I always worried about what Father might have threatened her with. Connie assured me she'd taken care of Lina."

"Connie?" Deirdre said with a frown. "She's involved in this?"

Harrison nodded. "Connie was still married to Father during the worst of this. She intervened on Lina's behalf, but she'd never reveal where you went, Ethan."

"Oklahoma," Ethan said. "I never knew how we got there, but we ended up in Oklahoma."

"Connie gave Lina money to help her get out of Chicago, and advised her to start over. She told her to stay as invisible as possible."

"My mother would never use credit. She worked cash jobs only. She didn't want to be found."

Harrison agreed. "I think Father threatened to take you away from her." He gave Ethan a look that was nothing short of pleading. "I didn't know, Ethan. I swear I didn't know."

"My mother got ill," Ethan said to no one in particular. "She didn't know what to do. She couldn't reach Connie."

"She was in Florida by then," Harrison explained. "No one had heard from Lina since she left, and Connie had lost touch with her." Harrison squared his shoulders. "Then Lina brought you back. She was so ill by then."

Deirdre concurred. "She looked awful."

Harrison went on. "I felt like I had finally been given a second chance to make things right. I told Father I was going to marry her."

"But you didn't," Abby said.

"Lina wouldn't," Harrison insisted. He nodded at Ethan's raised eyebrow. "I begged her. I swear I did."

"It's true," Deirdre told her nephew. "I was there for several of the conversations they had. Your mother didn't want you to become a Montgomery."

"Can you blame her?" Ethan's voice was so flat and emotionless, Abby felt like weeping. When she thought of the strife of his childhood, she realized how much richer her own had been.

"Not really," Harrison answered. "But I was concerned about my ability to protect you when she died."

"Your father didn't throw me out," Ethan pointed out.

"Connie wouldn't let him. And neither would I. I agreed not to formally adopt you if he'd let me make sure you were financially secure." Harrison's face registered his pain at the memory. "I will never forgive myself for how much I hurt you."

Abby studied him for a moment. "What about after?" she prompted.

"After?" Harrison looked at her.

"After your father died. What happened then?"

"Ethan, you were nine years old by then. And you already resented the hell out of me." Ethan didn't respond, so Harrison continued. "I didn't see any reason to make the matter worse than it already was. I—I didn't do all I could have. Maybe I was weak, or immature in a way—I don't know. I had no idea how to reach you. You were sullen and withdrawn."

"So you turned me over to Letty?" Ethan asked, his tone dry.

"It wasn't like that," Harrison protested. "I'm sure you don't remember, but I tried. I did everything I knew how to do, and you wouldn't respond to me. I'd never been a father before. Hell, I'd never had a father to speak of. I'd had a despot."

Ethan surged up from the arm of Abby's chair and crossed the office to stare out the window, as if he could no longer bear to watch as the story unfolded.

Harrison looked at Abby. "You already know the rest. Things went from bad to worse, and Ethan left home at eighteen."

"Tell Abby," Ethan said from the window, "where she fits into this."

Harrison dropped his head back against the sofa with a low groan. "The year after Lina left Chicago, I enlisted in the army."

"Harrison!" Deirdre stared at him. "Are you serious?"

"Yes." He nodded. "I was supposed to go to Vietnam. Father was furious."

"You were in college," Deirdre pointed out. "You could have been deferred."

"I didn't want that. I couldn't find Lina, and I hated Father for what he'd done to us. I wanted to go. I think," he confessed, "I wanted to die."

Abby's stomach had started to twist into knots. "You knew my father," she said. "Didn't you?"

Harrison shook his head. "Not then. Later."

Deirdre was confused. "But how—"

Harrison interrupted her. "Father was livid when he found out. He wasn't about to let me get myself killed. There had to be a Montgomery to run his empire." Harrison's laugh was humorless. "I think he secretly hoped it wouldn't be me—that maybe Connie could produce a second heir for him. But when she couldn't stand living with him anymore, he had to accept that I was his last hope. That's probably what killed him."

"But my father—" Abby insisted.

Harrison flashed her a faint smile. "Sorry, darling. I'm getting there. I enlisted, and Father was going to kill me before he let me leave. So he pulled some strings at the Pentagon. MDS was heavily into defense contracts at the time. Still, I never knew how he did it."

"Colonel Don Fisk," Ethan said from his position by the window.

Harrison turned to him in surprise. "What?"

Ethan faced them again. He leaned back against the window with his arms folded over his chest. Abby searched his face for something that might tell her what he was thinking.

"Don Fisk," he repeated. "He was a low-level Pentagon official with ties to the Chicago recruiting office." He looked at Abby, his gaze intent. "He knew Montgomery because of a few shady deals with defense suppliers."

Deirdre muttered a disgusted curse. "That doesn't surprise me. Father liked to make money—and he had no qualms about how he did it."

"We had several bids," Harrison added, "that

Fisk had fixed to ensure we came in low. Father gave him a kickback on every contract the Pentagon awarded us."

"So when the old man needed help to bail out his son"—Ethan waved his hand in Harrison's direction—"he called on Fisk."

Harrison nodded in agreement. Ethan continued. "At the time, Abby, your father was working in the recruiting office here in Chicago. Fisk pressured him to rate Harrison ineligible. I'm sure he was threatened."

"They turned me down," Harrison told Abby. "I never knew why."

"Did my father know why Fisk was involved?" Abby asked Ethan.

"Not at first," Ethan said. "But Don Fisk got greedy. He realized that Harrison's father was in a position to ease his transition into retirement."

"He called my father," Harrison said, "and told him that if he didn't arrange for his early retirement and a high-paying job with a defense contractor, he'd reveal what he'd done on my behalf."

Deirdre's laugh was derisive. "I can imagine how well Father responded to that."

"He didn't take threats well," Harrison agreed. "He decided the only thing to do was to get rid of whatever evidence Fisk had. So he had your father put on an active-duty roster and sent to Vietnam."

"Three years after I was born," Abby recalled. "My mother told me."

Harrison leaned forward on the sofa to bury his face in his hands. "It all went away for a while. While your father was gone, Fisk had no recourse but to keep quiet." His face had paled. "I think Father hoped your dad wouldn't return."

"But he did," Abby said.

"Yes," Harrison answered, "but by then Fisk had already left the Pentagon for his own tour in Vietnam. I'm certain Father pulled strings to arrange that."

"What happened when Dad returned?" Abby asked.

"Montgomery was still nervous," Ethan explained. "MDS was heavily invested in the defense industry, and with the antiwar movement growing, he didn't want to draw any negative attention. As insurance, he offered to pay your father ten thousand dollars a year to keep the issue quiet."

Abby's eyes widened. "My father took money?" She looked at Harrison. "Did you know this?"

"Yes," he confessed, and shot Ethan an angry glance. "I didn't think you needed to know that."

"She has a right," Ethan said, his tone utterly devoid of feeling. "Finish the story."

Harrison's sigh was harsh. "He took money, Abby. And stock tips. Father made sure he could invest the funds and turn it into a neat little fortune. That's how he purchased the restaurant—

and the house. His retirement pay never would have allowed him to do that."

Abby felt shaken. She rubbed her eyes with her thumb and forefinger. "All this time," she said to Harrison. "You've always known this."

"Yes," he said.

"And when he was killed? Did you know why?"

Harrison shook his head. "No, I didn't."

"There was a lot of money involved," Ethan said.

"Yes." Harrison rubbed his hands on his trouser legs. "Jack Lee had begun passing stock tips to his war buddies. Those poker games in the back room of the restaurant—" He shook his head. "They didn't play poker, Abby."

"Illegal trading?"

"Yes."

"I see." Her blood had started to run cold. "The jack of spades," she said softly.

Harrison gave her a sad look. "Do you know what that means?"

"No. Dad said he'd picked up the nickname in Vietnam."

"Not exactly. My father was part of a group of men who'd made their fortune off the military-industrial complex. For reasons I never fully understood—maybe they thought of themselves as high-stakes gamblers—they used playing cards to distinguish themselves in correspondence. Father was always referred to as the king of spades."

"And my father," Abby said, "was the jack?"

"Something like that. Jack Lee used the jack of spades as his calling card. Everyone in his inner circle knew what it meant. After my father died, Jack developed enough contacts to keep his investments going, but pressure was starting to mount."

"The Feds got suspicious," Ethan said.

"The investigation—" Deirdre glanced at Harrison. "That wasn't an IRS audit, was it?"

"No," he concurred. "The year before your father's murder," he told Abby, "federal investigators came to see me about alleged insider trading and the possible involvement of some of our top executives. The Justice Department had initiated a crackdown on all white-collar crime. Every successful company in the country—and especially those with ties to the defense industry—was suspect."

"Dad was implicated?" Abby asked.

"His name came up. The investigators felt sure they could get him to wear a wire, use him as an informant."

"Oh, my God." She shivered. "He agreed, didn't he?"

"Yes. But something went wrong. The night of the murder, the entire case was coming to fruition.

I think they were expecting to blow things open. Your father and his friends met in the back room like always."

"They let him get killed." Abby's heart was pounding so hard, she could hear the blood pumping in her veins. "No one protected him."

Harrison's face showed his anguish. "I never could find out exactly what happened. By the time I heard about it, the facts were buried somewhere in the federal case files." He held out his hands in a helpless gesture. "I knew that my father—and I, to some extent—was at least partially to blame. The only thing I could do was to give you a job and try my best to protect you."

Abby sank back against her chair in disbelief as a string of random memories assailed her. So many things made sense now. The endless red tape she'd encountered during the investigation. The way important evidence had apparently been overlooked. The confusing circumstances surrounding the murder and the apparent ambivalence of the Chicago police. She struggled to assimilate everything Harrison had told her.

"There's something I don't understand," Deirdre interjected. "You said earlier that someone was blackmailing you, Harrison. What is that about?"

He looked absolutely defeated. "A few months ago, I got a letter threatening to expose all of this. The person was going to tell you," he said to

Abby, "about your father's involvement. I didn't want you to find out like that. I thought a one-time payment would take care of it."

"The blackmailer got greedy," Ethan said.

Harrison nodded. "He wanted more. And soon I saw that there was only one honorable way out." His gaze turned pleading as he regarded Abby. "I've made a lot of mistakes in my life. I've done some terrible things." He glanced at Ethan. "You may never forgive me for some of them, and I suppose you've got a right to that. But for the first time in thirty years, I felt like I had the chance to redeem myself. I kept thinking about Lina telling my father to go to hell and take his money with him. She wouldn't have let some bastard blackmail her."

He sighed. "I knew the only way out of this situation without hurting either one of you"—he glanced apologetically at Deirdre—"or without exposing the entire nasty mess to the family, was to liquidate the company. If I'd sold it then, there would still be enough capital left to make me vulnerable to the blackmailer. But if news of the devastation of the Montgomery fortune got out, I'd be free of it."

"You were willing to lose everything?" Deirdre said.

"I knew you'd all be protected. I've spent years ensuring that everyone would have sufficient assets to live in comfort. There might have been some trimming, but no Montgomery would have suffered."

"So you were deliberately sabotaging your accounts?" Abby asked.

"Yes," he replied. "And well enough so that no one noticed." He looked at Ethan. "Until you."

Abby thought that over. Had she not brought Ethan into the picture and subjected Harrison's business ventures to such close scrutiny, he probably could have gotten away with it. The stock would have dropped far enough to warrant an unfavorable sale, and though he would have lost most of his stake in the company, he wouldn't have been destitute.

Suddenly she realized there was still one question as yet unanswered. "Then who left the jack of spades at my house, Harrison, and why did it turn up now?"

Fourteen

Rachel brushed one hand over the tablecloth in an absent rhythm. "Ethan?"

"Hmm?" It was Sunday night, and in the wake of Harrison's confession, his relationship with Abby had settled into an uneasy calm.

Abby had been understandably overwhelmed by yesterday's events. Ethan had never intended for her to learn the truth from anyone but him, but in the end, it seemed best that Harrison himself had delivered the blow. Ethan had come to Chicago ready to show Abby the evidence he'd accumulated. He'd already known the majority of Harrison's story, having pieced together the missing information about Jordan Fisk from his conversation with Hansen Wells, and the truth about her father's hand in Harrison's deferment from

Carter Jameson. His plan had been to lay it out for her, piece by excruciating piece, taking care to paint a picture she could live with.

He had not been prepared to open the wounds of his own past, especially not when Abby already had him reeling. Harrison's story had hit him with the force of a five-star hurricane. Fresh on the heels of the way Abby had forced herself through his defenses and stormed the door of his emotional restraint, he'd been unable to defend himself from the memories Harrison had evoked.

The tone in Harrison's voice when he spoke of Lina had left Ethan feeling starkly alone. He'd finally had to put physical distance between himself and Abby by moving to stand at the window, abandoning her to face Harrison's truth on her own. Ethan had spent the time shoring up what was left of his defenses so he could face the desolation he'd experience when she realized he'd been investigating her—and had known details he hadn't revealed. He'd been prepared for her rage.

Instead, she'd retreated into a contemplative shell that both alarmed and disconcerted him. He didn't know how to interpret the shifting emotions he saw in her gaze, nor the turmoil that seemed to shimmer just beneath the surface. She was hurting, but he was unable to offer her solace. If he pushed her too hard, she might demand answers from him that he could not yet give her. He

was no more ready to talk about Harrison's reve-
lations than she, and so he let the subject drop,
though it hung over their heads like the sword of
Damocles.

He was more determined than ever to answer
the question she herself had asked: why had this
come up now? Abby had seemed to take it for
granted that he would share her bed, but she'd
been distracted and edgy. He hadn't made love to
her. And she'd withdrawn even further today. By
the time Rachel returned from her weekend away,
things had grown unusually tense.

"Did you want something?" he asked.

Rachel was sitting at the table, watching him
through narrowed eyes. "Are you and Abby, you
know, doing it?"

He raised one eyebrow. He should have been
prepared for this, he thought in retrospect. "That's
a very personal question."

She didn't blink. "Are you?"

"I'm not sure I'm going to answer that."

He saw a flash of irritation in her expressive
eyes. "I'm not a little kid—you know? I know how
things work."

"I guess you probably do."

"But you aren't going to tell me."

"I'm not telling you because it's none of your
business—not because you aren't old enough to
understand."

Rachel's gaze turned shrewd. "You *are* doing

it!" she exclaimed. "I thought so." Ethan didn't respond. She continued. "I was kind of sure after the Memorial Day thing, but when I got home tonight, it was really obvious. She was just acting weird."

"Weird?"

"You know—like she's in outer space or something."

Ethan decided not to ask how that had contributed to Rachel's conclusion. Rachel shrugged. "Abby hasn't really been with a lot of guys before. She doesn't go out much."

"I know that."

"It's sort of my fault. I mean, after our parents died, Abby had to take care of me and everything." She lowered her gaze to the table, whose grain pattern she rubbed with her thumb. "There aren't a whole lot of guys willing to put up with something like that."

"I don't think your sister regrets any of it," he said carefully. "Except that you didn't have a chance to know your parents."

Rachel didn't respond for a long time. When she looked at him again, he noticed the sadness in her hazel eyes. For the first time, he clearly saw her resemblance to Abby. He'd been looking at that same sad expression for the past twenty-four hours. "She was a freshman in college when it happened," Rachel told him. "She was going to be a lawyer."

He hadn't known that. He added it to his growing list of Abby's secrets. "She would have been a good one," he said with a slight smile. "She argues well."

A small laugh escaped Rachel. "God, you can say that again."

"She quit college after the murder," he said. It wasn't a question.

"She had to go to work. If she hadn't—" Rachel shook her head. "Things would have been different."

"Do you know how much your sister loves you?" he asked.

"Yeah, I know. It still makes me feel bad sometimes."

"It shouldn't. She doesn't regret any of it."

Rachel frowned. "It just doesn't seem fair, is all. I mean, Abby's never had time for guys and stuff. Except for LuAnne, she doesn't even have a lot of friends. She had to leave work and, like, pick me up at day care or take me to the doctor or something. And she doesn't date—like hardly ever. I mean, there's that one guy from the company, David Wilcox, but that's not like a *date* date."

Ethan was beginning to be awfully glad he was having this conversation. "No?"

"Uh-uh. There just, like, friends, you know? I mean, if Abby needs a guy to go with her to some foundation function or something, she calls David."

"Have you met David?" he asked.

"Sure. He's a loser. He's got beady eyes, and his clothes are, like, sick—you know?"

Ethan decided he didn't need interpretation for the teen slang. It stood nicely on its own. "So you don't think Abby was serious about him?"

Rachel snorted. "Are you kidding? Abby would never go for a guy like that." She shook her head. "But it's different with you. She likes you." Rachel gave him an affirming nod.

"I like her too."

"She gets all, like, hairy when you're around."

"Hairy?"

"You know. Like at Carlton's party. She, like, *swooped* on Harrison the minute he got cranky. The last time I saw Abby do that was when one of my teachers told her I needed therapy. She gets all crazy and defensive—like she wants to deck somebody."

"Ever seen her do it?"

"Slug someone? No. But I've seen her come close a couple of times."

"Your sister is pretty fierce about the people she cares for."

"And you," Rachel said. "She's fierce about you."

Ethan nodded. "I've noticed."

"So I was just wondering . . . I mean, if you guys aren't doing it, then what *are* you doing?"

"There's more to a relationship than sex," he said bluntly.

"I know."

"Glad to hear it."

She drummed her fingertips on the table. "I wasn't talking about that. I just want to know what you think is going to happen with you and Abby."

The look of determination in her eyes finally made him realize what Rachel was after. She was asking what his intentions were toward her sister. Ethan thought it over, then sat up straight in his chair. "I'm deeply involved with your sister," he told her.

"How deeply?"

"Long-term deeply."

Rachel contemplated his answer. "What are you going do about it?"

"We haven't decided yet. We're working that out."

"You live in California," Rachel pointed out.

"At the moment."

Her eyes widened. "Would you move here?"

"I don't know. How would you feel if I did?"

"It could be okay. Kind of weird, maybe. It's always been me and Abby."

Not a ringing endorsement. "Do you remember anything about your parents, Rachel?"

"Not really. It's always been harder for Abby."

"Do you remember anything about the night they were killed?" he asked carefully.

She shook her head. "Sometimes I think I should. Everybody said I was supposed to be really freaked or something. That whole closet thing—" She waved a hand. "I don't know. It's like it never really happened to me."

"No bad dreams?"

"No. I'm not even afraid of the dark."

"It's okay, you know—not remembering," he said gently.

She looked away. "It might have helped them catch the guy if I could have told them something."

"They put a lot of pressure on you, didn't they?"

"I guess. I do remember that we went to the police station a lot. I didn't like it there."

He could well understand that. "People would ask you a lot of questions."

"Yes. And they usually wouldn't let Abby stay with me."

Ethan could only imagine the terror that a three-year-old child must have felt. "When did it stop?"

"Abby made them. She had this huge argument with this one guy who was around all the time. She told him he couldn't talk to me anymore."

"And things got better."

"Yeah. Abby went to work a little after that. I was in day care a lot. She made me see a shrink for a while, just to make sure I wasn't, like, totally freaked."

Ethan nodded, thoughtful. "Do you ever talk about this with your friends, Rachel?"

"It comes up sometimes. I mean, nobody else ever had anything like this happen. They start asking a lot of questions when they realize I don't have parents—just Abby."

Just Abby, he thought. The center of her universe. No wonder his relationship with her sister made Rachel nervous. "You're always going to have Abby, you know," he told her.

"Sure. I know." She didn't sound convinced.

"Even if you get stuck with me in the bargain, it doesn't mean you won't have Abby."

She scrunched up her face. "I understand. It's just that . . . I don't really know what to do. I mean, Abby's never had a boyfriend before. Not like a real one. So it's kind of different."

Ethan heard the slightly wistful note in her voice and recognized it immediately. Loneliness. How well he knew the feeling. Rachel had had Abby to herself for a very long time, and the thought of sharing Abby was making her understandably anxious. "I can understand that."

"You're okay, though. It's not like you're a creep or anything."

He bit back a smile. "Thanks."

Rachel shook her head. "I didn't mean it like that."

"I know."

"My friend Barb, her mother is divorced. And Barb says that when her mother started seeing her stepfather, they kind of expected her to stay out of the way a lot." She pinned Ethan with a look too shrewd for her thirteen years. "Barb was always making plans to come over to our house and stuff—like she didn't want to be home on weekends."

"Must have been a pain for Barb."

"Yeah. I wouldn't like that," she told him.

"Then don't do it." He held her gaze. "No one wants you to."

She seemed to process what he'd said. "But, um, don't you guys want to, you know—"

"Sometimes," he admitted. "But I'm not going to kick you out of the house because of it."

"Oh."

A fragile bridge of trust seemed to have spanned the gulf between them. "However," he added, sensing that Rachel had exhausted the line of questioning, "there are a couple of rules."

Her expression turned wary. "What kind of rules?"

With a slight smile and a bit of surprise at his insight, he placed both of his palms on the table. "For starters," he said, "boyfriends have to be fed."

Rachel looked momentarily confused; then he saw her lips begin to twitch. "Fed?"

"Yes. That's a secret about men, Rach—you might as well learn it now. We're always less cranky when you feed us."

"Are you telling me that you're dating Abby so I'll cook for you?"

"No, but it's a definite plus." He tilted his head to one side. "I mean, think of the money I save not having to take her out all the time."

Rachel giggled. "Yeah, but you have to fly in from California."

He shrugged. "A small price to pay for your cooking."

"Wait until Abby sticks you with the grocery bill."

That made him laugh. "Expensive?"

"Huge," Rachel told him. "Monsieur Billaud only knows recipes with gourmet ingredients. I'm glad he pays me for working in the restaurant, 'cause otherwise there's no way we could afford the food." She gave Ethan a conspiratorial look. "Did you know that you can spend eighteen dollars a pound for certain kinds of steak?" She sounded horrified.

"I've heard."

Rachel shook her head. "I mean, Monsieur Billaud is really cool, mostly, but he's kind of freakazoid about stuff like that. I kind of have to seriously doubt that a T-bone from some butcher named Gastôn is really all that different than a T-bone from Sam's Chop Shop."

"It's probably not. You're paying for the fact that he has a French name."

"Whatever. That's just bogus."

Ethan laughed. "Rachel, you're going to make some guy a great wife someday."

She shook her head. "I substituted cheaper pork loin once, and Monsieur never even knew the difference."

"No kidding?"

Her expression was sheepish. "No. There was this pair of shoes I wanted—Abby told me I had to pay for them myself."

"So you used the pork money?"

"Yeah. I figured I could always just pretend like I screwed up the recipe."

"But you got away with it."

"I did, but I was way too nervous to ever try it again. Harrison had to go to a lot of trouble to get me these lessons. Monsieur didn't want to do it."

Ethan could well imagine. "And Baldovino wants to do it even less?" he asked, recalling the upcoming cooking competition.

"Baldovino likes older students. He probably won't take me," Rachel said pragmatically. "I mean, I can't study with him full-time because I have school, so he'd have to make special arrangements for me. It's a pain."

"But Billaud made it work."

"He did—and if the competition goes well, we'll see. I'm kind of nervous about it."

"When is it?"

"Next week. I should hear this week if they're even going to let me enter. Monsieur Billaud says there's a chance they won't, but the rules don't say you have to be eighteen or something, so it's kind of a technicality."

"Hi, Rach." Abby breezed into the kitchen from the living room. "Sorry, I was on the phone."

Rachel held Ethan's gaze for a second longer. The new camaraderie they'd established remained fast. She glanced at Abby. "That's okay."

Abby crossed to the sink to dump the contents of her glass. "Did you have fun with Kelly?"

"Yeah. Her parents are cool."

"Sorry it rained all weekend," Abby told her. "I guess you didn't get to go out on the lake."

"I didn't mind. They have this killer kitchen. Their refrigerator is the size of my closet."

Abby laughed. "I'm sure they ate well, at least."

"They can't wait to have me back."

"I'll bet."

Abby still hadn't looked at him, Ethan noted. She put the glass in the dishwasher, then glanced at her sister over her shoulder. "It's probably time we thought about dinner. Do you want to eat here or out?"

Rachel grinned at Ethan. "Out," she said. "Definitely out."

* * *

By the time Rachel was in bed that night, Abby knew she could no longer put off the inevitable conversation with Ethan. She hadn't been the only one, she'd realized, left reeling from the confrontation with Harrison on Saturday. Ethan had to be struggling with demons of his own.

"I think you have to talk to the police," Ethan told her as he stared moodily at the fire. Friday's thunderstorm had chased in a cold front, and though the rain had cleared today, there was an unseasonable chill in the air. Ethan had started a fire in her living room.

Abby tucked her feet beneath her on the sofa. "And tell them what?"

He sat on the opposite end of the sofa with his feet resting on the coffee table. His expression was brooding and fierce when he looked at her. "That whoever tried to break in here knows something about your father's murder."

She nodded. "And they'll try to pull the case files, then they'll discover the same thing I did ten years ago: nobody wants the truth to get out."

"How can you live with that?"

"How can I fight it?" she countered.

"We're going to get answers."

"Maybe." She glanced at the fire. "Maybe they'll be answers I don't want."

"I'm sorry you had to find out like this."

"How long have you known?" She couldn't quite keep the condemnation from her tone.

While Harrison's duplicity had stung, she'd understood his motives. With Ethan, the picture was less clear.

He sighed. "I suspected, but I wasn't able to fit all the pieces together until this week."

"That's what you were going to tell me at dinner Friday night, wasn't it?"

"Yes."

"It wasn't a complete surprise, you know—at least not the part about the money."

"I didn't think it would be."

"After my parents died, it took a really long time for the insurance issues to get straightened out. At the time, I didn't think about where all that money came from. I mean, they weren't wealthy, but the insurance money, and the sale of the house and the restaurant, left me and Rachel very secure."

"When did it sink in?"

"When I bought this house." She glanced at him. "I paid cash for it. Harrison found it for us, and helped with all the negotiations and the legal end of things. Eyebrows were raised when I turned up with that much cash."

"How old were you?"

"Twenty-five."

He nodded. "People started asking questions."

"A lot of them. I had to take a good look at my financial status for the first time, and things started to seem odd to me. I talked to Harrison about it. He assured me nothing was out of the ordinary."

"But you didn't believe him?"

She still remembered the conversation she'd had with Harrison that day. There had been something about his tone of voice that hadn't quite rung true. Abby hadn't pressed him, but the seeds of doubt had been firmly planted. "Not entirely," she admitted. "But I was no expert, and I wasn't sure I even wanted to know what it all meant. I did try several times to get to the bottom of it, but I never succeeded."

"Harrison should have told you the truth."

"Probably. But maybe I wasn't ready to hear it then."

"Were you ready now?"

"It doesn't matter," she said softly. "Does it?"

They lapsed into an uneasy silence. Abby gathered her courage and continued. "I guess that's why I don't see the point in talking to the police. What are they going to do?"

"Someone tried to break into your house, Abby. You can't ignore that."

"I'm not ignoring it, but I don't think I need to freak out about it either. I'm sure it was a warning and not a threat."

"Abby—"

"I mean, *really*, Ethan. I scared the guy off with an umbrella. If someone were trying to hurt me, it would have taken more than a whack across the nose to send him fleeing."

"He still threatened you."

"I know, and I'm not taking it lightly, but I'm certainly not going to cower. I refuse to do that."

He looked irritated. "The police can protect you."

Her laugh was humorless. "Do you really think the police are going to find out anything if your investigator can't? How much are you paying that guy, anyway?"

The remark hit its target. She saw him flinch. "It's not what you think," he told her. "After you came to San Francisco, I did ask Charlie for some background information. It was what he *didn't* find that worried me."

"What are you talking about?"

"All the pieces fit together until he got to your parents' murder. That's when things started to fall apart." He drummed his fingers on the back of the sofa. "Did you know that some of the people the police interviewed in the investigation, the people who were supposed to be your parents' close friends, barely knew anything about you? And no one knew Rachel had been in the closet that night."

"The police wanted to keep that part of it quiet—to protect her and the case. They weren't sure the killer knew she'd been there, and either way, it seemed wise not to let it get out."

"You had no one, did you?"

The absolute desolation in his voice made her heart ache. She shook her head. "It wasn't like that. It's true that Dad's poker friends weren't around, but the veteran community took in Rachel and me. That's like having an instant extended family. They handled the funeral arrangements, everything. Dad was buried with military honors, and I have no idea who cut through all the red tape to make that happen so fast. I was so devastated, and so young. I wasn't paying much attention."

"And by the time you could, the case was cold," he guessed.

"It was like hitting a stone wall. The police made a couple of token attempts, but nothing went anywhere. Finally, they just stopped calling. Then they stopped returning my calls. I sent a few letters, but what else could I do?"

"I'm sorry."

She took a deep breath and forged ahead. "I had to let it go or it was going to consume me. I don't know why this business has come up now. My guess is that when you started asking questions, somebody got really nervous. If Harrison was trying to drain the company like he says—"

"He was," Ethan assured her. "I've had a group of people working on this, and there's no other explanation."

"Was he breaking the law?" she asked.

"No. He's too smart for that."

"But the stockholders—"

"The law doesn't require a company to turn a

profit. They could have gotten out whenever they wanted. Most of the money he lost was his own."

"Oh." She stared at the fire again. The flames danced in merry torment—contained, but slowly and irrevocably eating away at the logs. Just like the anger that consumed Ethan, she thought glumly. "So he just sells now, and nothing happens."

"It's not quite that simple, but yes, eventually that'll be the outcome."

"And then it will be over." She let the words sink in, for his benefit and for hers. She turned her gaze to him. "Knowing who's responsible for my parents' death isn't going to bring them back. It would just give me someone to hate."

"You have a right to closure," he insisted.

She managed a sad smile. "I hate to break this to you, but there's no such thing as closure, Ethan. I never stop missing them. I never stop wishing things were different. I never stop hating what happened, or grieving because I lost them. But I can't have them back. Being an orphan is no fun, no matter how old you become. I can let that destroy me, or I can let it make me stronger." She shook her head again. "I used to think that if I only knew who had killed them, I'd feel better. But would I?"

"You had a right—"

She interrupted him. "No, really. Would I? I mean, then I'd have to know why he did it, or who he did it with. Now I find out that he was probably doing it for someone else. Would I have to see that person's face too? Would it change anything if I did?"

"Abby—"

"The answer is no. I had to face that fact one day or I would've gone crazy."

"Someone knows the truth," he pointed out.

"Someone knows part of the truth," she amended. "I doubt anyone but my mother and father really has the entire story. And they'll never be able to tell me." She reached out and laid a hand on his sleeve. "I can't spend my life worrying about that."

He turned toward her and she felt the energy flowing through him. "Good God, Abby, how can you just let them get away with it?"

The anger, she realized, was coming from somewhere deep within him. Here was the nine-year-old boy who'd lost his mother and been left with a distant and unemotional father. For years he'd been struggling to conquer the rage, but it was beginning to get the better of him. She scooted closer to him so she could place her hands on his chest. His heart was pounding a mad rhythm. "I wasted too much time being angry and afraid," she said softly. "I thought revenge would make me happy, and then I realized that every day I spent waiting for it was another day I had thrown away. Dad wouldn't have wanted me to live like that."

"You had a right to know," he insisted.

"Maybe." He frowned, and Abby smoothed the creases from his forehead with her fingertip. "Being angry won't bring them back, Ethan." His eyes glittered at her. "She died," she said carefully, waiting for him to absorb her meaning. "Your mother died and left you alone. It wasn't fair."

His hands closed over hers in a bruising grip. "Abby—"

Abby held up a finger to his lips. "It's all right that it made you angry. You can still be angry." Tears stung her eyes when she thought of all he'd lost, how he'd never felt the freedom to shake his fist at God, how no one had embraced him and let him weep. "But you have to feel it," she said. "You have to be willing to feel it." Silence. She pressed on. "If you don't feel it, Ethan, you can never be alive again."

The firelight sharpened the lines of his face. His sterling silver gaze had turned almost black. Abby stroked his cheek with gentle fingers. "I'll go there with you," she promised him. "You can't scare me."

An inarticulate groan seemed to rip out of him as he pulled her to him in a fierce embrace. "God, Abby—"

"I'm so sorry," she whispered, stroking his hair.

Tears were streaming from her eyes now. "I'm so sorry."

His body shuddered against her. She laid her cheek on the top of his head and tried to absorb some of his pain. "Ethan, please," she whispered. "Please let me share this with you."

He turned his face into the curve of her neck. She sensed the struggle in him and dug her heels in for the onslaught. "Please don't shut me out," she told him. "Fight for it, and I'll help you get there."

"You don't know—" he began.

She cupped his face in her hands and forced him to look at her. The pain in his eyes was fathomless. "Yes, I do," she insisted. "Let me love you. Please, just let me love you."

He groaned and covered her mouth in a kiss that released a tempest. Abby clutched his shoulders and hung on as the storm set loose its fury.

Fifteen

Abby punched the button on her intercom the following afternoon. "Yes, Marcie?" She told her assistant.

"Detective Krestyanov is here to see you."

Abby darted a quick glance at the clock on her desk. She was expecting Ethan at any minute. "You can send him in," she told her assistant. "And if Ethan gets here, ask him to join us."

"Sure."

"Why didn't you tell me about this earlier?" the detective asked as he threw open the door to her office.

Abby rounded her desk and waved a hand in the direction of the stuffed chairs. "Hello. Would you like to sit down?"

He shook his head. "No time. I've got to meet

my partner downtown. I got your message about that playing card."

Abby had called him that morning and left a voice-mail message. "I take it the lab didn't turn anything up?"

"No." He scowled. "And it's the damnedest thing. I went to the evidence room to look at the card myself. They've sent it out of state to another lab."

She wasn't surprised. "Oh?"

"Until you called this morning, this was nothing more than a routine attempted break-in. Why the hell would they do that?"

"You couldn't access the case files on my parents' murder either, could you?"

"Sealed," he confirmed. He started to pace. "I'd like to know just what the hell I'm getting myself into, Ms. Lee. I haven't run into this much—"

"Am I interrupting?" Ethan stuck his head in the doorway.

Abby smiled at him. "No. I'm glad you're here."

The detective swung around. "Maddux. Do you have that file for me?"

Ethan nodded and handed him the large envelope in his hand. "This is everything I've turned up in the last few weeks, plus the information we got from Harrison."

Krestyanov stuck the envelope under his arm. "All right." He turned back to Abby. "I talked this over with Detective Garrison, and we're going to look into it. We won't be able to do much before we have to run it by the department."

"When you do," Ethan pointed out, "they'll tell you to drop it."

"I figure that too." The policeman ran a hand through his already rumpled dark hair. "I'll see what I can do, though, and I'll get back to you."

"I'd appreciate that," Abby told him.

"All right." He nodded to Ethan on his way out the door. "I'll be in touch."

The door swung shut, and Abby wasted no time. She wrapped her arms around Ethan's waist and hugged him hard. Late in the night, when they'd lain fully spent and exhausted, Ethan had gathered her to him so closely, she'd felt their heartbeats merge. The feeling had been so intimate; her heart had almost overflowed with love for him. Tears had followed. When first one, then another salty drop had plopped onto his skin, Ethan had eased her away and looked at her with concern. It had taken her several minutes to persuade him that she was crying for his loss and not her own. He'd offered to finally share all of it with her today.

"Thank you for coming," she said.

He crushed her to him. "You don't have to do this," he assured her.

"You do. And I want to." She stepped away from him and reached for her purse. When she took his hand, his fingers closed hard on hers.

As they moved through the outer office, Abby spoke to her assistant. "I'll be out for the rest of the day, Marcie. If anything urgent comes up, refer it to Deirdre."

Marcie's jaw nearly dropped. "Deirdre? Are you kidding?"

Abby shook her head. "No. It's time she started earning her way as event chair."

They made the cab ride in silence. Ethan fought a growing sense of alarm as they neared the gates of the public cemetery. He hadn't been here since the day Letty had brought him to his mother's funeral. At that time there had been Letty, a priest she had hired, and him. Today he had only Abby.

Something had broken loose inside him last night. There in Abby's living room, he'd finally lost the war. True to her word, she'd accepted all of it. He'd made love to her with a fierce intensity that had left him drained and breathless and unaccountably cleansed.

Abby had refused to let him retreat to safety.

Rather than passively riding out the storm inside him, she'd spurred it, urging him higher and faster. When he'd tried to slow the pace, she'd demanded more. She'd stripped him of every vestige of restraint and civility, forcing him to give full release to the turmoil he'd buried for so long. Once, she'd sunk her teeth into his shoulder, and the not-so-subtle nip had fought its way through another barrier. He'd lost count of the peaks and valleys she'd shown him. By the time he'd emptied himself for the last time, he'd lain in her arms feeling as weak as the day he was born.

Abby had stroked his shoulders and whispered her love in his ear. It had simultaneously shaken him and strengthened him. When she'd wept over his sorrow, he'd felt humbled by the sacrifice. She had renewed him, and with that realization had come an even more pressing one: he could never give Abby what she deserved until he was ready to lay the past to rest. He wasn't sure he had her courage.

She had kissed him and promised to give him some of hers.

His fingers tightened on hers briefly before he released her hand to reach for his wallet. He gave the cabdriver a fifty-dollar bill and asked him to wait. Except for a few lone visitors, the cemetery grounds were deserted. Abby paid a vendor at the entrance for a small bunch of flowers. Ethan put his arm around her shoulder and led her to the place he hadn't been to in nearly thirty years.

He found it odd that he'd never forgotten the way through the winding paths, as if every step had been permanently etched on his brain.

When they reached the tiny marker for Lina's grave, Abby handed him the flowers. He held them for a long time and simply stared at the piece of granite. He had always believed he would hate Harrison Montgomery at this moment—that everything the man had done and failed to do would well up inside him until he boiled with it. Instead, he pictured the haggard look on Harrison's face when he'd talked about Lina. Had she known, Ethan wondered, that Harrison had loved her?

Had she known that he'd never married because, Ethan now suspected, a part of his heart was buried in that grave?

"What do you remember?" Abby asked softly.

Ethan continued to look at the small stone. "She had red hair," he said. "Dark red. It was long, but she always wore it up. I never saw it down except at night." His chest had started to ache. "Sometimes she let me braid it."

Abby wrapped her arms around his waist. He absently stroked her back. "She laughed a lot. She had a great laugh."

"Like you."

"Mine is rusty," he confessed. "I don't use it as much as she'd want me to." He sifted through the memories again. "She liked butterflies. Once, she took me to a butterfly arboretum so we could see them. I wanted to catch one for her. That's when she taught me the lesson about letting wild things be free."

"Like her."

"Like her," he agreed. "She could have let Harrison's father destroy her."

"She had your strength."

"A lot more. She wouldn't have hidden from her feelings for this long."

Abby's arms tightened around him. "What would she tell you if she was here?"

He thought about it for a long time. "My mother was never afraid to feel things, even when it hurt. She loved Harrison." He'd never admitted that before. "Even though he disappointed her, she loved him. And me. I always knew that she loved me."

He closed his eyes for a moment. A soft breeze ruffled his hair and rustled the leaves of a nearby shade tree. He heard the sound of a bird whistling from the branches, as if it sensed that the stormy weather of the past few days had finally passed, and it felt free to sing again.

In so many ways, he thought. He could visualize the clearest picture of Lina's face that he'd had in years. "Love her," she seemed to be telling him. "For God's sake, Ethan, have the courage to love her."

"I will," he whispered to the wind.

Abby slipped out of his embrace and faced him with tears in her eyes. She took the flowers from him and stooped to put them on Lina's grave. Gently, she cleared away the leaves and twigs that had gathered around the stone. She pulled each flower from the bunch and placed it with excruciating care. When she was done, she stood beside him again and linked her fingers with his.

"Someone will come by here now," she told him, "and see that and know that you loved her."

Abby gasped when Ethan pressed a kiss to a particularly sensitive spot near her collarbone. They were in his hotel room. She wasn't really sure when they'd decided to go there. Sometime after they'd left the cemetery, the mood between them had undergone a subtle shift. He had looked at her with an overwhelming tenderness, and she'd nodded, understanding the silent inquiry.

Ethan smiled against her skin. "Want me to do it again?"

Abby threaded her hands in his hair. "I might expire if you do."

He laughed and kissed her deeply. She wrapped her arms around his neck and returned the kiss with equal fervor. He'd lingered over her endlessly that afternoon. He'd taken her places she'd never even dreamed of, then driven her higher as he'd lavished attention on every inch of her flesh. Her body felt both pampered and exhausted. When he lifted his head, his eyes were filled with the same tenderness she'd seen earlier. "Thank you, Abby."

She smiled at him. "I'm the one who got all the attention today."

He shook his head, his expression rueful. "You know what I mean."

She did. She stretched with the contented luxury of an overfed cat. Giggling, she remembered telling him how she'd felt like the slowest and fattest gazelle in the herd. "What are you laughing about?" he asked her.

"Gazelles," she said enigmatically. "And panthers."

Ethan entwined his hands with hers and pressed them to the pillow. "You're amazing."

"You're not so bad yourself," she assured him as he lowered his head.

The jarring ring of his cell phone on the nightstand interrupted them. He looked over at it with disgust. "I should flush that thing."

"It might be important," Abby told him.

He shook his head and kissed her. "Not more important than this."

The phone continued to ring, insistent and demanding. Finally, he tore his mouth from hers with a muttered curse and reached for it. "Maddux," he barked.

Abby watched his expression change from frustration to determination as the voice on the other end identified itself. He rolled away from her and sat up in bed. "How do you know?" he asked the caller.

Abby placed a hand on his shoulder. Ethan nodded at whatever the caller was telling him. "Fine," he said. "We'll be there in fifteen minutes." He hung up the phone and tossed it on the nightstand.

"Ethan, what is going on?"

He held out a hand to her. "We only have time for one shower, so it'll have to serve both of us."

"Who was that?" She let him pull her from the bed.

"General John Standen. He wants us downtown for a briefing."

"I don't understand," Abby said an hour later as she listened to John Standen talk to Detective Nick Krestyanov. "You think the person who tried to break into my house is connected to the center? How do you even know about this?"

Carter Jameson patted Abby's hand. "Ethan asked us to look into it."

She shot Ethan a look of surprise. He nodded. "My investigator had already turned up evidence that your father's military connections might have somehow played a role in his murder. I asked a few questions."

"I knew your father," Carter said, "when he worked at the recruiting office. I used to volunteer there just to take my mind off things. I didn't put you together with him until Ethan started asking around."

Abby frowned. "But the break-in—"

"After that night," Ethan said, "I came down here to see what I could find out."

John Standen concurred. "We began to really dig around. Most of the older veterans in this town still remember your dad's restaurant. It wasn't hard to get some answers."

The detective snorted. "*I* found it hard enough."

Carter laughed. "You didn't know how to ask the right questions."

Abby rubbed her eyes, hoping to clear her head. "And you think someone here knew why my father was killed?"

"A lot of money got passed around by the Feds after your dad's murder, Abby," the general told her. "People who barely knew the man were encouraged to remember deeper friendships."

"And his friends disappeared."

"Damn bunch of cowards," Carter muttered.

John continued. "But to a man, everyone remembered one thing about the weeks following his death." He looked at Detective Krestyanov. "There's a fellow named George Dryden. He's been here several years."

"Keeps to himself," Carter added.

"He's got a nephew who pulled some strings to get him in here. This is one of the better places around, and the waiting list is long."

"You think Dryden is behind this?" Krestyanov asked, writing the name down in his notepad.

"No," John said. "It's Dryden's nephew. We never met the guy until the other day. That's when the whole thing came together."

Carter nodded and slammed his hand down on the arm of his wheelchair. "If I hadn't been confined to this damned thing, I'd have slugged the guy."

"Do you have a name?" the detective asked.

John reached for Abby's hand and enfolded it in his own. "Abby knows him. David Wilcox."

"Why," Abby insisted later that day, "couldn't it just be a coincidence?" They were seated in Detective Krestyanov's office, where he was making phone calls about David Wilcox.

Ethan shoved a diet soda into her hand. "Honey, listen to me—"

"But I've known David for years. He's always been a friend."

That didn't surprise Ethan. David Wilcox would have made damned sure he could keep an eye on things. He'd been managing his uncle's money for him for years—a worthy chunk of cash Ethan was willing to bet could be traced to Abby's father. The last thing he'd appreciate was for information to surface that might stop the free ride he'd been getting from his uncle's assets.

"Try to look at this logically," Ethan urged.

"I don't *want* to look at it logically," she protested.

Ethan rolled his eyes and gave up trying to argue. The detective finished his call and nodded briefly at Ethan. "Okay. We're going to set up surveillance. If what you say is true, he's going to feel a little desperate as soon as he gets the news."

"Good." Ethan had persuaded Harrison to circulate rumors through his company executives about the reason for the planned sell-off. The news of the MDS breakup had already gone public that morning. If Wilcox suspected that Harrison was onto him, he'd have to act. "I called my office in San Francisco. They're making sure that the right people start calling the MDS corporate office for answers. Wilcox is going to feel the heat pretty damn quick."

"We can keep him under surveillance for a while," Krestyanov promised, "but something will have to bring this to a head soon. If one of the Feds was really responsible for getting Abby's father killed, we won't be able to get the guy unless we move fast enough to outsmart them. The roots of this are deep."

Abby shook her head. "I just can't believe—" She exhaled a heavy breath and asked the detective, "Do you think Rachel and I are in any danger?"

"Not right now," he said, "Wilcox is in this for the money. If he tried to break into your house, he most likely just wanted to scare you. If the man, or men, responsible for your father's death knew we were investigating this, that would be a different story."

Ethan frowned. "How do you know they don't?"

"The inner circle is really tight. The two of you, me and my partner, my boss, and your two vet friends—that's it. Nobody in this group is talking. As far as Wilcox knows, it's just about the blackmail. He has no reason to know anything about the federal case."

"He'll panic soon," Ethan agreed. "He'll try to contact Harrison again when he does."

"Harrison has agreed to wear a wire if necessary," Krestyanov told them. "But frankly, I don't think we'll need it. I have the previous threats he got—he turned them over to me. All I need is evidence proving that Wilcox is behind the blackmail."

"I still think we should take precautions," Ethan said.

"So do I." The policeman looked at Abby. "There's no point in being deliberately foolish. Is there somewhere you and your sister can stay for the next few days?"

"Yes," Ethan said. They'd stay with him. In San Francisco. Where he could lock the doors and put armed guards around the place. No one was going to hurt her.

Abby glared at him. "I'm not moving out of my house."

Krestyanov leaned forward. "Ms. Lee, I think you should consider—"

"I'm not doing it. I can send Rachel to a friend's house for a few days, but I'm not going to let him scare me out of my house."

"*Abby.*" Ethan's frustration was mounting.

"No," she said firmly. "I won't do it."

He studied the set of her jaw. This was the same woman who fought fiercely for her loved ones and clung to him in the night with a tenacity that robbed his breath. She wasn't about to back down without a fight.

"Fine," Ethan announced. "Then I'll move in."

As the week wore on, Abby found her fuse growing shorter. She and Ethan had explained the situation to Rachel, who had agreed to stay with her friend Kelly's parents. Access to the kitchen, no doubt, had played a major role in her acquiescence. Rachel had received her acceptance notification for the Baldovino event, and since the date was little more than a week away, her mind was fixed on preparing for the competition. The chance to experiment in the gourmet setting was more than she could resist.

Abby spoke to her daily, and she and Ethan drove out to see her twice that week. But as the weekend approached, with still no move from David Wilcox, Abby became increasingly more anxious. Ethan had been unfailingly patient with her moodiness. She supposed there were some advantages to his long-practiced habit of staying on an even keel. At least it freed her to feel like a basket case as long as one of them was thinking soundly.

But there were signs that he, too, was beginning to feel the pressure. For the past two nights their lovemaking had taken on a new tone, a slightly desperate edge that made Abby feel like the clock was ticking. She told him she loved him—she gave him everything she had—and though he was a generous and considerate lover, he still managed to keep her slightly at arm's length. She cautioned herself to be patient. He'd had years to practice insulating himself, but she couldn't fight her fear that once the case was resolved, Ethan would have no reason to stay in Chicago.

Detective Krestyanov had informed them that afternoon that he wasn't certain how much longer he could justify the extra surveillance on Wilcox if something didn't break soon.

She was in her office with Deirdre late Friday morning, pouring over the last of the contracts for the fund-raiser, when Marcie buzzed through on the intercom. "Yeah, Marcie?"

"Sorry, Abby, but Dave Wilcox is out here. He wants to see you."

Abby and Deirdre exchanged looks. "Tell him I'll be right with him," Abby said. Deirdre pulled a cell phone out of her pocket and dialed Harrison's private line.

"He's here," she said simply, and flipped the phone shut. With a brief nod, she sat down across from Abby. "Nerves, darling. Calm nerves. Just make the little ferret confess and he'll squeal."

Despite herself, Abby had to fight a smile. Deirdre was enjoying herself more than she'd ever imagined. Harrison's plea that Abby give her the event chairmanship to raise her self-esteem had obviously been right on target. And Abby had been pleasantly surprised at the friendship she'd been able to develop with his sister in spite of, or perhaps because of, her unique eccentricities.

"I should call Ethan," she told Deirdre. "He'll be pissed if I don't let him know."

The other woman laughed and punched his number on her phone. She gave Ethan the same terse message, then gave Abby a thumbs-up.

Abby hit the intercom button. "Okay, Marcie. We're ready."

David Wilcox sailed into her office full of his usual charm. He greeted Deirdre with a look of surprise. "Mrs. Cornwell, or is it Everson now?" He took her hand in both of his.

"It's back to Montgomery."

"I'm so glad to see you. It's been too long."

Deirdre, dressed in a turquoise suit with white pearl buttons, gave him a feline smile. "It certainly has, David, darling. What have you been doing down there in Harrison's accounting department? Working for slave wages, no doubt?"

His smile didn't falter. He laughed, and Abby wondered why she'd never heard the hollow ring to it before. He turned to Abby. "How have you been, Abs? It's been a while."

She had to squelch the urge to scowl at him. God. *Abs.* Had the man always been this obnoxious? Rachel had always thought so. "I've been busy, David." She noted the softness to his face and the slightly flushed look of his skin. Once, she thought him handsome in a boyish kind of way. "You know we've got the fund-raiser coming up."

He nodded. "And the Baldovino event. I just cleared the paperwork for the sponsorship."

Abby stared at him. "MDS is sponsoring the Baldovino this year?" Harrison hadn't mentioned it. The competition was a week away.

David nodded. "We got word from upstairs about a week ago." He sat in the chair across from her desk. "We were a little surprised—you know, things being what they are." He pushed his glasses up the bridge of his nose and gave her a rueful look. "But then, we just cut the checks. No one pays us for our opinion."

Abby gazed closely at David's face and wondered if she was imagining the slightly bluish color beneath his eye and across his nose. It was almost imperceptible, but could easily have been a latent bruise from the strike of her umbrella. She decided her imagination was playing tricks on her. "So what brings you up here?" she asked him.

"Well"—he looked a little sheepish—"actually, I was wondering if you wanted me to go with you to the fund-raiser this year—and maybe the Baldovino thing. We hadn't talked in a while, but—"

Deirdre's laugh interrupted him. "David, darling, obviously you all are completely out of the loop down there. You've been spending too much time with your nose in Harrison's books."

Did he flinch? Abby wondered.

"Sorry?" he said, looking blankly at Deirdre.

"Abby and Ethan Maddux are, er, together. I'm sure Ethan will be going with her."

"Oh." David blinked, and he seemed to square his shoulders. "I had no idea." He studied his manicured fingernails. "It's not a big deal. There's actually this woman in Accounting I was thinking of taking. It's just that you and I always had plans—"

That was a bit of an overstatement. Abby hardly considered the handful of casual dates she'd had with him a commitment. "I'm sorry," she told him. "I didn't think to tell you."

"So . . . Ethan Maddux." His expression turned unpleasant. "I imagine that must make things interesting upstairs."

There were few, Abby knew, who worked at MDS who weren't aware of the legendary feud between Ethan and his father. There were also few who were crass enough to gossip about it. She was starting to feel the same sense of anticipation she

had when she knew a spider was lurking somewhere in her kitchen. She was ready for him to
crawl out of his hiding place so she could enjoy
the satisfaction of squashing him. "You could say
that."

"I knew Maddux was offering up advice on the
financial situation, but I assumed, what with the
buyout and all, that—"

Deirdre clucked her tongue. "Ethan's interest in
MDS didn't go much farther than this office." She
indicated Abby with a wave of her hand. "Abby
did persuade him to take a look at things, but he
and Harrison agreed the best course of action was
to sell." Deirdre sighed dramatically. "It's really
been quite sweet to see the way this has brought
them back together."

David's gaze narrowed on Abby. "Oh?"

Abby nodded. "I wouldn't say things were
completely mended between them—" The door to
her office burst open, and Ethan and Harrison entered, laughing about a shared joke. Abby regarded the scene with amazement. Deirdre's
smile turned positively wicked.

"Oh, sorry," Harrison said, looking at David. "I
didn't realize there was someone in here besides
Deirdre."

Ethan rounded the desk and leaned over Abby's
chair to kiss her. It started as a brief peck, but when
he took a second taste, it had her heart racing. "All
right?" he asked quietly against her lips.

"So far," she whispered.

He raised his head. "We came by to see if you two wanted a break from all this paperwork." He indicated the clutter on her desk. Abby just stared at him. He and Harrison seemed positively chummy. David had to be shocked. Only Deirdre appeared to be taking it all in with a delicious satisfaction.

"Baldovino is so grateful for our sponsorship money," Harrison explained, "he's invited us all to lunch at his restaurant. Ethan and I hoped we could persuade both of you to join us."

"How cozy," Abby drawled. Ethan shot her a knowing look.

"Can you spare the time?" Deirdre asked Harrison. "I'm sure things are getting hectic around the office."

Harrison shrugged. "We're making the press statement this afternoon. That should take care of it."

Abby watched David's face during the interchange. Nothing seemed to register. He stood, though, and gave her a brief smile. "Well, I for one have plenty to keep me busy. I'll see you at the Baldovino event, I suppose, Abby."

"Yes, David, I suppose you will."

Sixteen

Ethan glanced around the crowded interior of the Navy Pier Festival Hall and scowled. The Baldovino competition was in full swing. Spread throughout the exhibit space, chefs representing different Chicago restaurants and those operating individually were demonstrating their techniques and pushing their menus. The space was too open and too crowded. He was having trouble keeping an eye on Abby.

Rachel was steadily working at Monsieur Billaud's booth, and while Abby stopped by there regularly, her foundation contacts and her innate flair for fund-raising kept her working the crowd.

Pio Baldovino was notoriously flamboyant, and the event reflected his unique style. Not to mention, Ethan thought dryly, a complete lack of common sense. The decor and theme of the competition looked like a Las Vegas version of King Arthur's feast. The chefs' white hats bobbing above the crowd helped create a frenzied activity.

Near the front of the hall, he spotted Detective Krestyanov. The woman with him, Ethan knew, wasn't his date, but a fellow detective who'd come along to provide him and Detective Garrison with backup in case things turned ugly. Ethan had not yet spotted David Wilcox.

Deirdre, he noted, was doing her best to hold court near the front of the Festival Hall. She wore a sapphire-blue costume that had enough feathers and sequins to pass for a Mardi Gras float. A group of adoring young men, clothed in garish tunics and wearing assorted pieces of armor—none of it appropriately period—surrounded her, hanging on her every word.

His aunt seemed to sense Ethan's scrutiny and shot him a look across the wide hall. A tilt of her head helped him locate Abby, deep in conversation with an older couple. He relaxed slightly and took a sip of his club soda. Abby was talking about the foundation. He knew that because she was using her hands to manipulate the air in front of her, something she did when her passions were evoked. There were plenty of other things she did in the throes of passion, but this was the only thing she did in public.

In the past week, he'd become acutely aware of

her idiosyncrasies and moods—as if the fabric of her life were sewn irrevocably onto his. He never got tired of watching her. The feeling had begun to make him a little edgy as he realized a growing need to bind her to him. She was becoming crucial to his existence, and he hadn't been able to fight the fear of the past few days that once things were settled with Wilcox, she would no longer need him in her life.

He'd known from the beginning that Abby wasn't the type to accept anything less than an absolute commitment. She'd want everything from him, and he wasn't sure he had it to give. He frowned as he watched her, fighting the urge to stalk across the ballroom and take her away with him. Maybe if he took her somewhere isolated, where he could have her undivided attention for two or three weeks, his gnawing hunger might abate.

Abby appeared so elegant in a simple black dress that hung low across her shoulders. On a sex-appeal scale, he'd have to say the look paled only slightly compared with the filmy nightgown she'd worn two nights ago when she'd deliberately seduced him at her kitchen table. It hadn't been much of a challenge, he admitted. He'd succumbed to the temptation in less than five minutes.

Abby turned her head slowly and made eye contact with him. The sweet longing he saw in her gaze stole his breath. He sent her a wordless promise that said he was hers for the asking. She seemed to ponder him for a moment, then excused herself from her conversation and headed toward him.

Abby was skirting the perimeter of the room, making her way toward him as quickly as propriety would allow. Every few yards someone would stop her for a greeting or a question, and she'd dart increasingly agitated looks at Ethan, who watched her with growing satisfaction. His hands were tingling with anticipation as he thought of touching her flesh—she'd have goose bumps. She always did when she was in this shivery, anticipatory mood.

"Maddux, is that you?" He felt the hand on his arm a split second after he recognized the voice. "I didn't have the chance to talk to you earlier."

Reluctantly, he pulled his gaze from Abby to rest it on David Wilcox. The weasel had a gigglylooking blonde on his arm. His eyes reflected the bright sheen of alcohol. "Hello, Wilcox." He looked pointedly at the drink in his hand. "Enjoying yourself?"

"You bet." David awkwardly patted his date's hand.

Ethan saw Krestyanov out of the corner of his eye. The detective was observing the exchange closely.

"So, Maddux," Wilcox continued, "it must have

been a blow to you, not being able to bail old Harrison out of MDS."

Ethan raised an eyebrow. "I wasn't trying to bail him out," he said. "Didn't you hear Harrison's press statement this afternoon? I would have thought the news would be all over the place by now."

The deliberate insult wasn't lost on David. He visibly bristled. "We heard, yeah. Something about blackmail because of his military deferment. That's why he decided to sell."

Ethan shrugged. "That's the quickest way, they say, to foil an extortionist."

"Don't suppose you've got any idea who the blackmailer could be?"

"Harrison hasn't told me, but I think he has an idea. He's been in touch with the police."

The color seemed to drain out of David's face.

"Hello, David." A breathless Abby stepped neatly between them. Ethan curved his arm around her waist. "I'm glad you could make it."

Wilcox stared at Ethan for a moment longer, then swung his bleary gaze to Abby. "Hey, Abs. How's your sister doing with her little chef thing?"

Ethan felt Abby tense. He tightened his arm and said smoothly, "Rachel's doing very well. Her mentor thinks she has a genuine chance of getting accepted into Baldovino's program."

The microphone squealed, and Ethan darted a

look at the stage. Pio Baldovino had begun making introductions. Ethan glanced meaningfully at Krestyanov. The detective spoke a few words to his female partner, then headed toward Harrison. The woman made a beeline for Monsieur Billaud's booth.

Abby laid a hand on Ethan's upper arm. She gave him a none-too-subtle shove toward the door. "If you'll excuse us, David, Ethan and I need to find Harrison. Baldovino has asked him to make a speech tonight about his sponsorship plans."

"Sure, sure," David said. "He's here, then?"

"Oh, yes," Abby assured him.

"Hmm." David's eyes narrowed. "I'll have to try and find him. I'd like to thank him for inviting us lowly accountants."

Ethan made the mistake of not budging at Abby's evermore insistent pressure on his arm. The look she gave him told him if he didn't yield, she'd gladly bring her high-heeled foot down on his instep.

He'd seen that look before. So he indicated the door with a sweep of his hand and followed her out of the crowded ballroom. The view, he had to admit, was prize-winning. He made a leisurely inspection over her hips, past her narrow waist, and up her spine until he reached the froth of honey-blond curls, neatly held in place by a shiny black rod. She'd done that just to tease him. When she'd slipped it into place with a coy glance at him in her mirror, she'd known that for the rest of the evening he'd have his mind on plucking that rod out.

Abby rounded a corner into a semisecluded corridor, then jerked open a door. Grabbing his arm, she pulled him inside the semidarkened room. They were in an unused section of the Festival Hall, behind the stage where the speeches were being made. The room was cluttered with tables and stacked chairs. On the other side of the dividing wall were Harrison Montgomery, his blackmailer, and two thousand spectators.

"I can't breathe," she told Ethan.

He eased her into his arms. "It's almost over. Wilcox is drunk and stupid—he'll make a mistake."

She shivered. "Krestyanov told me earlier that he wanted me out of the hall so David could make his move."

"I agree." He stroked her back. "Krestyanov had signaled Harrison. His partner was headed for Rachel when we left. Everything's going to be all right."

"I didn't think it would feel like this."

"I know, baby. It's okay."

The sounds of the speeches and the applause carried through the dividing wall. Laughter cascaded over them as Ethan rocked her against him.

Abby's fingers curled into the lapel of his tuxedo jacket. "How long are we supposed to wait?"

"Until the detective comes to get us. The quiet rumbling from the ballroom had begun to escalate. Ethan lifted her chin. "Have I told you lately that you're the bravest woman I know?"

She gave him a half laugh for his troubles. "No, I'm not. I'm shaking like a leaf."

The week had been hard on her. The interminable waiting had exacted a high price on her peace of mind. He'd done what he could to help her through it, but with the moment finally at hand, he knew she was feeling the pressure. The voices were beginning to sound agitated. Abby glanced at the dividing wall with a frown. "What do you think is happening in there?"

The question was followed by a burst of applause. Ethan pressed a kiss to Abby's temple. "Baldovino's sponsors are congratulating themselves."

"Rachel seemed to be doing well," Abby said. "I hope whatever happens with David doesn't cause too much of a disturbance."

As if on cue, a shrieking scream emanated from the ballroom. Abby gave Ethan a startled look, then took off at a run.

The scene in the Festival Hall confirmed her worst fears. David had obviously used the distraction of the speeches to approach Harrison with his demands. Somehow the argument had escalated out of control, and soon the assembled crowd had grown more interested in watching the spectacle than in listening to the collected wisdom of Baldovino's corporate sponsors.

Abby had no idea when things had turned physical, but David's glasses lay smashed on the floor and Harrison's face was red with fury. Detective Nick Krestyanov was standing to one side with his hand inside his tuxedo jacket where his firearm was holstered. He was waiting, Abby knew, for a confession. Two thousand witnesses would make a fairly ironclad case.

"Damn you, Montgomery," David was saying. "Why the hell couldn't you just do what I told you to? Everything would have been fine."

Harrison scowled at him. "You spineless bastard."

David's face was as flushed with rage as Harrison's. The two were standing near one of the enormous display units featuring cakes and pastries and themed decor. David looked around and seized a gold sword—à la Excalibur—from its resting place inside a large cake. The crowd gasped. David brandished the icing-smeared sword with theatrical finesse. "All you had to do," he said with low menace, "is what I told you to do. I told you where to find the money. I told you how to get it."

Deirdre had worked her way through the crowd and now stood next to Harrison. "David," she said chidingly, "be a nice boy and put that down."

The words seemed to enrage him. "Shut up," he barked. "Just shut up."

Harrison mopped his sweating brow with his handkerchief. "Don't talk to her like that."

David's laugh was bitter. "Why the hell not? What have I got to lose now?"

"You should have thought of that when you tried to blackmail me," Harrison snapped.

David stalked forward with the sword. "It would have worked if you hadn't been so damned stubborn." He slashed the air and bits of frosting plopped onto the carpet. "You sold the company and bankrupted yourself just to avoid paying for your mistake."

Abby saw Detective Krestyanov step forward.

"Your uncle made plenty of money off my mistake," Harrison said coldly.

David swore loudly. "You arrogant asshole!" He charged forward with the sword. Deirdre extended her foot and tripped him. He stumbled, then fell heavily into the display table, crashing into a giant pie. The crowd shrieked as the pie crust gave way beneath his weight and the entire concoction collapsed onto the floor. From inside the cavernous display unit, birdcages tumbled open, releasing a swarm of blackbirds into the crowded ballroom.

Four and twenty, Abby guessed, of the large birds shrieked and fluttered above the crowd, adding to the cacophony of noise. Krestyanov had lunged forward and pushed David facedown on the floor. He was cuffing him and quietly reading him his rights amid the chaos.

Abby watched the scene unfold with a growing sense of horror. One of the birds had evidently developed a fixation for Baldovino's hair and was tangled in the jet-black coiffure. Baldovino was yelling orders into the microphone while two young men dressed like knights tried to free the hapless bird from his hair.

The detective hauled a handcuffed David to his feet and shoved him in Abby's direction. Deirdre, she noted, was observing the entire display with thinly disguised glee. Ethan draped his arm over Abby's shoulders. "Do you think," he whispered in her ear, "that Baldovino is going to announce the winners soon?"

She gave him a chilling look. The more Baldovino resisted the bird, the more hopelessly tangled it got. To add to the confusion, event security was trying, somewhat vainly, to restore order and calm to the hall. They were aided and abetted by the costumed knights, most of whom, Abby suspected, moonlighted as exotic dancers.

"Oh, God," she groaned. "When he finds out we're responsible for this, Rachel will never be able to show her face again."

Ethan's fingers curled around her elbow. "There's always San Francisco."

Before she could respond to that, Nick Krestyanov pushed a sputtering David in front of them. David glared at Abby. "All you had to do was mind your own business," he told her angrily. "Everything would have been fine."

She felt fury rise in her and turned the full force of it on him. "You tried to terrorize me, David. You're a weak, pathetic little man who took advantage of your uncle and everyone else around you."

Without giving him time to respond, the detective shoved him hard. "Go," he barked. "I'm sick of looking at you." His partner eased forward and guided David out the door. Krestyanov looked at Abby. "I'll be in touch, Ms. Lee. If you want us to pursue—"

She shook her head. "No, it's over." She slid her hand into Ethan's. The stakes of pursuing the truth any further were higher than she wanted to pay. "I'm really ready for it to be over."

He hesitated, then said, "I'll see you soon." He nodded in the direction of the booths. "Tell your sister I'll taste that meal she promised when the ambience is a little calmer."

Abby watched him leave amid a swarm of guests who streamed through the exit as the birds swooped down and began to settle on the buffet table.

Ethan squeezed her hands. "I'll handle the birds," he told her. "You take Baldovino."

Baldovino yelled again. Abby groaned and started forward. "I don't care what you have to do to them," she told Ethan. "Just get rid of the damned things so we can grab Rachel and scram out of here." Finally, Baldovino's knights freed the bird from his hair. It joined its companions near the ice sculpture. As the birds picked at and pranced around the hors d'oeuvres, Abby made her way determinedly toward Monsieur Billaud's booth. She saw Rachel deep in conversation with Deirdre. On the stage, Baldovino had collapsed dramatically onto a chair and sat fanning himself in a near swoon. Harrison bounded onto the platform and seized the mike.

"Ladies and gentlemen, please . . ." His voice had little effect on the tumult in the room. "Please, if you'll just remain calm."

Behind him, Baldovino shrieked, "Calm? My God, it's worse than an Alfred Hitchcock movie."

Harrison gave him a quelling glance. "Pio, please. We have everything under control."

Abby eased around the debris from the fallen pie and continued weaving through the crowd toward her sister.

Ethan, she noted, was rounding up the security staff and issuing instructions while making vague gestures in the direction of the buffet table.

Several reporters had shoved their way toward

the front of the stage and were snapping pictures of Baldovino and Harrison.

"Montgomery," one of the reporters yelled. "Do you have a comment on this?"

"Who was that man?" another asked.

Harrison held out his hand to quiet the storm. "Please, please. I'm sorry this had to happen. If you saw the statement I issued this afternoon, you know that I have decided to sell MDS and all its subsidiaries as a result of the blackmail threat I've been under for the past several months."

"Was that the blackmailer?"

"Yes," Harrison confirmed.

The crowd noise escalated. Abby was a few feet from where Rachel and Deirdre were still engaged in an intense discussion. She was relieved to see that her sister didn't look overly distressed by what had happened here.

The microphone squealed as Harrison started to speak over the din in the ballroom. "Ladies and gentlemen, please. I think we have everything under control. I'll be happy to answer any questions you may have, but I don't want us to forget why we're here tonight. Pio Baldovino works hard all year to bring this competition to our city and provide opportunities for aspiring culinary artists across the country. We came here to support and encourage them—" He glanced at the buffet table, where Ethan and the security staff had managed to net the bulk of the birds. "Although you'll probably want to avoid the buffet." He won a be-leaguered laugh for that.

He glanced at Baldovino, who still sat in a boneless heap on the chair. "Pio, I have to hand it to you. I attend fifteen to twenty of these benefits a year. I've never been to a more memorable one." This was met with more laughter and scattered applause. Harrison continued. "I regret that my personal situation put a pall on the festivities, but I think you all should know what Pio told me earlier. Thanks to your support, this event has raised over half a million dollars for Chicago's public schools and enrichment programs." This time the applause was louder and sustained. "So I'd like to thank everyone for coming, for your support of Pio's work, and I encourage you to come again next year." He chuckled. "I'm sure you'll want to tell your friends this is an event not to be missed."

The crowd roared its appreciation. Harrison switched off the mike. He caught Abby's eye and gave her a sad smile. She blew him a kiss, then made her way toward Rachel.

Rachel and Deirdre were laughing. "God," Rachel said as Abby reached them, "can you believe this?"

Deirdre patted Rachel's arm. "It'll be the talk of Chicago for years."

Abby regarded her sister closely. "I'm really sorry, Rach. I know how much this meant to you."

Deirdre shook her head and pointed to where

Ethan finally had the birds back in their cages and on the way out of the ballroom. "Things aren't nearly as bad as they probably seem, Abby. You'll see."

Another hour passed before the staff had cleared away all the debris. By mutual consent, Baldovino and his board had agreed to wait until the next day to announce the winners. Fortunately, the tasting portion of the competition had concluded before David made his move.

Ethan had insisted that Abby and Rachel leave with him shortly after Harrison's speech had concluded. They'd met Harrison and Deirdre at a small coffee shop near the MDS building. An exhausted Abby sat beside Ethan with a wet linen napkin draped over her forehead. Rachel, he noted, seemed buoyant. The night at Festival Hall hadn't taken the same toll on her that it had on her sister. Deirdre, too, seemed energized, while he sensed an undercurrent of anger in Harrison. It echoed his own. Ethan was beginning to see how much he had in common with his father.

Rachel and Deirdre were rehashing the events with glee. Abby groaned and leaned her head against Ethan's shoulder. "What did I do to deserve this?" she asked him.

"You know what part I liked?" Rachel said, drumming her fingers on the table. "I liked the part where the crow landed on Baldovino's hair."

"It was a blackbird," Abby said with another groan.

Beside her, Ethan's chuckle was warm and rich. "You have to admit, Abby, it was a priceless moment."

"Did you see all those reporters?" Deirdre asked. "The publicity should be spectacular."

"I've never seen so many cameras in my life," Rachel remarked.

"Great," Abby said. "Maybe we'll make the front page of the *Tribune* tomorrow."

"Can't you see it?" Ethan exclaimed. "A full-page spread of Baldovino with that bird tangled in his hair and the caption, 'Can you find the old crow in this picture?'"

Harrison continued to stare broodingly into his coffee. Rachel erupted into a fit of giggles. Deirdre's shout of laughter sounded slightly more sadistic. "Serves him right. That man is so histrionic."

Harrison regarded his sister stonily. She laughed and patted his arm. "I know, darling. You're thinking I've got no right to comment."

"You seemed to enjoy yourself tonight," he said.

"I did," she agreed. "Immensely. I wouldn't be a Montgomery if I didn't love spectacles."

Abby pulled the napkin off her forehead. "Rach, are you sure you're all right? I didn't want this to ruin the night for you."

Rachel shrugged. "I'm fine. Aunt Deirdre and I had a long talk about it."

Deirdre patted Rachel's hand. "Just remember what we talked about, dear. No one's going to forget your first competition."

Rachel nodded. "And it wasn't like I expected to win or anything. Cripes, there's always next year."

"If Baldovino lets us come next year," Abby muttered.

"He will," Deirdre said confidently, "for the right amount of sponsorship money."

Rachel nodded again, emphatically. "And frankly," she continued, "I really don't think it was all that bad. I mean, everything was basically okay until that stupid David and the birds."

"He's behind bars now," Harrison said moodily.

Ethan linked his hands behind his head. "And he's going to stay there."

"And we have notoriety," Deirdre said. "Nothing is better than having notoriety."

Abby sighed. "Why don't I feel comforted?"

"Oh, come on, Abby," Rachel protested. "It was hilarious."

Abby frowned. "If you say so."

Harrison set his coffee cup down and pinned Ethan with a shrewd look. "So what are you going to do now?" he asked him in an abrupt change of subject that had the impact of a nuclear bomb.

Ethan felt Abby go still beside him. "What do you mean?" he asked.

"You've got no reason to stay in Chicago now. The case is closed. Wilcox is through. MDS is as good as sold. When are you heading back to San Francisco?"

"I haven't decided yet," Ethan replied.

Harrison held his gaze. "I've never tried to give you fatherly advice, and I won't start now. But at least listen to the voice of experience." He shook his head. "You don't always get a second chance. It might seem like too much of a risk right now, but if you don't take it, you'll regret it for the rest of your life."

Seventeen

Of all the qualities the man had to recommend him, Abby thought—and they were many—what appealed to her most about Ethan Maddux was his incredible passion.

Abby strolled into his San Francisco office and studied him from behind. He was on the phone, staring out the window at his prizewinning view of the San Francisco Bay. It had been a week since she'd seen him. After that night in the coffee shop, he'd stayed in Chicago long enough to ensure that the charges against David Wilcox stuck.

But she'd felt him withdraw. Rachel had come back home, and Ethan had moved back to his hotel room. Day by day, little by little, she'd watched as he'd carefully reconstructed the walls around his heart. She'd spent a long time convincing herself that she couldn't accept him on those terms. She wanted everything, or nothing at all.

Deirdre had been the one to convince her that "nothing at all" was an awfully high price to pay for not being willing to compromise. They had met for lunch yesterday, ostensibly to discuss the final arrangements for the fund-raiser. With smart-bomb precision, Deirdre had pinned Abby to the wall. "You look terrible," she'd told her.

Abby had shrugged. "I haven't been sleeping well."

Deirdre had laughed. "I can imagine. Missing someone in your bed?"

"Deirdre—"

She'd shaken her head. "For God's sake, Abigail, are you going to mope about that man or are you going to fight for him?"

"He made his choice."

"He did not," the older woman had insisted. "He left the choice up to you." She'd leaned across the table and lowered her voice to a conspiratorial whisper. "It's a thing men do to avoid taking responsibility. I should know. I've had five husbands."

"And you yourself said that the Montgomerys can't commit to one person."

"I was wrong about the men, evidently," Deirdre admitted. "I had no idea Harrison felt so deeply about Lina. I don't know how I missed that."

"He loved her."

"So much that he never married."

Depressed by the conversation, Abby had picked at her meal. Deirdre hadn't relented. "Ethan is so much like his father."

That had gotten Abby's attention. "He is not."

"Yes, he is, dear. That brooding nature. All that pent-up angst." His aunt's eyes sparkled. "No wonder you think he's so sexy. What woman wouldn't?"

Abby drew a deep breath. "He made absolutely no indication that he's interested in continuing his relationship with me."

"Except that he fled back to San Francisco hoping you'd chase him."

"Don't be ridiculous."

Deirdre's expression turned serious and concerned. "Abby, are you really going to let pride stand in the way of getting what you want?" She paused. "You love him, don't you?"

"Madly," Abby confessed.

"Then fight for him, darling. He's just waiting for an excuse to tell you he can't live without you. Sometimes men need help seeing that."

"I don't know what to do."

Deirdre had reached into her purse and produced a first-class ticket to San Francisco. "Your plane leaves in an hour. You won't have time to pack." She handed Abby an envelope. "Harrison sent you this to cover whatever you need to buy."

There was a thousand dollars in cash in the envelope.

By the time Abby arrived in California, her stomach was tied in knots. It was after seven, and she'd asked her cabdriver to take her to the Maddux Consulting offices, thinking she'd find a hotel nearby and confront Ethan in the morning.

But the light in his office was on. She'd seen him silhouetted against the window. The security guard in the lobby had taken pity on her babbling explanation and admitted her into the elevator. She'd passed Ethan's secretary on the way out. Edna had waved her into his office with a muttered "Thank God you're here," and now she was back where it all began.

Uneasy, she moved quietly toward his desk while she listened to him issuing quiet instructions over the phone. She'd forgotten how much she missed the sound of his voice.

Her gaze fell on a pencil near the corner of his desk blotter. The eraser had been chewed off. Abby found her confidence restored in that small piece of evidence, which meant he hadn't completely forgotten her. With a slight smile, she picked up the pencil and began coiling her hair. Ethan finished his conversation.

"Hello, Ethan," she said softly before he had a chance to replace the receiver in its cradle.

He spun, eyes wide, and slammed the phone down on his desk. "Abby."

She still had her arms above her head in an effort to insert the pencil into the coil of her hair. She froze. His eyes registered a sea of turmoil. "What are you doing here?" he asked.

Not exactly the response she'd hoped for, but not a denouncement either. She finished securing her hair, then lowered her arms. "Fighting for you," she said quietly.

He stared at her. Abby gathered her courage. Deirdre was right. Pride made terrible company on lonely nights. She rounded the desk and placed her hands on his chest. "I've had some time to think things over."

"You don't—"

She tugged at his tie. "This long-distance thing isn't working for me. First of all, my phone bill is going to be huge. And now that Harrison has a buyer for MDS, I may not even have a job. The foundation is on solid financial footing, but the buyer may want to bring in his own people."

"Honey—"

She gave him a shove and he toppled into his chair. "So I'm thinking of relocating." Ethan watched her warily as she pushed him farther back in his chair. "I've heard California is a pretty nice place. My sister kind of likes the cuisine."

His eyes glittered. "What are you—"

Abby pulled his tie off. "But I don't know. Do you think I could be happy here?"

"Abby, I can't—"

She pressed her fingers to his lips, her expression turning serious. "I know. And I should have realized that. Ethan, I love you. I didn't think it was possible for me to love anyone as much as I love you. I spent a lot of time thinking that maybe I couldn't let anyone be that important to me."

He looked a little shaken. She smiled and smoothed the crease from his forehead with her fingertips. "I wanted you to do all the work. I wanted you to take all the responsibility away from me by demanding that I be with you." She shook her head. "It wasn't fair to you, and it's not fair to me."

"Honey—"

"No." She quieted him. "Deirdre made me see this. If I'd convinced you to do that, I would have always wondered if you really meant it. Did you really love me because you couldn't help yourself, or did I just manipulate you into it? I never would have known." She took a deep breath. "I don't need you to be wild about me. I'm wild enough for the both of us."

That remark seemed to galvanize him. He captured both her hands and pulled her onto his lap. "Abby, listen to me. I've been going crazy without you."

"You didn't call—"

"I was giving you space."

"I didn't want space."

"My mistake," he admitted. "I've been driving

myself and my staff crazy so I could get back to Chicago. My pilot is waiting for me at the airport."

Her heart tripped into double time. "Good thing I turned up, then," she quipped. "I saved you a trip."

"I was kind of hoping I could wrangle a meal out of your sister."

"I could maybe make you a tuna sandwich from what's in the mini-bar in my hotel room. Does that count?"

Ethan's eyes filled with tenderness. He swept a hand over her hip, then jerked open his top desk drawer and took out a small velvet box. "I was going to beg you," he told her and flipped open the box. A diamond winked at her.

She looked deeply into his eyes and framed his face with both hands. Tears stung her eyes. "I don't need that. I just need you to love me."

With a low groan, he crushed her in his arms and covered her lips in a kiss filled with promise. "I do," he whispered. "You can't imagine how much I do."

"Then marry me," Abby said and laid her hand alongside his face. "Marry me and spend the rest of our lives showing me."

Ethan kissed her again. "Are you sure you want to take a chance on a Montgomery?"

"Absolutely sure," she told him. "I've been miserable without you."

"Abby—" He plucked the pencil from her hair

so it tumbled over her shoulders. "I can never tell you how much you mean to me. You gave me my life back."

Her eyes started to tear again. He tenderly kissed each one and whispered, "You are the love of my life. I've been waiting for you forever."

Epilogue

Ethan gently adjusted Rachel's veil at the back of the church. He had a tightness in his chest he'd grown to recognize over the past eight years as the wellspring of emotion Abby had helped him find. He'd had it at his wedding. He'd experienced it again when each of his three sons were born. He'd felt it countless times just looking at his wife and wondering how in the world he could have deserved her.

And now Rachel was getting married, and the emotion was back. He hoped he didn't embarrass himself when he walked her down the aisle. "You look gorgeous," he told her.

She fidgeted, but smiled. "Thanks. I'm really nervous."

"Don't be. Just enjoy the moment." The man

Rachel was marrying was a chef at the restaurant where she now worked. Soon they'd open their own place. Ethan liked him, primarily because the poor guy had survived the rigorous scrutiny he'd endured from Ethan and Harrison.

"Ethan?" Rachel said.

"Hmm?" He finished adjusting the fine lace.

"When you married Abby—how did you know? I mean, that she was the one. The only one."

He heard the slight thread of anxiety and took Rachel's hand in his. He carefully considered his words, not sure he could express what he was just beginning to understand himself. "Being with Abby was magic and humbling at the same time. She makes me feel alive—and sometimes better than alive. It's—" He searched for the right words. "It's like a paradox. I could live without her if I had to, but I'd never want to. She sets me on fire, and she's the place I go when my soul needs refreshing. I never have enough of her, but I'm always right on the verge of feeling too much." He shook his head. "That probably doesn't make any sense."

Rachel had grown teary. "That's exactly how I feel about Mike."

"Then it's love," he assured her. "That's how you know."

"Ready?" Abby asked them from the doorway. Ethan noted the mistiness in his wife's gaze. "Scott's getting ready to walk me down to the front. I'll signal the organist to start the prelude."

Rachel hurried across the room and hugged her. "I love you, Abby." She glanced at Ethan. "I'll go wait for you at the back."

He nodded. The tightness in his throat had increased. He went to Abby and took both her hands in his and raised them to his lips. "I mean it just as much today as I did the first time."

She brushed away a tear from her eyes. "Me too. I love you, Ethan."

"More every day," he told her.

Abby gathered herself together with a slight smile. "And Deirdre said that no Montgomery can commit to a single love for a lifetime."

He grinned at her. "Then I must have gotten it from my mother, because you're my one and only."